THE VENERY

JC MENVIELLE

The Venery by JC Menvielle

Published by JC Menvielle

jcmenvielle.com

Cover by JC Menvielle

ISBN: 979-8-9991310-0-3 (print)

Printed in United States of America

1st Edition

For my wife

Prologue

Z eya opened her eyes to the dim, candle-lit bedchamber. Bleary-eyed, she attempted to see what had disturbed her tranquil dreams. Eventually, she focused on her wombsister who was leaning over her excitedly.

"Zeya, are you awake? Zeya!"

"Meleya?" Zeya asked groggily.

"Yes, Wombsister, wake up! Something is happening! Many sisters have gathered in Father's chamber, let's go and see," replied Meleya.

Zeya slowly sat up and rubbed the sleep from her eyes. She slid off the bed and was jarred awake the moment her bare feet touched the frigid stone floor. "What hour is it? Where is Mother?" she asked.

"In Father's chamber with the others. We should sneak in and see what they're doing, but you must be very quiet, understand? Just like when you try to sneak past me while we play Hide from the Greishic," Meleya answered.

"OK, I will be as quiet as I can."

Meleya slowly opened the door to their bedchamber and looked down the hall to see if anyone was there. If they were caught outside of their chamber at this hour, their mother would be very upset. Seeing no one, she motioned for Zeya to follow her, and the two wombsisters crept slowly down the hallway. Lit braziers adorned the stone walls, and Zeya appreciated both their light and warmth on the cold night.

As they got closer to their father's bedchamber, Zeya heard voices and sobs. She watched as Meleya noiselessly entered the chamber. Zeya was always impressed by how silently her wombsister was able to move, and Zeya hoped when she was older, she would be able to move in the same way. She went into the chamber and mimicked her wombsister's stealth as best she could. Thankfully, no one seemed to notice either of them enter. Zeya slid next to her sister, who hid behind one of the many standing woven panels that decorated the room, and waited. She could hear the voices of the other women in the room as she peered through the panel. Her father was lying in bed and many women stood around him. Zeya wasn't surprised to see him in bed. Her father had been lying there for as long as she could remember.

"How can we possibly survive now?" one of the women asked, with fear in her voice.

"Do not be worried, we will find a new source soon," came another voice.

"We haven't had so much as a rumor of a Venery in a very long time, and I don't expect there to be one soon. The Sisterhood is finished. Vesta help us all," replied the first woman.

"Then this really is the end? How many sisters are currently with child? Not enough, I am sure of that," a third woman spoke. "Besides, even if we had another male, it would take too long for the next generation to come of age. The Greishic's numbers grow far too quickly and the beasts will overrun us in a matter of years!"

"Sisters, calm yourselves!" Zeya's ears perked up when she heard her mother's voice. "We have had dark days in the past, and we will continue to have dark days in the future. It is sad that this would happen in our time, truly, but we all knew Yareil's life was nearing its end."

"But Freila," someone spoke, "with no one to replace him, the Sisterhood will fall into disarray and ruin. Once word of his passing spreads, the people's faith in us will be shaken."

"Do not be foolish, Sister. There is still time." Zeya recognized Gilza's voice. Due to her age, everyone saw Gilza as the wisest sister, and so when she spoke, ears listened. "We have many sisters who currently have children growing inside them, not enough to contain the Greishic, sure, but enough to have hope. Do not forget, there are many young sisters that have yet to ripen. We have always found another buck, and this time will be no different."

"Gilza is right," Zeya's mother replied, "We still have a few years before desperation fills our hearts. I am certain we'll have found a new male by then." Zeya's mother turned toward the woven panel where they were hiding. She seemed to lock eyes with Zeya's. "Meleya, Zeya, come out here, please."

Zeya nearly yelped in surprise at her mother's call, but managed to cover her mouth and muffle any sound that would have betrayed their presence. How could their mother know they were there? Zeya had been very quiet when they entered the chamber, just like her sister had told her. For a moment, she thought about staying behind the panel in hiding. Maybe her mother was only guessing they were there and didn't know for sure?

"No reason to stay hidden now," Meleya told her. "Looks like the Greishic found us. We're dead." Meleya stood up, dusted off her nightgown, and jumped out from behind the panel with her arms spread out dramatically. "You found us, Mother!" she exclaimed.

This made Zeya giggle, and she too jumped out from behind the panel, trying her best to imitate her wombsister. Zeya's grin quickly transformed when she realized their audience was not at all pleased.

"This is no discussion for the ears of children!" one of the women exclaimed loudly.

"And why not?" demanded their mother. "Are they not the future of the Sisterhood? Does this not concern them even more than it does us? It is never too early for our daughters to learn of what threatens us."

"Freila speaks true," Gilza replied. "Our young need to know the future they will inescapably face. Attempting to shield them from the harsh realities will only serve to hasten the Sisterhood's downfall."

Freila nodded to Gilza, then knelt down, and took both of their hands. "My dearest daughters, your father is dead. He has passed into Vesta's warm Embrace where he will remain for all eternity. This is a very sad moment for us all. With his passing comes change to the life we all know."

Zeya stared at her mother, confused by the tears she saw welling up in her eyes. She could not understand why her mother was sad. It's not like her mother and father were close. And why did her mother think she should feel sad? Zeya barely even knew her father. She could only really remember meeting him a few times, and he always just stared at her with empty eyes, almost as if he was looking right through her. Her father stayed in his chamber all day, and anytime Zeya would get close to the doorway, the sisters who guarded him would chase her away. So why did her mother's eyes hold tears?

"Meleya, you have already been taught some of this, but Zeya has not. Your father was not only your father. He was also the father of every young sister you know. He was the father of the sisters Meleya's age, of those your age, and even the father of some sisters who are, right now, growing in their mothers' wombs. Many years ago, I took his seed into my body and with it created first your wombsister, Meleya, and then you. The other mothers also took his seed and did the same when they created their daughters, those you know as your sisters.

"His death has now led us into uncertain times. You are too young to have learned of the dance we must do to bear more sisters, but just know that it cannot be done without a man. Your father, Yareil, was the only man in this world known to us. Without another, we are not only unable to produce more sisters, but are also unable to produce another man. Unless we find the next man, the cycle we have all known for many generations will come to an end, and with it, our very way of life."

Zeya stared at her mother. She had never realized her father was that important! Had she known, she would have tried much harder to know him. Zeya felt herself being overwhelmed by an intense sadness. He had been the only man, the only father. She and Meleya were alive because of what he had given to Mother. She felt her face growing hot as tears began to well up in her eyes.

"Do not worry, my child," her mother soothed. "All is not lost. Some of your sisters are out in the world right now, looking for another male. They were Blessed by the goddess and will surely find one."

Zeya's mother pulled her close in a secure embrace. After a moment, Zeya also felt her wombsister join in the hug. Zeya sniffed and asked, "But Mother, what if they don't? What if they don't find another Father?"

"Well, my daughter, if that happens, the Sisterhood will cease. We will live out our days as we are. There will be no more baby sisters born into this world, and sadly, you will never know the blessing of carrying a child within you or of giving birth to one. You will never feel the warmth inside you as you watch your daughters grow. But do not worry, I am sure it will not come to that."

Meleya suddenly pulled away from the embrace. "Mother, I will find him! I will find the next Father, and I will bring him to the Hearth and save all the Sisterhood!"

Her mother looked at her, a smile growing on her face. "My dearest Meleya, if you are chosen by Vesta, given her Blessing, and sent on the Venery, then there is little doubt in my mind that you *will* be the one to find him."

I

The Council of the Jurisa

"No! Not like that, Zeya!" shouted Preza. "You must keep your ears, eyes, and mind ever-watchful if you are to survive a Greishic attack. They rely on their numbers to overtake us. Fighting the Greishic is very different from fighting on the training grounds! You left your flank open, and are just begging them to slash you with their claws."

Zeya rolled her brown eyes at Preza's criticism as she gripped a blunted dagger in each hand. She had heard this same lecture many times before. Just because they had grown up together, that did not give Preza the authority to talk down to her as she would an unripened child. Zeya had ripened years ago and was certainly no longer a child.

"Distance is your ally, if your surroundings offer it," Preza stated. "Do not hesitate to move away from your foes whenever possible, especially if they are grouped together. The Greishic may not be cunning, but a group of them could defeat even the most celebrated of warriors."

They were engaged in their daily practice session at the Hearth's training grounds. Preza was a great warrior, and even though her teaching method annoyed Zeya, she was still honored to have her as an instructor. Of course, she would never tell the woman that.

Taking Preza's words to heart, Zeya broke off and put enough space between the two of them in preparation for her next attack. The large, muscular woman noticed Zeya's change in tactics. Preza shifted her stance in anticipation of Zeya's assault and adjusted her grip on the large blunted practice axe she held in her sizable hands.

"Careful, Zeya!" Meleya, who stood nearby, called. "Preza knows all your tricks, she'll be ready for you."

"Don't give her aid!" roared Preza.

Zeya launched forward and swiftly closed the distance between them. She bent down as she drew near in what appeared to be preparation for a leap. Preza raised her axe, ready to meet Zeya in the air, but this was precisely what Zeya was waiting for. Instead of launching herself toward Preza, she shifted her weight and propelled herself to the side, toward Preza's unguarded flank. Realizing her error, Preza twisted her body and began to bring her axe down to meet the unexpected feint. Zeya also anticipated this, and she waited for the axe to move far enough out of the way, then hurled one of her daggers directly at Preza. Surprised, and unable to bring her axe back up in time to defend herself, Preza resigned to a wince as the blunted dagger struck her hard in the chest.

"Ha! I can't believe you fell for that one!" Meleya laughed.

Preza looked down at Zeya, who stood crouched and ready for a counterattack. "Very good, very good," she said. "But you already ignored what I *just* told you. Were I Greishic, you would have killed me, sure. But another beast would have quickly taken the place of the dead, and you'd be at a disadvantage, absent one of your weapons. Just how many daggers do you plan to carry?"

Zeya shrugged and brushed her dark hair from her face. "If I desired to hold my weapon until I entered Vesta's Embrace, I'd carry something with more heft, like your axe or Meleya's sword."

"Just be mindful, Zeya. You are unlikely to survive against a single Greishic if you are caught without a blade in hand, even if the beast itself is also unarmed."

"That's why she has me." Meleya walked over to them and put her arm around her wombsister's neck. "It'll take more than a few Greishic to take us both down."

Preza smirked at the two wombsisters. "Well, I'll be with you too, but overall, I'd feel much better if I was fighting alongside someone who actually held on to their weapons."

"I'll try and remember that." Zeya smiled at the large woman. "But I make no promises."

Preza ran her fingers through her short blonde hair and sighed. "Vesta, help me."

Meleya laughed. "Divine intervention won't save you from us, Sister."

A woman in a gray cloak approached the three women. Her garb signified her as one of the venaren, a sister who served the Council of the Jurisa. The venaren gave a slight bow before speaking. "Selfa Zeya and her companions, you are all hereby summoned to the chamber of the Jurisa. Details are contained within this missive." The woman handed Zeya a note, hastily bowed again and walked away.

"What do you think Mother wants with us this time?" Zeya wondered, looking at the sealed note in her hand with hesitation.

Meleya grabbed the note from her wombsister's hand and tore it open. "This appears to be an official summons, I don't think it is only Mother who has requested our presence."

"Truly?" Preza snatched the note from Meleya and read it. "Aye, it's official. We are to appear before the whole council. It doesn't say why."

"A Venery, then?" Meleya asked, stroking her light brown hair woven into a side braid.

"It's likely." Preza handed the missive back to Zeya, then looked the two wombsisters over before sniffing in disgust. "Sisters, if we are to appear before the Jurisa, we should visit the baths first."

* * *

Freila sat at a large gilded round table in the chamber of the Jurisa. The four council members had been meeting more frequently as of late. The council chamber walls were adorned with flags bearing the Red Flame as well as tapestries and paintings, most depicting coition and birth. The stone walls were inlaid with precious stones that matched the gems found on the chairs the council members sat in. A large statue of Vesta, her outstretched hand clutching a brazier, lit the substantial room. Beyond the council table, a sizable glazed window provided a majestic view of Vulna, the capital city of the Sisterhood. Freila always found the decor to be rather garish. She saw the ostentatious room to be little more than a distraction from reality. A simple room with four wooden chairs and a table would be sufficient for the conference of four women.

"More frequent Greishic sightings reported from Haralda," Cereila commented as she shuffled through the reports on the table in front of her. "Captain Layna states that her scouts now expect to see the creatures on this side of the Reypar River. Something Haralda has not had to worry about for some time."

"Their numbers grow while ours dwindle. Will it be time or the beasts that finally end us?" Gilza pondered. "Worse, their numbers are growing far too quickly for us to contain them within the Greenwood. Were there any reports of casualties from Captain Layna?"

Cereila shook her head. "None in this report, thank Vesta."

"Time will end us, then," the eldest council member concluded. "The Eyas and Ezas are the only women of proper birthing age, but even the Ezas' wombs shrivel with each passing day."

"Do not forget there are still a few Ynas with ripened wombs," Sieyna commented. "I am certainly not one of them, but surely there are a few young enough to still bear a child."

"And die in the birthing process." Gilza sighed. "No. If the next male is found, I would not waste his seed on your generation, Sieyna."

Sieyna nodded before turning her attention to Cereila. "And what news of Selfa Delreza? Have you received any word on her progress?"

"Yes. But the news is not good." Cereila turned her attention to the next parchment and squinted at the small writing before raising a small pair of spectacles to her eyes. "It would seem Selfa Delreza found no male after performing a complete investigation of the village. According to her message, she believes the rumors were a fabrication designed to wreak havoc and cause unrest within the Sisterhood."

"Maddening!" Sieyna exclaimed. "What would any sister have to gain in spreading such deceit and wasting the valuable time of a selfa?"

"Maddening indeed," Freila replied. "I am sorry, sisters, it would seem the report that was brought to me was rife with falsity."

"Do not blame yourself for the failure, Freila," Gilza replied. "Vesta willing, the next Venery will succeed."

"I appreciate your words, Gilza. Still, I cannot help but feel partially at fault for the lost time. I vetted the information myself, and it came from a seemingly reliable source."

"Sisters," Sieyna began, "I must once again repeat that we should postpone the next Venery. With Delreza returning from Noor, we are left with nought but an inexperienced selfa to send to Rolier. Worse yet, she is young and possesses very little first-hand knowledge in true combat."

"Inexperienced?" asked Freila, looking at Sieyna sharply. "Inexperienced in what? The inability to find a male? I am not certain that experience in failure is a trait we want our selfas to possess."

Sieyna glared at her. "Not knowing what to look for or how to question the villagers rightly will surely decrease the likelihood of success. Just because she's your daughter—"

"Sisters, enough!" interrupted Gilza. "While Selfa Zeya would not be my first choice, we cannot wait until Selfa Delreza's return, nor can we send Selfa Reila. She is far too old. It will be a long and arduous journey across the Greenwood, and the Selfa must depart soon. There must be another male out there. I refuse to believe that Vesta would forsake us now after sustaining our numbers for this long."

"I agree with Gilza," Cereila spoke up, "It matters not who is sent on the Venery. All that matters is that we find the male and bring him safely back to the Hearth. Selfa Zeya was chosen by Vesta just as Selfa Delreza was. If she was granted the goddess' Flame, then she must have an important role to play in our survival."

A gentle knock came from the large wooden door of the chamber, it creaked open, and a venaren entered.

"Forgive the interruption, Mothers," the gray-cloaked venaren said, bowing before them.

"Yes, Child, what is it?" questioned Gilza.

"The Selfa and her escort are here and ready to see you."

"Is it that time already? Dearest Vesta, where does it all go?" Gilza replied. "Very well, send them in."

The venaren nodded and left the room. A moment later, Zeya, Meleya, and Preza entered, bowed, and stood at attention. Freila looked at her daughters with pride and Preza with respect. Preza, who she had only partly raised after her mother, Veyna, was killed, turned out to be as fine a sister as any. Unfortunately, her pride in seeing them standing there brewed with a deep sadness in her heart. Even though she knew they would succeed, a part of her still held regret for it being her own blood sent on this crucial quest.

"Selfa Zeya, where is your signate?" Gilza's chastising voice interrupted Freila's thoughts.

"I... uh." Zeya's face reddened as her brown eyes darted around the room in a panic.

"Oh, I have it, Wombsister!" exclaimed Meleya. "Sorry, I meant to pin it to you after we finished dressing, but I forgot." Meleya reached into her pocket and pulled out Vesta's Leaf, a large silver pin that signified to all that Zeya was a selfa of the Sisterhood, and with it, she had the authority of the Jurisa to act on their behalf.

Sieyna scoffed as Zeya fumbled to pin the silver leaf to her breast. "This is to be the savior of all womankind?"

"Selfa Zeya," Freila spoke in a loud, commanding voice as she rose from her seat, "you have been trained better than this. Vesta's

Leaf is not some trinket to be worn as jewelry for when you so choose, it is an official emblem of the Sisterhood. See that you do not neglect to wear it again."

"Yes, Mother."

Freila gave her daughter a stern look.

"Mother Freila! Yes, Mother Freila," Zeya replied hurriedly.

"Very well." Freila returned to her seat. Better that she be the one to scold her daughter than any other member of the Jurisa, especially Sieyna.

"Selfa Zeya," Gilza began, "we have received several reports that lead us to believe the next male is being hidden in the remote village of Rolier. Being that you are currently the only selfa fit enough and within a week's journey of the Hearth, we the Jurisa have deemed it necessary to send you on the Venery to the village of Rolier."

Freila saw the eyes of both her daughters widen at this news. She couldn't be certain, but Meleya's green eyes appeared to widen with excitement, while Zeya's seemed to with dread.

Gilza continued, "We have already discussed and chosen a route for your journey, but we are leaving it up to you and your escort to make any necessary adjustments. You will leave in the morning, so see that you have been adequately outfitted for this journey. We will provide you with supplies and horses when you depart. Find the male and bring him back to the Hearth. He must be protected at all costs, do you understand, Selfa Zeya?"

"Yes, Mother Gilza."

"And you two," Gilza turned her gaze to Meleya and Preza, "This will be a perilous journey. As her escort, you must ensure the Selfa reaches Rolier safely. Are the two of you still bound to the oath you made to the Selfa? Will you protect her against all dangers, even at the cost of your own lives?"

"Yes, Mother Gilza," Preza and Meleya answered in unison.

"Very good. Cereila has our missive for you. Take some time to look it over and get familiar with the path that lies ahead. We will meet you when you depart in the morning. You are dismissed."

Freila eyed Zeya closely as she stepped forward and accepted the sealed parchment from Cereila. There was no betrayal of emotion on her daughter's face and no trembling of the hand. The flash of dread she had witnessed was completely gone. It seemed Zeya was able to maintain control of her emotions, after all. Good. That would surely be a boon on this journey. None of them had faced such a trial as this before, and the burden on both their body and minds would be great.

She watched as her daughters bowed and left the chamber, so confident in their exit. Freila could not help but feel pride swell within her heart once more. She knew they would succeed, they would be the ones who would save all of humankind.

"The Selfa still has much growing to do, but she seems capable," Cereila stated, after the chamber door closed.

"Agreed," replied Gilza. "Every selfa must begin without experience. Freila, what are your thoughts? Do you think your daughter is capable of success? Will she be able to bring the male back to the Hearth?"

"So long as they make it through the Greenwood securely, I have little doubt they will succeed in finding the male."

"She does have the advantage of a small retinue," Sieyna stated. "I pray stealth will see her safely through the Greenwood and safely past the abominable Greishic. May the goddess guide them on their path."

"On the topic of the Greishic, let us discuss the report we received from Regent Vuleila in Memier," Gilza replied. "Most worrisome that the beasts appear to be approaching the Paling with more frequency and aggression than usual."

"Vuleila has been exaggerating Greishic attacks ever since she became Regent of Memier," Sieyna remarked. "We never received any such reports from the previous Regent. I suspect she only desires more women and arms to strengthen her position on the Eastern Plateau."

"Exaggerations or not," Freila began, "it is imperative that the city not be breached. Allowing the Greishic to roam freely across the Eastern Plateau would devastate already dire circumstances. Not to mention how it would affect the Venery and safety of the male."

"What is it that Regent Vuleila would like us to do with this information?" asked Gilza.

Cereila brought her spectacles to her eyes and once again read the report in front of her. "As of yet, she has requested no aid. It seems her intent was simply to keep us informed."

Gilza thought for a moment. "Very well, send a response. Tell her we appreciate the information she has provided, and that we desire to receive more reports as necessary."

"Should we offer her aid?" Cereila asked.

"Not as of yet. If she requests it, we will consider it, but until then, we will not risk sending any more sisters through the Greenwood than absolutely necessary. As of now, the future of the Sisterhood weighs on the shoulders of Selfa Zeya and her companions."

II

Vulna

"It's about time!" Meleya exclaimed as the three of them exited the Hearth into Vulna, the capital city of the Sisterhood. "I've been waiting years for you to be sent on the Venery. I never would have bound myself to you had I known it would take this long, truly!"

"Don't be filled with too much excitement, Meleya," Preza replied. "This will be no easy task. We will be heading through the heart of Greishic territory. It is one thing to fight them on the borders of our lands. It is another to face them on their own soil."

Zeya remained silent as Preza and Meleya conversed. She was trying to overcome the fear that had been rising up inside her ever since she had received her decree. Although she too was excited to finally have a chance to leave the Hearth and explore the world, Zeya had always dreaded the day her first Venery would come. One of her biggest fears was failing the Sisterhood as a selfa.

"Come now, Wombsister, show us the missive!"

Meleya interrupted her thoughts. Zeya pulled the parchment out and broke the wax seal stamped with Vesta's Flame, the symbol of the Hearth. Taking time to read it carefully, she handed it to Preza, who quickly read through it.

"It would seem the route is what I expected," Preza stated. "We are to travel east by the main road, resupplying in Solren. We then proceed to Haralda. Upon leaving the outpost, we will leave our horses behind and travel on foot down into the Greenwood. We will continue through the forest and across the Reypar River's multiple distributaries, until we reach the Eastern Plateau and the gates of Memier for resupply, respite, and mounts. It will then be a few days' ride from Memier to Rolier.

"Fortunately, the return journey should go more swiftly. A riverboat will be supplied from Rolier and will take us down the Yeren River until it bends south. Once there, we will meet back up with warriors from Haralda and have added security until we return to the Hearth with the male."

"Why not just spare some soldiers to help us cross the Greenwood?" Zeya asked.

"We would risk drawing the attention of a Greishic horde if we traveled through it in too large a group," Meleya replied. "The three of us should be able to slip through nearly undetected if we tread with caution."

"What's the Greenwood like, Preza?" asked Zeya.

"About what you'd expect. It's not much different from the neighboring forest. Trees, rocks, and moss. As for the beasts, Vesta only knows. On one occasion, I have successfully traveled through without so much as laying eyes on a single one of the creatures. On another, my party stumbled upon a wandering horde and was forced to fight until we were able to flee." Preza paused and stared somberly down the city street. "I was nearly taken, and we lost a third of our number that day."

"Glad they didn't get you," Meleya replied, gripping Preza's arm.

Preza tore her eyes from the street and met Meleya's gaze. "As am I," she murmured, then huffed suddenly. "Well, let us get outfitted for the journey. And it seems the time has come for you both to cut your luscious locks."

Surprise showed on Meleya's face, and she gripped her side braid. She stroked it nervously. "I am not ready for that."

Preza shook her head. "Your hair is far too long. Cutting it could very well be the difference between life and death. Zeya, what about yours?"

Zeya brought a hand to her hair defensively. "Perhaps once we reach Solren."

Preza grunted. "Fine, then follow me to the best weaponsmith in all of Vulna."

They continued down one of Vulna's busier streets until they reached their destination. It was a dilapidated looking weapons shop on the outskirts of the Artisan District. The bell above the door drew the shopkeeper's attention as they entered.

"Ah, welcome, Preza! Oh, and Selfa Zeya as well, what an honor!" the shopkeeper exclaimed.

"Hail, Sister," replied Preza. "We have come with a writ from the Hearth and are in need of the best weaponry you are able to offer us."

"Truly? Well, which of my wares might you be in need of?"

"I, for one, desire a new battle axe," Preza replied. "A set of daggers for the Selfa, and a sword for her wombsister."

"I do not require a new blade," Meleya stated.

"You sure? The Hearth is paying and an upgrade never hurts. Do not be fooled by the building's appearance, this really is one of the finest craftswomen in the whole city."

"I am certain. Any other piece of steel would be a downgrade from my beloved sword."

"Very well. Shopkeeper, show me your finest axes!" Preza exclaimed.

Zeya looked around at the many weapons of great quality hanging on the walls. It was surprising just how high-end the weaponry was in contrast to the building's exterior. She glimpsed a weapons case containing daggers and approached it. One set, in particular, caught her eye. The grips were a deep crimson that tapered down to the pommel. The pommel itself held a highly polished silver leaf. The double-edged blades glistened in the waning sunlight that flooded through the nearby window. Zeya lifted the glass cover on the case and pulled one of the daggers out, admiring it.

"True blades for a selfa," the shopkeeper said. "Those were a special order made many years ago. Unfortunately, Selfa Ineila fell in battle before she had a chance to carry them."

"They are incredibly well made," said Zeya as she balanced the dagger on the tip of her finger."

"Aye, put my heart and soul into those blades, I did. Was tempted to remove the leaf on the pommel, just so I could sell them without the emblem of the Selfa, but somehow, I never could. It just didn't seem right. They were made for one such as you, Selfa Zeya." The shopkeeper gave Zeya a slight bow.

"Well, I think we've all found what we came for," Preza said. "Shopkeeper, can you have them polished, honed, and delivered to the Hearth by the morning?"

"Of course."

"Excellent. Now, if you'll excuse us, I need a drink!"

"Selfa Zeya, if you can spare one more moment of your time?" the shopkeeper asked.

Zeya looked at Preza, who shrugged. "Yes, what is it?"

"Forgive my asking, but is there to be a Venery? Will we finally have another man who will provide the Sisterhood with the seed to strengthen our numbers?"

Zeya studied the tradeswoman, seeing the shimmer of hope in her eyes that was so common in all the sisters who spoke to her. "Unfortunately, I am unable to discuss official matters of the Hearth at this time." The shopkeeper's face showed obvious disappointment at the response. "However, I will say that it is unlikely that the Hearth would have the need to outfit us with such exemplary weaponry if our business was not of the greatest import."

The shopkeeper smiled. "Thank you, Selfa Zeya. May Vesta guide your path and see you safely back from your journey. Alé volás, Sister."

The three left the weapon shop and continued down the street until they reached the lively Pleasure District. Shouts and jeers of jubilation could be heard coming from the nearby taverns, many overflowing with patrons. The exterior crowds were so jumbled, it was difficult to tell which establishment they were patronizing. Eventually, they reached Preza's favorite, Reigart's Embrace. While it was not nearly as bustling as the others in the area, the tavern still had a good number of patrons inside. As they approached the door, they were stopped by a comely young woman, who was obviously a chamber companion.

"Evening, sisters, interested in a lick?" the woman asked.

Preza smiled. "Maybe after dinner, Love. I'm starving."

"What about the two of you?" The woman paused, noticing Zeya's silver leaf pin. "First one's free, for the Selfa."

"Perhaps another time," Zeya answered.

"Shame. Never been with a selfa before, and I'd have loved to feel that Vesta's Flame you got inside you."

Zeya smiled politely before the three of them entered Reigart's Embrace, and Preza quickly pushed her way through to the bar.

"Barkeep, three pours of your best mead, and as much mutton as you can spare!" Preza turned and looked at Zeya and Meleya expectantly. "Well, aren't you going to order anything?"

"We'll just have some wine, thank you, barkeep," Meleya answered.

Zeya always had to hold back laughter anytime she witnessed Preza outside of the Hearth. Although both Preza's dedication and duty to the Sisterhood were unwavering, once she was off-duty and loosened her buckles, she really loosened them.

They ate their meals mostly in silence, but it wasn't long before more eyes began to take notice of Vesta's Leaf pinned to Zeya's breast. She cringed when the word selfa finally reached her ears.

"Pay them no heed, Wombsister," Meleya said, noticing Zeya's discomfort. "The sight of you simultaneously fills their hearts with hope and gloom, but I doubt any will approach you with inquiries of your business."

"I know," Zeya replied. "Still, I do not like to look upon the faces of those I will disappoint if I fail."

"Hey!" Preza roared abruptly. "Have ya never seen a selfa before? Vesta's tit! If ya used your eyes to watch for the next male instead of gawking at the Selfa, we'd all have a child in our belly by now!"

Startled and somewhat offended by Preza's profane language, the patrons of Reigart's Embrace quickly went back to their drinks and meals.

"That ought to give us peace for a while," Preza stated with a big smile on her ruddy face.

"Ten coin says one of Preza's oral assaults would keep even the Greishic at bay," Meleya teased.

The smile on Preza's face briefly faltered before returning. "Doubtful, Love, but be that as it may, there's only one thing I plan on orally assaulting tonight." Preza's eyes shifted to one of the nearby chamber companions.

"Preza!" Zeya exclaimed in surprise. "Have some subtlety."

Meleya laughed. "She carries a battle axe near as tall as you, and you think she possesses subtlety?"

"I can have it if I desire, but I expect this to be our last night free of subtlety, at least for a while. And I, dear sisters, intend to put it to its proper use," she replied with a chuckle.

"Don't forget, we'll be passing through Solren in a few days," said Meleya. "They are known for their... hospitality."

"Oh, believe me, I have not forgotten that," Preza replied. "But I doubt I can wait that long. A woman has her needs. So, if you'll excuse me, sisters, I will see you in the morning."

Preza rose from her seat and staggered over to find a companion for the evening.

"Well, guess it's just you and me, Zeya. Up for an evening stroll?"

Even though Zeya did not much feel like it, she did not want to disappoint Meleya and agreed.

The two wombsisters left the tavern, and the brisk night air sent a shiver through Zeya. Meleya guided them away from the noisy crowds until they reached an overlook that offered a scenic view of nearly the entire city, including the Hearth. Even though she resided there, the sight of the Hearth never ceased to amaze Zeya. She stared at the building for a long while, its color-less walls gleaming, even in the waxing moonlit night. The massive dome-shaped structure stood at the center of Vulna, demonstrating to all the strength of the Sisterhood. Adjacent to the Hearth, the spiraling tower of the Aviary rose high enough to loom over the city. Zeya remembered visiting the Aviary once with her mother. She had never ascended so many steps in her life. Her legs ached for days after that journey. All because her mother insisted she learn of the divebirds and how the Sisterhood communicated. After they had finally reached the top, her senses had been accosted not only by a cacophony of cries from the birds but also from the unpleasant stench emanating from their droppings. After that, Zeya saw no reason to ever make the climb to the Aviary again.

"You've been pretty quiet since you were given the missive. How are you feeling?" Meleya asked.

"Fine, just overwhelmed by the surprise today, that is all."

"Are you certain? You appear to be holding something back."

"Yes, dear Wombsister, I am sure."

"I am glad of it. And it was a surprise, wasn't it? We've known for so long what fate would befall us, and yet, my mind was not as prepared as I thought. Do you think you'll be able to find the next buck?"

"I hope to Vesta I will. Assuming he even is in Rolier."

"I am sorry, Wombsister. All this talk and I forget, the weight of the Venery surely pulls heavier on your heart than it does on mine."

Zeya hesitated before meeting her wombsister's eyes. "Think nothing of it, Meleya. I do wonder though, do you think we will survive this journey?"

"I cannot say with certainty. Just thinking of crossing the Greenwood fills my mind with all the horrors I've heard concerning the Greishic." Meleya paused. "Still, Preza has fought against the Greishic before, and she appeared confident in our ability to make it through."

"True. Regardless, I do feel safe knowing that you and Preza are joining me."

"Don't forget, Wombsister. Preza and I feel safe knowing your blades travel with us as well."

"Thank you." Zeya looked at her wombsister somberly. "Although, I think I would feel much safer if we had a fourth traveling with us." She then smiled mischievously. "Do you think Preza would be willing to invite her chamber companion on the Venery too?"

Meleya laughed loudly. "Oh, Zeya, you jest, but I would not be surprised if she did! But as for a fourth, do not forget, we will also have Heyfic with us."

"I was not certain if you intended to bring him."

"I do," she replied. "Besides, if I tried to leave him behind, he'd tear free from his cage and come find me anyway."

Zeya smiled, "It'll be good to have him around. That I can say for sure."

III

The Venery

The following morning, the three sisters stood in the courtyard of the Hearth, making their final preparations for the Venery. It would take many days to reach Rolier, and that time could be extended if they faced any significant delay. Attempting to avoid the Greishic in the Greenwood would undoubtedly be an obstacle, but Zeya hoped it wouldn't add too much time to their journey.

Zeya slipped her leather cuirass over her head and tightened its buckles, then did the same with her bracers. The leather armor would provide moderate protection against Greishic claws, and any other wild creatures they may face on their journey. She shifted her body, feeling the broken-in cuirass move comfortably with her. Satisfied, she inserted Vesta's Leaf into its designated location on her armor and fastened it. Zeya looked up at her wombsister who stood near her horse, feeding Heyfic.

Perched on the saddle of Meleya's horse, the large dark-feathered hawk had been Meleya's companion for nearly ten years. The two were nearly inseparable. Meleya and Zeya had found him one day while exploring a nearby cliffside in the wilds. He had been wounded and was splayed out on a rock, helpless as the carrion eaters moved in. Meleya quickly scared them off, brought him back to the Hearth, and nursed him to health. From that time onward, he would become agitated if they were apart for too long.

Eventually, the shopkeeper entered the courtyard, pulling a cart behind her. "Apologies for my tardiness," she said. "The streets are crowded this morning." The shopkeeper reached into her cart and pulled out a large, cloth-wrapped battle axe and handed it to Preza. She then gave a box with an intricate carving of Vesta's Leaf to Zeya.

Zeya looked at the box, taking her time to appreciate the craftsmanship of the carving. It matched the silver leaf on her breast nearly identically. She opened the box and took out her new daggers. They were gorgeous. Far more now than when she initially saw them at the shop. They glimmered, even in the early morning light that filtered through the gray skies.

"Thank you, shopkeeper. These blades are some of the finest my eyes have ever looked upon. They will surely be a boon on this journey," Zeya stated, while binding the daggers' sheaths to her belt.

The shopkeeper bowed deeply. "I am honored to have even a small part to play on the Venery, my Selfa."

Preza grunted nearby, as she flourished her new axe through the air, feeling its weight. She swung it in what appeared to be an uncontrolled and thoughtless motion, but Zeya knew from experience that Preza always maintained strict control over her weapon, and it was foolish to think otherwise.

"Still the best weapon's craftswoman in all of Vulna," Preza declared in admiration.

"I thank you for your compliment, Sister," the shopkeeper replied. "I pray that my weapons will help protect you all on your journey, wherever it may lead." The shopkeeper bowed again and exited the courtyard with a smile.

A short time later, the door to the Hearth opened, and all four members of the Jurisa appeared. A group of venaren accompanied Freila, Gilza, Cereila, and Sieyna. The Jurisa approached the three sisters and looked them over.

"My daughters, I am proud of you," Freila said. "You not only possess the look of preparedness, but also the look of confidence. Precisely what you will need to succeed on the Venery."

"Sisters," Gilza began, "you are about to embark on what will not only be the most important journey of your lives, but also the most challenging. Go now and do the will of the Sisterhood. Retrieve the male hidden in Rolier and bring him back to us. He may truly be our final hope. May Vesta see you swiftly and safely through the Greenwood."

"Thank you, Mother Gilza," Zeya stated as she bowed. "We will do our best to find the male and bring him back to the Hearth."

"Your best? Child, do not use such indefinite language in the presence of the Jurisa, nor in the presence of the Sisterhood." Gilza looked at Zeya, her faded eyes full of chastisement. "You *will* find the male, and you *will* bring him back to the Hearth."

"Yes, apologies, Mother Gilza. We *will* bring him back to the Hearth."

"See that you do, Child."

Freila stepped forward and gave Zeya a firm hug. During the embrace, she whispered so softly into Zeya's ear, no one else could hear. "I know you will, and I know you will save us all." Her mother released her and moved on to embrace Meleya. "Daughter, I know it is your duty to protect your wombsister for the Sisterhood, but please, also see that you protect yourself for me."

"I will, Mother."

"And Preza, I have no doubt you will guide and guard them well. See that you also keep yourself safe." Freila paused, looking up at Preza who stood tall before her. "My heart is filled with pride. Pride of the powerful and determined woman you have become. Were your mother still here, I know she would feel it as well."

Preza bowed her head. "Thank you, Mother Freila."

Freila walked over to Meleya's horse and held a piece of dried meat out to Heyfic, who accepted it graciously. Petting the dark-plumed hawk, she spoke to it, "You, Heyfic, may your umber eyes be ever-watchful, and your golden beak ever-keen." The hawk bobbed its head as it swallowed the meat. He then let out a loud screech, showing his appreciation.

"Very well," Gilza said, turning to the courtyard gate that led out into the city. "Sisters, open the gate!"

Loud cheering erupted from outside the courtyard as soon as the gate began to open. Zeya stared in amazement at the massive crowd of sisters that lined the road before her. There were thousands of them. It seemed nearly every sister in the city was present. She mounted her horse and nudged it forward. Preza and Meleya followed her.

"I guess word got out," Preza stated in awe.

"The shopkeeper, you think?" Meleya asked.

"No, she is trustworthy. My guess is one of the venaren. Or maybe one of the Hearth's servants," replied Preza.

"All these sisters are here for us?" Zeya asked, still in shock.

"For you, Wombsister. For the Venery."

Zeya halted her horse and stared at the crowd in hesitation. The crowd grew quiet, and Zeya realized in horror that they expected her to speak. She took a hurried breath and nudged her horse forward into the city, hoping her movement would quell any calls for a speech. The crowd cheered even louder than before at the sight of her entering the streets, on her way to the Venery. She felt panic. She wanted to turn her horse around and flee right back into the Hearth. Her senses were inundated by both the sight of the crowd and by the cheers that erupted from it. Suddenly, a dark shape soared past her as Heyfic flew above the city, screeching as the crowd began to chant.

"Hail, the Selfa! Hail, the Sisterhood! Hail, the Venery!"

Many called to her, wishing her well, asking her questions, but she continued onward, careful to keep both her eyes and her horse on the path toward the city gate. The crowd seemed endless. The multitude of sisters began to fall in behind her as she passed them, following her to the city gate.

"Steady, Wombsister." Zeya jerked her head left, startled at the nearness of the voice. Meleya had moved up alongside her.

"Your first trial," Preza said, flanking her on the right.

"This is... madness!" Zeya exclaimed.

"Do not worry, I doubt they'll follow us all the way to Rolier," chuckled Meleya. "And if they do, they'll offer great protection from the Greishic."

"How should I..." Zeya trailed off.

"Sit straighter in your saddle. Let your body do the talking," replied Preza. "They have only come to witness the Selfa embarking on the Venery. Do not show concern. Project confidence."

Zeya did as Preza advised. Sitting straight did help her feel more confident, though she wasn't sure if she was projecting it as much as she should be. Her heart continued to race faster and faster. These were them. These were the sisters whose faces would darken with contempt and despair if she were to fail the Venery. She looked ahead, just a short distance more to the city gate. Hearing another screech overhead, she looked up and saw Heyfic, circling above. He swooped down and landed atop the city gate. The gate opened as they approached, and upon crossing the threshold, Zeya felt herself let out a breath she hadn't realized she had been holding. The crowd did not follow beyond the gate, thank Vesta, and eventually, the cheers died as they moved further from the city.

* * *

Freila stood with the other Jurisa on one of the upper levels of the Hearth. She witnessed the crowd that went all the way to the city gate, but could barely make out her daughters since their figures blurred with that of the masses. Freila began to wonder if she had made the right choice in having them sent on this journey. It would undoubtedly be full of hardship, and they would not return the same women, if they were to return at all. She concluded there was no use in worrying about it now. Plans were in motion, and what would come to pass would come to pass.

"Such hope fills the city of Vulna," Sieyna said. "May the Venery not fail."

"Do we know who spread word of the Selfa's departure?" Cereila asked.

"No," replied Freila, still looking out at the crowd in awe.

"Though in the past, we have found it best for the Selfa to sneak out quietly, this inordinate display has certainly boosted the morale of the city," observed Gilza.

"Better for the Sisterhood to be optimistic than the alternative," replied Sieyna. "Hope breeds tranquility. Still, if this Venery fails, the backlash will be disastrous. Many more years without a buck to provide us with his seed will no doubt cause the masses to rise up in revolt and drag us screaming to the gallows. I am not sure about any of you, but I would like to keep my gullet intact."

"Selfa Zeya seemed rather shaken at the beginning of the Venery," Cereila commented.

"She did," replied Gilza. "Not a great start for her, or for us."

Freila finally broke her gaze from the spectacle and turned to face the other women. "She was caught greatly off guard by the crowd. Zeya is young and has not fully grown sure of herself. However, Meleya will not allow Zeya to give up or give in to thoughts of hopelessness. She will be a guiding force that will see them to Rolier and back. Likewise, Preza will protect the two until her death. There is no horde of Greishic that will cause her to turn tail and abandon her sisters. So long as they are with each other, they will not fail."

"Good," replied Gilza. "Now, let us discuss our plans for the male once he is returned to us. After all, getting him here is only one portion of the great obstacle the Sisterhood must surmount."

"We must send only the most trustworthy of soldiers to meet them when they disembark from the Yeren on the return journey. Better not to risk a sister trying to take the male for her own," Freila said.

"Any estimates of his age?" asked Cereila.

"Impossible to say for certain," Freila replied. "My source was not specific with that information. If he is from Yareil's seed, he could be as young as fifteen. However, I would think it difficult for a ripened male to be hidden from the Sisterhood for so long. There is always the possibility that the mother's womb was blessed by the goddess, and she was allowed to carry him without the seed of a man, as was written in the days of old. If that is the case, then we may yet have a few years before he ripens."

"Regardless," Gilza began, "we must keep him safe and secure until we are ready to harvest his seed. We should be mindful not to drain him too quickly. The last male gave us fewer than thirty years of seed. We must do everything we can to ensure this one endures longer. We cannot fail in our duty. It will be difficult for the Sisterhood to survive if we are forced to wait another fifteen years before a new male is found."

"We may not have another fifteen years, much less thirty," Sieyna replied. "The Greishic's numbers continue to grow. We need a new generation of sisters, and we need them soon. I say milk him for all he's got and get as many sisters with child as we can."

"It is a balance, Sieyna," responded Freila. "We must manage this resource wisely."

"And if the Greishic overtake us then who will there be to manage this resource? This male should be a stopgap. We only need him to quickly produce another and then we can continue to increase our numbers as the Sisterhood has done in all the generations before us."

"Sieyna, your assumption is that he will produce another male soon. Historically, that is very rare," Freila replied.

"Truly," Gilza replied. "Let us hope to Vesta that this time will be different."

IV

Vesta's Flame

A day's journey later, Zeya finally felt the fear of failure beginning to subside. Save for the occasional traveler, the road was mostly empty once they left Vulna. This allowed Zeya to focus her mind away from the magnitude of the task at hand. She took some time to admire the beauty of the wilds that surrounded them. It was near sundown, and the day's light filled the world with a serene glow. The road to Solren would see them through a lush plain, containing a diversity of plant and animal life. Beyond the plain lay the Sol Forest, its dense trees provided a bounty of resources to both Vulna and Solren. Zeya had never traveled beyond the edges of the forest, so she was looking forward to finally passing through it.

"Probably best we set up camp for the night," Preza called. "No use fumbling around in the dark trying to find wood."

"A fire sounds lovely," replied Meleya. "The air is beginning to chill already."

"A bit of timber gathering should warm you up then. Thank you for volunteering. Zeya and I will tie off the horses and set up camp."

"Hey, last I checked, it was Zeya, not Preza leading the Venery. Zeya, what say you?"

"Well, I would hate for you to be cold, dear Wombsister. Probably best you go and find us some wood!" Zeya laughed.

"Fine, fine, I am going." Meleya dismounted and stormed off in mock anger.

"The days are certainly getting colder," remarked Preza. "I wonder if we'll see snow on this journey. I hope not."

"Indeed. The last thing we need is something else to slow our progress."

Preza looked at Zeya, studying her. "Aside from being unable to find the male, what worries you most about the Venery, Zeya?"

"I am unsure if I have an answer for that. The risk of being killed or captured by Greishic weighs somewhat on my mind, but I haven't given it much thought. There have been other concerns up until now."

"Getting taken by a Greishic should be at the forefront. If that happens, we will fail. I suggest you prioritize your fears. At least that will help turn your mind from thoughts of failing to find the male."

"You really know how to make a girl feel better, don't you?"

"I am not on this journey to placate your fears. I am on this journey to make sure you survive. The rest is up to you," Preza replied.

"I know, Sister. I appreciate your words, I am sure they will help, somehow."

After Meleya returned with the wood and got a fire going, the three women reclined on their bedrolls. They sat in silence, absorbing the warmth and staring into the flame, mesmerized by the sparking embers that crackled and rose toward the sky. Heyfic too, who was nestled alongside Meleya, gazed deeply into the fire.

"How are you feeling, Zeya?" asked Meleya after some time.

"Warm now, thanks."

"No, I meant concerning the Venery. I imagine the shock of all of Vulna turning out to see you depart has worn off by now."

"It has, mostly. I do not think I will ever forget the faces of all the sisters filled with so much hope and joy."

"They will be far more joyous when we return with the male," Preza stated.

"Yes, when we return," Zeya repeated softly.

"Do not worry, Wombsister. You have Vesta's Flame within you. Being blessed by the goddess surely will count for something," Meleya replied, noticing the nervousness on Zeya's face.

"It will if I still possess it," she replied. "I have not felt Vesta's Pull since the night I became a selfa."

Meleya nodded. "I remember that night well, but it would be great to hear the story again. I doubt we'll have a better time for it."

"I too would like to hear it," Preza said. "I have never heard it first-hand, only from your mother."

"It was a few years after Father... after Yareil died. I remember waking up in the middle of the night to a sensation overwhelming my entire body. It felt as though there was a fire blazing in my chest. My body felt hot, not as if I was taken by fever, but as if someone had placed a piece of burning coal inside me. It was strange though, it did not hurt. I could feel the heat, but no pain.

"I rose from my bed, unable to tolerate the discomfort any longer, and moved to lay on the cold chamber floor in an effort to alleviate the heat. It was then that Meleya awoke, and I remember seeing her peer over the edge of her bed quizzically. I cannot blame her. I must have looked absurd lying on the stone floor at such a late hour.

'Zeya? What is wrong?' she asked.

'I don't know, I feel hot like there is something burning inside me.'

She climbed down from her bed and touched my forehead gently with her hand. 'You do not feel at all hot to my touch, Wombsister.'

'But I do! All over my body, it feels like I am circled with fire, inside and out!'

'Zeya, your eyes! They are shining blue!'

"It was then that I felt the Pull. I rose up, barely aware of my actions, and began stumbling toward the chamber door. I remember Meleya grabbing me, trying to hold me back.

'Zeya, where are you going? And your eyes, why did they change?'

'I... I have to find it.'

'Find what? Wombsister, you are worrying me. You are not acting yourself. Please stay here while I get Mother.'

"After Meleya left, I tried to stay, I really did, but I couldn't. The Pull was too great. Something was calling to me. I couldn't hear it, but I could feel it. I opened the chamber door and blundered out into the hall. The Pull lessened slightly as I began making my way to the Hearth's western exit. I reached it and was about to open the large door to the city when someone grabbed me from behind. Startled, I twisted around and saw my mother, her eyes filled with concern.

'Zeya, what is wrong? Why are you wandering the hall in the middle of the night?'

'I don't know, Mother. I feel as if something is tugging at my heart, telling me I need to go, telling me I need to leave the Hearth.'

"I was surprised that my mother simply nodded and bowed her head gently, 'Zeya, you must follow what you feel in your heart, you mustn't ignore it. You have been chosen. Follow the Pull wherever it may lead you. Meleya and I will wait for you here.' She then bent down and kissed my forehead. 'Alé volás, my daughter.'

"I wanted to ask her many questions, but the feeling inside was overwhelming and all I could do was follow its draw. I went through the door and out into the city. It was so tranquil at the late hour. I did not see any sisters until I reached the West Gate. There were two guards on duty, and one of them stopped me.

'Where are you off to so late, Little Sister?'

'I must... I must go out into the wilds. I feel something is calling to me. My mother said I should follow it.'

'Oh, your mother did, did she? Tell me, who is your mother? She should know better than to let such a young sister out on her own so late at night.'

"I hesitated, I did not want Mother to get in trouble. But then I realized she was more important to the Sisterhood than this guard was, and this guard could not have my mother punished.

'My mother is Freila of the Hearth,' I said defiantly. The guard stood straight in surprise. She looked as if she wanted to question me further, but then decided against it and signaled the other guard to let me pass.

"I continued through the gate and onward into the wilds. The light of the moon lit the wilds enough for me to find my way, but it didn't matter. I was not using my eyes to find the path. It was not long before I sensed my destination. A large outcropping of boulders, not far from the city, is where I was being led. I approached the large stones carefully and felt the Pull begin to subside. After searching the area for some time, I began to lose heart. The sensation had weakened, and there was nothing of note among the rocks. I began to turn back toward Vulna, deciding whatever had called me here had left. But the moment I turned to leave, I felt the Pull strengthen once more. My body seemed to move without my permission, almost as if I was being dragged. I did not resist, and eventually, my feet took me to one of the boulders that was encircled by all manner of brush. I hadn't noticed before, but there was a gentle wind escaping from the rock. Crouching to the ground, I realized there was a hole partially obstructed by the foliage. It was just large enough for me to fit through, so I moved the brush aside and slipped into the opening.

"I was surprised the cave was not at all dark inside. There was a faint red glow that was bright enough for me to see by, and I had no trouble moving through it. I soon realized the origin of the red light and the source of the Pull were the same. I continued forward, the light growing more brilliant with each step. Finally, I reached the chamber which held the source. Within its center, there was a depiction of a woman, carved in stone, standing with both arms out, as if she desired to envelop me in an embrace. In her left hand, she held a ball of red flame, and its radiance burned so bright that I could not look directly at it. In her right, she held the emblem of the Selfa, the silver leaf.

"It was then that I understood. It was the goddess, Vesta. She had awoken me in the middle of the night, calling me to this holy place. I felt drawn to the silver leaf and cautiously approached the statue. I knew she held it in offering to me, and I knew I needed to accept it. I reached forth, took hold of the emblem, and pulled. Vesta's Leaf came loose easily, but the moment it was free from Vesta's grasp, a roaring wind reached my ears, then my body. I stumbled back and fell to the ground. Looking up at the statue of Vesta one final time, I witnessed the red flame in her hand transform to a blue flame, then suddenly go out. I screamed as darkness overwhelmed me.

"The next thing I remember was waking outside near the outcropping. I wasn't certain how much time had passed, but the sun was beginning to rise on the horizon. A dream. The cave, the statue, the flame, that was the first thought I had. But before I could settle on this conclusion, I realized I held something in my hand. I looked down and saw, clenched between my fingers, Vesta's Leaf."

They all sat in silence for a while before Preza spoke. "Pit. And you don't know how you got out of the cave?"

"No, I have no memory of traversing back through the cave. None at all."

"That is..." Preza trailed off. "That is quite a story. I have never been one of Vesta's faithful servants, but if anything like that ever happened to me, I'd go immediately to her nearest temple, abandon my worldly possessions, and sing her songs of praise until I was surrounded by more men than the number of stars in the sky."

"I don't know, Preza," Meleya replied. "I've heard you sing, and if that's what you have to offer the goddess, she is certainly better off without it."

"Your words wound me, Meleya. I have been practicing day and night as of late, would you care to hear?"

"Vesta, no!" blurted Meleya.

"Pity. I was going to sing a ballad I wrote about you, I call it, Meleya the Homely Hag."

Zeya laughed. "It sounds beautiful."

"It would be, if only I was permitted to sing!"

"You may serenade me after we find the male," scoffed Meleya.

"I shall hold you to that," Preza replied with a smirk. "Say, what were you doing while Zeya was off cave-diving for the goddess' treasure?"

"Very little, just sick with worry waiting for her return. I remember begging and pleading with Mother to let me go with Zeya. I could not understand why she would let her travel out on her own. I tried to explain to Mother that it was not safe for Zeya to be alone so late at night. I told her over and over until tears and sobs took my words. Mother just repeated again and again that this was something Zeya had to do on her own. This was for her and her alone.

"Being unable and unwilling to sleep, I stayed in Mother's bedchamber the rest of the night, my heart filled with worry. I did not fully understand until Zeya returned the next morning, holding *that.*" She pointed at the silver leaf pinned to Zeya's chest. "And here I always thought I would be the one to be Blessed and take up the title of Selfa."

"Though you were unable to be with me then," replied Zeya, "I am glad you are with me now. You too, Preza. I know I would have no chance of succeeding on this journey without the two of you."

"Well," Preza replied gruffly, "that's enough plucking heartstrings for one night, sisters."

Preza rolled over and pulled her blanket tight around her, falling asleep quickly. Zeya lay in her bedroll, eyes wide open, staring up at the night sky. She wondered how things would be if Meleya had been the one chosen by Vesta, instead of her. She supposed, if that were the case, the male would not only have already been found, but he would have been safe back at the Hearth as well. Regrettably, it was Zeya and not her wombsister that was Blessed.

V

The Village of Rolier

Keila lived on the outskirts of Rolier. She enjoyed the solitude her hut provided her, away from the hustle and bustle of the village. Not that Rolier was a busy village, but she never liked how most of the sisters of the village stared at her accusingly whenever she went out, almost as if she was the source of all their difficulty. She was a resident, same as them. While she may have originally come from Vulna, that should have no bearing on her right to live here. In her younger years, she had made a living as a carpenter in the capital. While she still enjoyed woodworking, she had grown weary of pouring her heart and soul into a magnificent piece only to have it be rejected by an empty-headed customer. Thankfully, in her retirement, she did not have to deal with commissions or patrons.

Keila was returning home from her weekly trip to the village market, humming and swinging the basket containing the day's purchases. She loved the location of her hut. There were only a few neighbors to deal with, and they typically ignored her. Well, most of them ignored her.

Keila entered her hut and headed for the kitchen. Reaching inside her basket, she pulled out a variety of fruits and began to crush them. "Mashing, mashing, mashing," she sang softly to herself. "Soft and smooth and pure, no chunks, no chunks." She scraped the puréed substance into a bowl. "It is now perfect for—" Her singing was interrupted by a knock at the door.

"Keila? I saw you come home, do you have a moment to chat?" asked the voice at the door.

It was Heleila. It was *always* Heleila. The one neighbor that just would not let her live in peace. She did not hate Heleila, in fact, she rather liked her. The woman often had compelling news to share, or at the very least, she kept Keila up to date on the comings and goings of the village. The problem was, Heleila always wanted to chat, and her chats were never brief. The woman could ramble on and on if no one attempted to stop her, and even when someone did, the woman did not always comprehend a subtle request to leave. Oftentimes, very blunt words were necessary to cull the incessant speech.

"A moment, please!" Keila set her fruit aside and looked around the inside of her single room hut. Everything was neat and orderly, as usual. Everything but her bed. Keila had spent a lot of time constructing her bed, and she had spent even more carving the intricate design into its posts. It was truly a work of art, possibly her masterpiece. But for some reason, her bed was never right. She moved over to it and straightened the coverlet. She lifted the pillow, fluffed it, replaced it, and then picked it up and fluffed it again, multiple times. After finally returning the cushion to her bed, she attempted to smooth the wrinkles from it. Keila was not entirely satisfied with the result, but she could see Heleila looking impatient through her front window. She took a deep breath, then went to the door and opened it.

"Heleila, what a pleasant surprise!" she exclaimed with all the false excitement she could muster.

"Hello, dear Sister! How are things?" Heleila asked, leaning on her cane. The woman had mangled her leg long ago, and it had never healed correctly.

"Oh, nothing worthy of note. I went to the market today and bought some fruit."

"It's been such a great harvest this year, the fruit has been far more succulent than usual!" Heleila paused, looking inside the hut. "Do you mind if I come in?"

Keila hesitated. If she let the woman in, there was no telling how long she would stay.

"I will not be long, heart to Vesta. I just heard some grand news and wanted to share it with you."

"Oh, of course! Sorry, I did not intend to be rude! Come right in." Keila moved away from the doorway and allowed Heleila to pass through. After closing the door, Keila turned to face her visitor and had to quickly stifle her anger as she saw that the woman was sitting on *her* bed.

"Thank you, I've been out all day, and heart to Vesta, my leg sure is acting up! I don't know if it is from the weather, or what! Sometimes I think about moving closer to the village, have you ever considered it? If I moved closer it would certainly be easier for me to get around, but of course, I like my privacy!"

"Not really, I like my peace as well. You said you had news?"

"Ah, yes, I sure do!" Heleila exclaimed and bounced on the bed in excitement. The sudden movement caused Keila's pillow to fall to the floor. "Oh, sorry, Dear." Heleila bent down to pick up the pillow.

"No!" Keila snapped, before catching herself. "I mean, I would not want to cause your leg additional discomfort." Keila bent down, picked up the pillow, and set it on the nearby table.

"Thank you. So, the news. Well today, I was talking with Mitilza, and do you know what she told me? She told me she received a divebird from Memier carrying an exciting message, and do you know what this message said? Well, according to her, the message said Memier received a different message from the Hearth, and *that* message told her that they should expect a selfa soon! Exciting, is it not? A selfa coming to the Eastern Plateau! Why, I don't think that has happened in nearly a generation! It would be so great to get to see one of Vesta's Blessed, wouldn't it?"

The revelation surprised Keila. A selfa crossing the Greenwood? That could only mean one thing, the Venery. The Hearth would not risk sending a selfa through Greishic lands otherwise. "Did Mayor Mitilza say where the Selfa's journey would end? Do you think she'll come here, to our humble village?"

"I asked that very question! You and I really do think alike, that's why I enjoy your company so much. Why, just the other day I very nearly got in an argument at the market because the vendor thought I was stealing! Can you imagine? Me stealing! It was all a misunderstanding of course, but—"

"What was her response?" interrupted Keila. The woman would have rambled on for ages.

"Oh, the message did not state the Selfa's final destination. I supposed they did not want to panic whoever may be hiding the male, assuming there is a male, and this is not all just born from desperation. I doubt the Selfa will come to our humble village, though. More likely she'll be ending the Venery in Memier, or maybe even Coratch. I know everyone in this village quite well, and no one seems the type to hide a male! Can you imagine, though? And if there was one? All this time, under my very nose! Imagine! But I'm sure the male is being hidden in one of the bigger cities. Those sisters in Coratch barely have any respect for the Sisterhood, who knows, maybe they've been producing children this whole time! I wouldn't put it past them."

"I find it hard to believe no one in all of Coratch would have reported such a defiance to the Sisterhood."

"True, true. But you never know! Some sisters live only to serve their own interests and desires. Not all are true to Vesta's teachings like you and I."

"Well, Heleila, please let me know if you hear anything else. I would very much like to know the road the Selfa might take."

"As would I! And don't worry, Sister, I most certainly will, I do hope they find the male. It is a real shame that so many ripe sisters of today have not had the honor of bearing children. It has been so long since the last one, I bet their wombs are just crying out for a child! I know my daughter, Vesta bless her, just cannot wait to fulfill her duty to the Sisterhood and bear four, five, maybe even six children!"

"How is Aadeya?"

"Oh, Aady's doing excellent as of late, very few fits, I think the new concoction I have been giving her is helping tremendously. Thank you for asking. I have even started allowing her outside our hut on occasion. Sunshine is good for a woman her age, it truly is. She's been cooped up in our small hut for so long, the poor thing, I fear she may be going mad! Why, just the other day I awoke to see her standing over my bed, I shouted from the fright! I thought she was an apparition, can you imagine? Imagine waking up to a figure standing over you. I don't even remember what she wanted, I was so startled!"

"I appreciate the news you brought me, Heleila, but unfortunately, I should be returning to dinner."

"Oh, I did not mean to interrupt your meal! By all means, please continue. I will leave you now."

The woman slowly rose, leaning heavily on her cane until she stood fully. She hobbled over to the door, and Keila quickly moved to open it for her. Once on the porch, Heleila turned to Keila one last time.

"You know, if my daughter's fits continue to abate, we would love to have you over for dinner. Poor thing barely gets any interaction with anyone who is not me! Imagine! Being stuck inside all day and having no one to talk to but me!"

"I would love to. Please let me know when the time comes. Thank you for the visit, Heleila. Goodnight." Keila quickly closed the door, hoping that would end the conversation. It did not.

"Oh, the pleasure was all mine," she said through the closed door. "We should do this again soon. I always have such an exquisite time visiting with you! And I'll mention it to Aady, about you visiting."

Keila listened through the door for Heleila's fading footsteps, and eventually decided it was safe to return to the fruit. She walked past her table to the kitchen, picked up the bowl of mashed fruit, and carefully took it over to her bed.

VI

Tales in the Forest

Zeya yawned loudly. She had not gotten very much sleep the night before. She tried to convince herself it was from sleeping outside on the ground instead of in her comfortable bed back at the Hearth, but she knew that wasn't it. The fear of failure grew with each passing day. No matter how much she tried to ignore it, she could not. Even when she did manage to fall asleep, she was tormented by waking dreams. She always woke up tired. It didn't matter how many times she told herself that everything would work out in the end, or how she tried to remind herself that plenty of Veneries had ended in failure before. Nothing eased her mind enough to provide her with restful slumber. She wondered if the other selfas carried this burden, and if it stayed with them long after the Venery had failed. She knew she should be feeling hopeful and excited for the opportunity to save the Sisterhood, but instead, her heart was filled with dread.

They were crossing through the Sol Forest, and its large coniferous trees filtered out much of the early morning light. Riding along, her eyes began to feel heavy. She attempted to keep them open, since drifting off on horseback was never wise, but eventually, the soothing clop, clop rhythm of the horses got to her and her eyes drooped closed. Suddenly, a distant sound snapped her fully awake.

"What was that?" she asked the others.

"What?" asked Meleya.

"A scream, didn't you hear it?"

Preza turned in her saddle and looked at Zeya. "I heard nothing. Did you, Meleya?"

"No. Was it animal or human?"

"I couldn't tell, but it sounded like it came from—" The cry came again, this time, unmistakably human.

Preza twisted toward the origin of the sound. "I heard that one. It sounds like someone's in trouble." She turned her horse from the road and rushed deeper into the forest.

As Zeya and Meleya followed, they heard the scream again, this time much closer than before. Soon they reached a clearing and saw a woman lying on the ground near the center. The woman's clothing was stained with fresh blood. They dismounted and sprinted over to her. Meleya crouched and tried to examine the woman's injuries.

"Sister, what happened?" Preza asked.

"Oh, thank Vesta," the woman muttered weakly. "I thought I was going to die here. My wombsister and I were attacked by brigands. We tried to fight them off, but I was wounded, and they carried her further into the forest, down that way." The woman raised her arm with much effort and pointed toward a nearby path. "My wombsister

was not taken very long ago, you can still catch them and save her!"
She winced from the effort of speaking.

Zeya looked over at the path, wanting to follow after the brigands and free the abducted sister, but she knew the delay would not be looked upon with favor by the Hearth. To the Sisterhood, their journey was far more important than the life of one sister. While she felt prepared to take on brigands, she had no idea of their numbers or their abilities in battle. If she were to fall here, so close still to Vulna, she would certainly be lauded as the worst selfa to ever live.

"What is your name, Sister?" Meleya asked.

"I am Loreza. But please, save my wombsister!"

Meleya nodded solemnly. "I am sorry, we cannot. We do not have the time to spare in the pursuit of highwaywomen. We are on an important and time-sensitive journey. We cannot help your wombsister. But what I can do is help with your wounds, and we can escort you to Solren."

"No, please!" Lereza exclaimed. "My wombsister, she is young, not older than fifteen! Vesta only knows what they'll do to her! I beseech you, save her!"

"I am sorry, Sister," Preza replied. "Our quest is from the Hearth itself. We cannot delay. Allow Meleya to tend to your wounds, and we will carry you to our horses."

"Half-witted cows!" The woman lashed out with a concealed dagger toward Meleya's throat. Meleya quickly shot back, barely managing to dodge the tip of the blade. In the confusion, Lereza leapt up and ran to a nearby boulder, drawing a sword that lay hidden behind it. Zeya heard Heyfic screech from overhead in warning as three other women who had been lying in ambush burst out and charged at the party with weapons drawn.

Meleya pulled her sword and moved to challenge Lereza. Preza and Zeya turned to study the advancing women.

"I will take the two on the right," Preza said calmly, pulling her two-handed axe from behind her back.

"Oh, sorry," replied Zeya, who had just launched a dagger pulled from her boot toward their attackers. The knife flew through the air and struck the right-most woman in the chest, sending her to the ground.

Preza sighed, "The *one* on the right, then." She charged forward.

Lereza lunged at Meleya with her sword, but she easily deflected the blow and countered with strike after strike, forcing Lereza to take the defensive. Meleya could tell immediately she greatly outmatched Lereza in terms of skill. The woman was soon gasping for breath as she attempted to block or evade Meleya's attacks. Before Lereza could fully recover from the previous assault, Meleya unleashed another flurry. A few of her strikes drew blood.

"Why would you prey on the kindness of your fellow sisters?" Meleya asked angrily. "Are we not all women of the Sisterhood?"

"We're just trying to survive in this Vesta-forsaken world," Lereza replied between breaths. "Being from the Hearth, I doubt you have ever wanted for anything. The rest of us have to *work* for it!" She leapt toward Meleya in a desperate attempt to land a blow, but Meleya spun and easily avoided the attack. Reversing her grip, she thrust her sword behind her and felt minimal resistance as the sharpened point entered Lereza's flesh.

"Alé volás, Sister," Meleya murmured as Lereza slowly sank to the ground.

Zeya quickly brought her twin daggers up, deflecting her foe's sword. As her enemy faltered from the parry, Zeya moved back and prepared for her attack. Rushing forward on the offensive, she stabbed, twisted, stabbed, twisted, then elbowed her opponent in the face. Stumbling back from the blow, the bandit repositioned herself, preparing for the next assault. The woman's eyes shifted to Zeya's chest and rested on Vesta's Leaf. She stepped back in astonishment and abruptly threw her weapon to the ground. She shouted to her companion to stop fighting. Distracted for a moment, the other bandit barely had time to dodge as Preza's heavy axe came down. Uncertain of what was going on, she too moved back and threw her weapon to the ground.

"Forgive us, we didn't realize you were a selfa! Had we known, we never would've attacked you." The bandit stared at Zeya, her eyes begging for forgiveness.

"That I am a selfa should not matter," Zeya replied. "I am no different from all your victims. I am your sister. How is it you see my life as more valuable than that of any other?"

"Corrupted Hearth or not, we would not dare harm a selfa. You are the only hope we have left in this world."

Preza advanced on the bandits, the adrenaline of battle fueling her anger. "Single-coin whores! Attack any of the Sisterhood and face the wrath of us all!" The two remaining bandits turned and ran, fleeing deeper into the forest. "May your wombs shrivel and fall out!" Preza roared after them.

"Should we follow?" Meleya asked.

"No, we have expended enough time on their ilk," Preza replied, breathing heavily. She began walking back toward her horse.

Zeya approached the woman she had killed with her thrown dagger. She had reacted on instinct when they were charging, she did not really have time to think. It had been her first true kill. Her stomach suddenly felt hollow. Now that the flame of battle was cooling, she realized her first kill had been a sister, not a Greishic. She bent down and slowly pulled her bloodied dagger from the woman's chest, wiped the blade clean, and returned it to the sheath on her boot. She found it difficult to break her gaze from the sister that lay upon the ground.

"It could not be helped, Wombsister," Meleya stated flatly.

"I know, but they were human, they were *sisters*."

Meleya shook her head. "They were enemies of the Sisterhood, enemies who preyed on the compassionate. This world is better off without them in it."

She was right, of course. The world was bad enough with the Greishic and the imminent extinction of the Sisterhood. Brigands and thieves did little but speed up their collective demise, but the thought did little to calm Zeya's heart.

* * *

The party continued along the road until late into the day, and Zeya noticed the forest's density was beginning to diminish, They were almost through the Sol Forest. Another day's journey, and they'd be in Solren. Zeya imagined how good a bath would feel, her bare skin soaking in the heated water of a bathhouse, a soft clean bed. Unfortunately, her fantasy was rudely interrupted as a loud screech from Heyfic sounded overhead.

"More sisters ahead," Meleya said.

"How many?" Preza asked.

Meleya shrugged. "Never could teach Heyfic to count."

Preza grunted.

"Should we get off the road and sneak around them?" Zeya asked. "There may be more brigands in this forest."

"That is up to you, Selfa," replied Preza, "but I think the likelihood of more criminals is low. To be honest, I am surprised we ran into any this close to Vulna. It may be better for us to creep in for a closer look before deciding our action."

Zeya considered this for a moment. The memory of killing one of her sisters was still fresh in her mind, but breaking camp with others loyal to the Sisterhood would certainly lift all their spirits. "Meleya, do you mind scouting?"

"Not at all, I think I hear their voices so they're near. I shall return briefly." She dismounted and headed toward Heyfic's call.

"How are you, Zeya? You've seemed shaken ever since the encounter with the brigands," Preza asked.

"I am well. Those women were enemies of the Sisterhood, they deserved what we gave them," Zeya replied

"Agreed, their mentality threatened the order that we depend upon for our very existence. Still, if I recall, that was your first kill, yes?"

"It was."

"So again, I ask you, how do you feel?"

Zeya hesitated before responding. "It did not strike my mind until after the battle, but I feel that my first kill should have been a Greishic, not a sister."

"I suspected as much, but those women were not our sisters. They forsook the Sisterhood when they chose to prey upon others. The status of respect and love we share with all our sisters did not apply to them."

"Even so, my heart will not swiftly move on from this."

"No. It will not. We all carry our deeds until we fall, and Vesta only knows if we must carry them beyond that. The only advice I can give is that, with time, it does get easier to bear these burdens. I pray we do not have to face more foes who have forsaken the Sisterhood, but if we do, the kills will get easier."

Zeya nodded. Preza's words did not help much, but it was good to know that the guilt she felt for killing another human was to be expected.

"There are five sisters ahead," Meleya stated, returning from her scout. "They are camped out just up the road, I would say violence is unlikely. There are two young sisters and one gammer among them. I must say, they had a cookfire going, and whatever was in the pot possessed the most tantalizing of scents."

"Well, Selfa?" Preza asked expectantly.

"May as well see if they will allow us to camp with them. After the day we've had, some friendly company would be nice."

The three approached the camp, and it wasn't long before Zeya smelled the cooking. Meleya was right, it did smell delicious. Since they had left the Hearth, the party had only been eating bread and dried meat. Whatever was in the camp pot reminded Zeya that their diet, although adequate, was far from gourmet.

"Hail, sisters!" Preza called out.

"Evening!" the old gammer returned with a smile. "We have not passed many travelers on the road, joyous to see some."

"Nice for us as well," Preza replied. "Do you mind if we share your fire?"

"Not at all, not at all. Please, warm yourselves. We just finished our dinner, and there is plenty left. You may help yourself to it if you're hungry."

"We thank you for your generosity, truly," Zeya replied, bowing graciously.

"Think nothing of it, Dear! I would not dream of turning..." The woman trailed off as she noticed Zeya's leaf pin. "Vesta, bless us! We are graced by the company of a selfa!"

Excitement spread through the group as they all took notice of Zeya's pin. She was bombarded with questions concerning the Venery, whether she thought they'd soon have the male, and when they'd be able to have his seed.

"Sisters!" Preza interjected. "Please, allow the Selfa to rest. We have a long journey ahead of us, and she needs every moment of respite available to her."

"Thank you, Preza." Zeya turned to the group. "Unfortunately, I am unable to discuss private matters regarding the Venery or the Hearth, but your excitement fills my heart with joy." Zeya hoped no one sensed her lie. Seeing the faces of the excited young sisters and the hopeful older ones did not supply her heart with joy. It filled it with more dread. More faces she would disappoint if she failed.

"I apologize for the behavior of the young," the elder replied. "We are traveling to Vulna, and never imagined experiencing such elation on the road."

"Think nothing of it," Zeya replied.

"Now please, help yourselves to our stew. May it warm your heart as much as you have warmed ours."

Zeya, Meleya, and Preza gleefully scooped the stew into their bowls and began slurping it down. It tasted even better than its scent implied.

The gammer turned to the others. "Now, who wants to hear the story of Diana's curse?"

"Grandmother!" one of the younger sisters whined. "We've heard the story so many times! Can you tell us a different tale?"

"No, Child, I cannot. This story is the only one you need remember. It is a reminder that going against Vesta's decree will not only bring you to ruin but also bring ruin to us all. A mistake we must never make again."

Everyone reclined in preparation for the story. Although Zeya had also heard this story many times before, she always enjoyed hearing it from someone new. The woman was right, it held great relevance to their lives, assuming it was actually true. It was hard to know how much truth there was in the ancient tales.

The old woman cleared her throat and began, "A time many generations ago, there was at least one man for every woman. Children were being born every day, and no one lived in fear of extinction. It was the man's job to hunt, the man's job to go out and explore, and the man's job to protect his family. Back then, the woman had one significant role. Children. She would grow them in her womb, birth them, and ensure they were fed. That was the extent of a woman's responsibility. She possessed an additional task when it came to her daughters. She was to make sure any daughters learned to do the same until they too came of age and birthed children of their own.

"This cycle continued on and on for many generations, until one day, a daughter named Diana was born. She was the youngest of five, and the only girl. Diana's mother took great care to teach her the traditions, to cook, to clean, and how to accept a man inside of her to produce children. But Diana had no interest in her mother's teachings. She repeatedly begged her father to let her join with her brothers when they went out to hunt, but he always refused.

'A hunt is no place for a woman,' her father would say. 'You must learn to be a nurturing mother to the children you will one day bear.'

"Diana tried to accept her role, she really did. But whenever her father and brothers would go out, her resolve to join them would strengthen. On many occasions, she attempted to follow them into the wilds, but each time she was caught and beaten for her transgression. Diana then tried getting into fights with her brothers to show she could be just as strong as they were. She won once, defeating the youngest of her brothers in what she saw as a fair fight, but her father did not care that she was the victor, only that her brother lost. He dragged her brother off and nearly beat him to death for being so weak that he had allowed a woman to defeat him. It was this that made Diana finally realize that her father would never allow her to do anything but be married off, and so she made the decision to flee into the wilds on her own.

"Diana managed to survive many days in the forest, but after that, was unable to find enough food to sustain herself. She had simply never been taught what was needed to endure in the wilds. Approaching starvation, she relented and returned home. She was welcomed, not with open arms, but with another of her father's beatings.

'Women are only fit for spitting out more sons!' he declared. 'Learn your place, or I'll trade you off the day you ripen, regardless of how trifling the dowry is!'

"A year to that day, Diana began to bleed. She remembered well her father's threat, and so she chose to hide her ripening. She was successful at concealing it for nearly a full year until she was caught by her mother while trying to dispose of a soiled cloth. Diana pleaded with her mother not to tell her father. She tried to convince her that they, as women, needed to fight this unjust cycle. But her mother was too set in tradition, so she immediately told her husband the news. Her father came in with a pleasurable look on his face, for he knew just the husband for her. Old Man Cheros' wife had recently been used up, and he was seeking a new woman with which to bear him more children. It was not long before the arrangements were made, and the day of the ceremonial exchange was set.

"The day before the exchange was to take place, Diana once again fled. She grabbed a bag of sundries that she had been stashing away and left. She hoped she would eventually find another village, one where the men and women would not force her to marry. Unfortunately, her father had anticipated her flight. He had been keeping a close watch on her and sent his sons, her brothers, out after her. Diana ran, she ran as fast as she could, but Diana did not know the wilds like her brothers, for they had been living their whole lives within it. They eventually caught her and tackled her to the ground. This struggle caused her to receive a large and unsightly gash on her face. Her brothers dragged her screaming back to their father as blood still poured from her wound. Upset by her damaged appearance, and fearful Cheros would no longer want to take a blemished bride, her father attempted to postpone the ceremony, hoping that it would give her face time to heal. He approached Cheros with this offer, but Cheros did not accept. He wanted a new wife, and he wanted one now.

"On the day of the ceremony, Diana, her father, and Cheros stood before the altar of Vesta, which contained her sacred blue Flame. Her father apologized for Diana's face, saying it would heal in time. Cheros studied Diana, his gaze lingering on her body for far longer than she was comfortable with, and stated he did not desire to possess her for her face. As long as her body was intact, they could proceed as planned. With no objections between the men, the ceremony continued. Her father spoke the words, as did Cheros, but when it came time for Diana to speak her acquiescence, she refused. She cursed her father, cursed her would-be husband, and most of all, cursed Vesta. Standing before the Blue Flame of Vesta, she swore she would never bear a single child, and especially not this man's.

"Diana continued to rant and blaspheme against the goddess until she was interrupted by a loud crack that sounded from the sky. Vesta's Flame flared and its color suddenly flashed from blue to red. The heaven's split open, and a thundering voice was heard, the voice of Vesta. Because of Diana's effrontery, she would be cursed. From then on, her husband would possess an insatiable lust for her. He would force himself onto her every night until she became with child. Diana's womb too, would be cursed. She would bear an increasing number of children, all female, who would also only be able to bear daughters. This would continue on throughout her bloodline until the time came that the world they all knew would end.

"After this curse was spoken, the breach in the sky closed, and Diana fell to her knees, crying tears of defeat.

"And so, it happened just as the goddess decreed. Months later, Diana gave birth to three daughters, then four, then five, and so it went. By the time Diana died, she had borne more than one-hundred daughters. All of her children grew, birthing daughters of their own. As the generations continued, those from Diana's line grew in numbers, while those who were not, waned. What few men remained were found and worshiped by the women, exalted above all, for it was their seed that sustained humankind.

"But a time came when no more men could be found. The women searched and searched, but none endured. In that time, when all had given up hope, one woman, the last of them with a child in her womb, gave birth. She birthed a man and named him Reigart, and he would be the one to preserve humankind for another generation. Many women claimed Reigart was theirs to raise until his ripening. A great battle was fought over him, and many women died. This reduced their already waning numbers further still. From then on, at least one new male was always found. The women would treat him as a god and take his seed into them in the hopes that one day Diana's curse would be broken, and the human race would return to a time when there would not be a persistent foreboding of demise.

"That was, of course, until Yareil. Yareil was the last male to be born, and the last man to give his seed. He was the last male to sire the young women of today. No man has been found since Yareil's death, and many sisters are beginning to accept that this may very well be the end."

Preza grunted after the woman finished the tale. "A good story, but if a man ever tried to keep me from doing what I desired, I would greet his face with my axe," she snapped.

"Indeed," the gammer replied. "Women back then certainly seemed more weak-willed than we are today."

"Or the men were worse," muttered Meleya.

"Regardless," Preza began, "I do not think we should all be subject to this curse that was bestowed upon one woman so long ago."

"So long as her blood beats in our hearts, we are all products of Diana's blasphemy, Sister," the woman replied. She then grabbed Zeya's hands and brought them to her lips, kissing them softly. "Yet, there is still hope, is there not? You have felt the Pull of Vesta leading you toward our salvation. Toward our next man. We may yet persevere."

VII

The Paling of Memier

Joreya was putting the finishing touches on her newest woodcarving, a miniature representation of a stallion. Inside her makeshift workshop, the flames of the nearby candles wavered as the wicks approached their ends. She was working on the horse's eyes, the most difficult, but also the most critical part of any carving. Many woodcarvers in the city neglected to add detail to the eyes, but Joreya knew that they were what made wooden sculptures truly come to life. She wiped her dark curly hair from her eyes and continued working, shaving minuscule flakes from the stallion's pupils until she was satisfied with the work. She set down the wooden animal and scrutinized it in the candlelight.

"Near perfect," she whispered aloud.

Joreya stood up as best she could, her improvised workshop possessed a very low ceiling, and even a small woman like herself could not stand straight without bumping her head. She peeked her head around the corner and saw through the distant metal grate that the sun had already set. In a panic, she threw open the small chest she kept in the room and placed the fresh-carved stallion gently inside. The chest was filled, nearly to the top, with carvings of all sorts and sizes. She closed the lid, blew out the candles, and began making her way down the tunnel to the exit. Although she could barely see in the dark tunnel, she knew the path quite well and could just make out the fading light of the city at the other end. Joreya approached a grate and peered outside, making certain no one would see her exit. It would not be good if anyone noticed her leaving her hide-away, especially not one of the city guards. They'd have questions she would not want to answer, and undoubtedly, her mother would find out. That would most assuredly ruin her plans to leave the city of Memier behind.

Pushing the loose grate, Joreya squeezed through a small opening and out into the city street, leaving the culvert behind. Since it was near curfew, there were few sisters out and about. The majority of them were likely in their homes preparing or eating supper. Joreya's mother would be furious with her for being late. She would undoubtedly bombard her with questions of where she had been all day, and why she had no coin to show for herself. No doubt her mother would beat her. Again.

She made her way through the city, following the Paling, a wall of massive wooden logs that jutted up from the earth. Not for the first time, Joreya stopped and stared up at it in awe. The amount of time and timber it must have taken to construct was daunting. The Paling completely enclosed the city and shielded it from the nearby Greenwood and any Greishic attacks. Two city guards in full steel armor took notice of her lingering and approached her.

"Sister, you should already be home," one of them stated flatly.

"I am sorry, I lost track of time, but I'm on my way now."

"The Greishic have been more aggressive than usual as of late, and Regent Vuleila has decreed all should be off the streets by nightfall to ensure their safety. Hurry on home."

"I will, thank you, Sister." Joreya gave a slight bow and ran the rest of the way home.

She reached the stone stairs that led up to her abode just as the curfew bell over the city square rang out. She stood there in the fresh evening air, debating whether or not to enter. Her mother would beat her tonight, there was no uncertainty regarding that. She could return to her workshop and stay there for the night, but that would result in a stronger beating. Her stomach growled. A reaction to the scent that was wafting from the open window. It was tantalizing. It would be Eleza's cooking, no doubt. Her eldest wombsister always prepared the most succulent of meals. She decided a chance at such a meal was worth the risk of a beating. Joreya climbed the steps to the upper level of the street and entered her home.

Inside, she saw all four of her wombsisters sitting at the table enjoying dinner. Thank Vesta, her mother was not there! Her wombsisters all froze when they saw her. Eleza raised a finger to her lips, signaling her to be as silent as possible. Joreya carefully approached the table, admiring the roasted meat as she took in its tantalizing scent. She sat down and reached out to tear off a chunk of the juicy vittle.

"Well, the little rat smelled food and came scurrying back home, did she?"

Startled, Joreya whirled and saw her mother, Rueila, standing at her bedchamber door. The woman's eyes were filled with disdain. "What makes the little rat think she deserves to eat? Half of her wombsisters worked all day to provide us with this meal, the other half worked hard to prepare it. Tell me, little rat, what did you do today? No doubt you were as useless as always."

"I have nothing to show for, Mother," Joreya replied softly.

"Squeak, squeak, I cannot hear you, rat. Speak up!"

"I have nothing to show for, Mother," she repeated more loudly.

"Truly? Why, I am simply shocked, *shocked* at this revelation! So why then does the useless rat think she deserves to enjoy a meal that the rest of us worked hard to provide?"

Joreya sighed. So there would be no dinner tonight after all. She rose from her chair and started toward her bedchamber, but her mother moved to block her path.

"And wherever do you think you are going?"

"To bed, Mother."

"Bed? No, as I said, your sisters worked hard on this meal, you will sit right back down and appreciate it while they enjoy it."

Joreya did not move.

"What are you waiting for, little rat? If you are lucky, I will allow you to lick the leavings from the floor. A real feast for a rodent such as yourself."

Joreya begrudgingly returned to her seat at the table. Her wombsisters did not continue with their meal.

"Mother, please let her have some, she's growing thin!" Eleza spoke up.

"You dare go against me, Daughter? And in defense of this miserable creature?"

"Mother, I did the cooking, and I must insist that Joreya, too, is fed."

"Oh, you *insist*, Eleza? Are you certain that you *insist?*"

Eleza hesitated.

"Because if you insist, then I will throw it all out for the dogs. If you insist that the little rat gets fed, I insist that no one gets any. So I ask you one more time, Eleza. Do you insist?"

"No, Mother," Eleza mumbled.

"You surely are related to the little rat, Daughter. Speak up!"

"I do not insist, Mother," she repeated.

"Very well, the rest of you may continue with your meal."

The table slowly continued eating.

Eventually, conversation began again around the table.

"I heard the Greishic have been attacking the Paling more often," her wombsister, Reya said. "Do you think they will be able to break through?"

"The Paling has withstood Greishic attacks for generations, as have the sisters that stand defending it," Joreya's mother replied. "It will not fall to those beasts."

"But what if it does?" asked Beya, Reya's twin wombsister.

"It will not. Regent Vuleila knows how to defend the city from attack. Pay no more mind to any of that. We are safe inside the Paling wall and always will be."

Beya looked ready to argue. "But Mother, surely it can't—"

"I said, pay it no more mind, Daughter!" Rueila yelled, interrupting her.

The meal continued until everyone except Joreya had their fill. There was plenty left over, but her mother took it to the refuse pot and scraped the remains of the succulent meal inside. She made sure Joreya watched her do this.

Joreya pondered trying to sneak a few pieces out of the waste after her mother went to bed. The refuse wasn't always filthy, and she had retrieved some good sized scraps out of it before. As she was debating when to make her move, a knock sounded at the door.

"Such impropriety!" Rueila exclaimed. "Who would be disturbing us at this late hour? Is it not past curfew?" She moved to answer the door.

While her mother was distracted, Eleza quickly passed Joreya some of the meat from the meal. "I saved you some," she whispered. "Sorry, it's cold, but hopefully, it still tastes good."

"Thank you, Sister!" Joreya whispered back. She scarfed down the meat, fearful her mother would turn around at any moment. It may not have been much, but it was delicious, and the flavor instantly lifted her mood.

"Hail, Sister!" a soldier proclaimed from the doorway.

"To you as well, Sister." Rueila replied. "How may our humble household aid the Sisterhood this night?"

"I have here a writ from Regent Vuleila. It states that any able-bodied sisters above the age of seventeen but younger than forty years are to assemble at the city square first thing in the morning, no exceptions. Please acknowledge your comprehension of this message."

"I understand," Joreya's mother replied.

"Thank you. Goodnight, Sister." The woman turned and went back down the stairs.

"Only sisters older than seventeen? It seems even the Regent thinks you are useless, little rat," Rueila growled.

"Why do you think the Regent is summoning us?" asked Gureya. "Do you think a male has been found?"

"I do not know, Daughter, but that certainly is a possibility."

"Oh, Vesta, I hope! I cannot wait for him to share his seed," Reya replied excitedly.

"Mind your tongue, Girl. I too was excited my first time, but when your body is worn and you are forced to carry another child all in the name of the Sisterhood, that eagerness will diminish swiftly." Rueila shot Joreya a hateful look. "I believed my days of childbearing were well behind me, but when the Tour of Seed once more came to Memier, I was bade to have another. Who would have thought I would not carry a daughter in my womb, but a rat." The room remained silent until Rueila continued. "Though Vesta did bless me with four wonderful daughters, so I suppose it was not all bad. Now, off to bed with you all. You want to be well-rested for the Regent's summons tomorrow."

They all got up and moved toward their bedchambers, but Rueila grabbed Joreya's shoulder before she could pass.

"Not you, little rat. If you do not make yourself useful in the day, I shall make sure you are useful in the night. Get to work clearing the table and cleaning those plates."

"But Mother, I didn't even—"

Rueila struck Joreya hard across the face. "Don't talk back, little rat! You will clean those plates, and if I see so much as a spot on any of them, I will beat you so hard you'll be unable to talk back, am I understood?"

"Yes, Mother."

"Very good." Her mother left the room.

Get out, I have to get out, Joreya thought. Selling her carvings was her only way out of the city and away from her mother. She took delight in knowing that she was close. Joreya had nearly saved enough coin to purchase provisions and a ride to one of the neighboring villages. She just needed one or two more good days at the market to make that a reality. Joreya was undecided where she would go. She'd love to travel to Vulna, but passage on a riverboat was very expensive and that would mean she would have to save even more. Crossing the Greenwood on foot was out of the question, since Joreya knew she would never make it through on her own. Coratch seemed like the next best option. It wasn't too far, only a few day's journey, but she wasn't sure the citizens of Coratch would appreciate her art enough for her to make a living. She had heard terrible things about the sisters in Coratch. Most didn't even follow the laws of the Sisterhood. Did she really want to end up in a place such as that? There was Rolier, but it probably did not have enough residents to where she could prosper either. It was a difficult choice to make, and one she knew couldn't be put off for very much longer. Anywhere was better than this.

"No better place on this side of the Reypar than Memier," she muttered to herself. At least, that's how the saying went. She imagined whoever came up with the adage had never met her mother.

* * *

Vuleila, the Regent of Memier, headed to the Paling for what seemed like the tenth time that day. This had never happened before, she was sure of it. The Greishic typically only were daring enough to attack the wall a few times a month, but she had already lost count on the number of times it had been this week. It was truly unheard of. Vuleila climbed the steps to the battlement and peered out over the Eastern Slope. In the darkness, she could barely make them out, but they were there. Those beasts. The Greishic were attempting to rush past the watchtowers and assault the Paling directly. While this tactic was nothing new, the frequency was. With so many beasts at once, the watchtowers were running low on arrows, and while the city had plenty to spare, actually getting them to the towers proved difficult when there was no respite from the waves of onslaught. It almost seemed as if this assault was orchestrated, but that was absurd! The Greishic possessed intelligence barely above a rodent. Strategizing an organized assault or siege was simply beyond their animalistic brains.

"Will they never cease?" Treya, Vuleila's aid asked. "Can you recall any such frequent attacks on the Paling in the past?"

"Not in my lifetime," Vuleila replied. "I've asked the scholars to consult the archives for any example of this behavior, but they have yet to find anything."

"Your writ has gone out, we will be ready to bolster our ranks tomorrow."

"Bolstered with citizens, not soldiers. Such little training will not protect them. Many will die," Vuleila replied somberly. "I cannot believe I will be throwing away the lives of so many ripened sisters."

"It was not an easy decision, but if the Greishic breach the walls, the city is finished," Treya stated. "Better to lose some ripened than all of them."

"And the divebirds, have they gone out?"

"Yes, as discussed. Two to the Hearth and two to Haralda, all with identical messages. If the number of requests for aid doesn't alert the Jurisa to the severity of this threat, then I doubt anything will."

"I wish we had requested aid sooner. I am uncertain if we can hold out until reinforcements arrive."

"There is something else." Treya hesitated.

"What is it?"

"We received word a little more than an hour ago that Selfa Zeya is headed here."

"A selfa! Oh, Vesta, and at the worst possible time!" Vuleila exclaimed. "Do they expect us to meet her in the Greenwood to help with safe passage?"

"No, it seems they are hoping her small group will be able to slip through mostly unnoticed," Treya replied.

Regent Vuleila again looked across the Eastern Slope. "If this keeps up, they'll have better luck scaling the cliffs. How many days before we can expect one of the Blessed to grace us with her presence?"

"I'd say between eight and fourteen days."

"Well, we'd better let the watchtowers know to keep an eye out. We absolutely do not want the Selfa being mistaken for a Greishic."

"I will be sure they are infor—"

"They are upon us! Take them down, now!" Vuleila shouted as she noticed a small band of Greishic approaching the Paling. The sound of arrows being loosed filled the night as multiple missiles cut through the air, many hitting their mark. Vuleila squinted in the darkness. Was that more movement? She grabbed a nearby torch and launched it out onto the Slope. Shouts erupted from the Paling as the pale light illuminated close to fifty Greishic, their filth covered bodies nearly invisible on the dark night. "Let loose, sisters! Let loose!"

The Greishic snarled and rushed toward the Paling wall. The barrage of arrows cut them down, but not quickly enough. Vuleila and Treya took up bows of their own and began firing into the darkness as well. A few of the beasts made it to the Paling and immediately began hacking away at it with their primitive weapons, hoping to breach it, but the Paling wall stood strong and they did little more than dent its thick timbers before they too were slain.

"How did so many make it past the watchtowers?" Treya asked incredulously.

"Pit if I know!" Vuleila replied. "What's worse is they were approaching with stealth. Stealth! Tomorrow we *must* line the Slope with well-fueled torches and we *must* replenish the quivers at the watchtowers. We may lose sisters doing this, but we will lose many more if the towers lack the arrows to cut down the continuous waves of these beasts."

"Yes, Regent. I will see that it is done."

"Thank you, Sister. Were all of the advisors told of the meeting tonight?"

"They were, and we are expected briefly. Most were understanding and did not complain," Treya replied.

"Most? Yelza didn't much like being awakened from her sleep, did she?"

"She did not. I nearly had to threaten to have the city guard drag her to the meeting. She was insistent that whatever it was could wait until the morning."

Vuleila smiled. "I would have liked to have seen her dragged through the city by the guard."

"As would I. Pity she confirmed her attendance after the threat."

"The woman is difficult, but she is wise. She often does bring perspectives I have overlooked. Not that I always consider them, but occasionally, I do."

Regent Vuleila looked out across the Eastern Slope one more time. The air was calm and the sounds of battle had subsided. The night did well to hide the Greishic bodies that littered the ground. What the night did not hide well was the sense of foreboding that Vuleila felt in her heart. She knew the next few days were going to be the most trying of her time as Regent, maybe even the most trying of her life.

Vuleila and Treya returned to the Regent's Keep just as the other advisors were arriving for the emergency meeting. Everyone in attendance looked haggard and some appeared to have rolled out of bed mere moments before their arrival. It was rare for such a meeting at this hour, but in these times, rarity crossed paths with occurrence more frequently.

"Why are we spending life that can create it? We should be sending out sisters more advanced in age!" Yelza, the Commerce Advisor, demanded. "Our young are our future, if a woman's womb is dry, then let her face the creatures."

"The beasts are strong. While we know some of our older citizens can hold their own, many cannot," Veneya, the captain of the city guard, responded. "How are we to decide which of those with dried up wombs should be sent to die? Or are you suggesting we send them all?"

"I am sure many would volunteer to protect their homes and daughters," Yelza replied. "I myself would gladly take up arms in defense of our future. While I know I would not last long, if I was able to save the life of a single ripened sister, I would do it gladly. I know I am not alone in this."

"Your heart is valiant, dear Sister, but I am not so sure your aging body would be able to last long enough to protect the city," Captain Veneya replied. "Our hope is that the young are able-bodied enough to hold the line, or at the very least, swift enough to retreat safely back behind the walls."

"Do you think our casualties will be low?" asked Nilza, who oversaw the city's foundries.

Treya shook her head. "Most of these women have never been soldiers. A few days of training will not give them what they need to stay alive. Our best hope is that our soldiers can hold the Greishic back. The conscripted sisters are only to be our last line of defense."

"Be that as it may, we are risking our very survival," replied Yelza.

"If the Greishic breach the Paling, none will survive," Vuleila finally replied. "They will flood through this city capturing or killing old and young alike. I am not against arming the older sisters, but I believe that to be a course of action we should take only if it becomes absolutely necessary. It is important that our resources are put to efficient use. As it stands, we do not even have enough weapons to arm all of our young."

"Nilza, how are the smiths doing?" asked Treya.

"Not as well as we would like. The forges have been running hot, nonstop. There simply isn't enough time," Nilza replied. "However, one of the blacksmiths suggested something to me, and I feel it was sensible enough to bring to this meeting."

"What did they say?" asked Regent Vuleila.

"The carpenters and woodworkers could fashion sharpened spears of wood with haste. Far quicker than the time it takes to forge a single sword."

"Sticks? We are to send the future of the Sisterhood against the Greishic with nothing but a stick?" demanded Yelza.

"Of a sort. Remember, the wood here is strong and we have plenty within our walls already. It is certainly better than sending them out empty-handed."

Yelza looked aghast. "We would be sending them directly to their deaths! Regent Vuleila, surely you aren't considering this?"

Vuleila thought for a moment before speaking. "Our plan is to form a defensive perimeter around the Paling. The vanguard would consist of our seasoned soldiers and city guards. If all goes well, the young sisters wouldn't even have to face a single Greishic in battle. They wouldn't even have to leave the safety of the Paling."

"And what do you think the likelihood that all goes well will be, Regent?" challenged Yelza.

"Vesta only knows. While I am confident in our soldiers, I know they will not be able to hold back a large horde of the creatures if they have to face one. Our last line of defense is a desperate tactic to save the Paling and the city, nothing more. My hope is that enough of the creatures have died off in their fruitless attacks that a major horde is unlikely, but that hope is small. Nilza, give word to the woodworkers. We need whatever weaponry they can offer us, wooden or otherwise."

"As you command, Regent Vuleila."

"And what of the Hearth? Do they intend to send us aid?" Captain Veneya asked.

"Not as of yet. I am afraid we underestimated the Greishic when we sent our last message," Treya replied. "Had we known their attacks would persist, we certainly would have requested soldiers sooner. With that said, I sent four birds earlier today, two to the Hearth and two to Haralda. I told them in no uncertain terms that if we do not receive aid soon, the city will fall. At this point, our best hope is that Haralda sends sisters into the Greenwood to wreak havoc on the Greishic camps, but I am uncertain they will do that without the Hearth ordering it. But when the Hearth does give the order, and Haralda draws the creature's attention away from Memier, it will provide us with some much needed respite."

"I pray to Vesta that they receive and act on our message soon," Yelza murmured. "I hate to send our daughters out to die with nothing but sharpened sticks."

"As do I. As do we all," Regent Vuleila replied.

VIII

Solren

"We will be in Solren before nightfall," Preza announced with glee. "Soon we'll be treated to a hot meal, a warm bed, and a beautiful woman to share it with!"

Meleya smirked. "Dear Sister, are we not good company? What do the Solrennians have that Zeya and I do not?"

Preza laughed. "I am afraid neither of you are able to provide me with what it is that I desire."

"Fair enough," Meleya replied. "Just be sure to make the Venery proud with your performance."

"I have yet to receive any complaints thus far, and I have no intention of changing that. The sanctity of the Venery will remain intact, do not be concerned, Sister."

"I am glad to hear it. For if you cause detriment to our reputation, I am certain the Hearth would be none too pleased! Imagine the outcry when the masses hear that Preza the Lover left her chamber companion unfulfilled."

Zeya chuckled at her sisters' banter. They could match wits as well as they could match steel. Their conversation reminded Zeya of her first time going to bed with a woman. She remembered the excitement that overtook her entire being and the nervousness that overtook her mind. The warmth she felt in her body was second only to what she had felt in Vesta's Pull. Still, somehow, the other woman's body had felt even hotter than her own. Even now, the memory of hands not her own caressing and stroking her bare skin aroused her. She especially remembered the sensation of their tongue upon her as it moved down her body.

"Zeya?" Meleya questioned.

"Huh? What?"

"Are you well, Wombsister? Your face has gone crimson."

"Oh, yes, sorry, I was just lost in thought."

Preza laughed. "It would seem I am not the only one looking forward to the hospitality of Solren."

Zeya's face grew even redder. "No, no, not that. I was just thinking of the warm bed we'd have tonight."

"Made even warmer by a sensuous companion, no doubt!" Preza jeered. "Deceit is not your strongest trait, Zeya. Find us the man, and I'll find you a woman!"

"In any case," Meleya began, "I remember the last time we visited Solren, it was when Mother was one of Father's guardians on what ended up being the final Tour of Seed."

"Really? I do not remember any of that! I thought I had never been this far from home until now," Zeya replied, her face finally returning to its normal color.

"You were too young to remember, maybe two or three years of age."

"Do you remember Father much, Meleya?"

"Not really. I had very little interaction with him, probably the same as you. He was nearly always locked up in his chamber."

"I remember him," Preza stated. "I remember the first time my mother took me to the Hearth to lay with him. I was shaking. Whether it was from anticipation or nervousness, I still do not know."

"What was it like?" Zeya asked.

"It was... different. I remember feeling so special, being chosen to take his seed into me. I was so certain I would birth the next male and be the one honored by all the Sisterhood. I remember thinking my wombsister, Vesta embrace her soul, would be so jealous when it was I and not she who birthed the next male. My fantasy was all for naught though. His seed did not even take to me. Not the first time, nor the third. After that, I was labeled barren and prohibited from laying with him ever again. Nothing but a useless vessel."

"But what was it like? Laying with him, I mean," Zeya questioned.

"It was fine. Yareil pretty much just lay there as I performed the Goddess' Dance, just as my mother had taught me. It seemed to go on forever, and my legs grew weak from the effort. Finally, he shuddered beneath me, and I felt his seed enter into my body. Immediately after that, his guardians came in, helped me down, and directed me to lay on a special bed that kept my legs raised high. Your mother was there, and she handed me a cup, instructing me to drink all of its contents. It was hard to drink lying on my back and the concoction tasted foul, but she insisted I not leave a single drop. When that was done, I was given various roots to eat, as well. I was told it would help with the permeation, whatever that meant. A lot of good all that did though. I guess some of us just weren't meant to bear children."

"Well," Meleya began, looking up at the sky, "seed aside, Heyfic is the only male I'll ever need." She extended a gloved hand and the noble bird answered with a cry and swooped down to land on her arm. She gently scratched the top of his head before releasing him back into the air.

They reached the entrance to Solren, a town consisting primarily of wooden structures with thatched roofs, and a bustling main street. The thoroughfare was packed with sisters trading in all manner of goods and services.

"Pork, get your pork, fresh off the pig!"

"Fresh baked pies, cherry pie, rhubarb pie, milkroot pie! Get them while they're fresh!"

"Armaments for sale, don't get caught by the Greishic without sturdy protection! Best on this side of the river!"

Zeya wondered if this was what Solren was like every day, and if so, how its citizens could stand to live with all the commotion. Vulna was a much larger city, but she had never seen anything like the mass of sisters that meandered before her. Well, besides the start of the Venery.

"Is this a town fair?" she asked Preza.

"Nope. This," she spread her arms forward dramatically, "is Solren!"

"Madness, more like! How many people live in this town?" Meleya questioned.

"Start counting if you really want to know. The Hearth has not had an accurate census in over a generation! Too many residential comings and goings."

As the three women approached the throng, Preza had to shout over the noise. "Get behind me, sisters, I will see us through the crowd!"

Zeya and Meleya followed closely as Preza pushed through the wall of women between them and their destination, the town hall. The mayor was expecting them, or at least she was supposed to be. It was a tight squeeze, even with Preza clearing the path. To Zeya, it felt good to be among so many sisters again, and it felt better still that none of them had recognized her as a selfa. She was invisible. No one noticed her pin, and no one noticed her.

"Coming through! We have urgent business with the mayor! Move aside! Move aside!" The large woman barrelled through the mass more forcefully as the crowd tightened around them. Zeya felt sorry for the sisters who were unable to clear the way in time and were nearly knocked over by Preza's bulk.

The crowd began to ease as the town hall came into sight. It was a sizable two-level structure that apparently also served as Solren's largest tavern. They entered the building and were surprised by how few women were inside. It seemed the establishment had been cleared out in preparation for a private event, but no sisters were there to meet them. Decorations adorned the walls and most of the tables had fine centerpieces and place settings.

"Oh no." Realization hit Zeya. "I hope this isn't for me."

"We are in Solren, dear Wombsister! They will make any excuse to throw a party, and the Selfa visiting during a Venery certainly gives them legitimate cause, for once."

"Hello!" a woman called from the landing above them. "We are not finished setting up yet. If you would please return in a little..." she trailed off and squinted at Zeya.

"Here it comes," Zeya whispered sheepishly.

"Oh, Vesta! You have arrived!" the woman exclaimed. "Neza, why was I not notified of the Selfa's arrival? Neza? Neza! The Selfa is here, and we are not yet prepared! Oh, the Jurisa will have my head! Ahhh! I apologize for the shouting, I seem to have lost my assistant! Neza! Neza?" The woman continued calling for her assistant as she rapidly descended the stairs and gave a bow, first to Zeya, then to her companions. "Apologies, apologies for our ill-preparedness! We were not expecting you until later in the evening." The woman turned to face upstairs. "Neza? Neza! Get down here, the Selfa has come!"

"It is quite all right, we do not require any celebration or fanfare," Zeya replied.

"Neza! Oh, for the love of Vesta! Have you gone deaf?" The woman turned back to Zeya. "Oh, nonsense, it is not every day a selfa passes through our humble town! Why, the only event that would trump this would be the birth of twin males!"

The tavern door opened and a sister entered. "Ah, there you are, Neza! I've been calling you and calling you! I thought you were upstairs, swear to Vesta! The Selfa has arrived! Contact the chefs and tell them the schedule has been moved up!"

"Yes, of course!" Neza swiftly turned and ran from the tavern.

"And Neza! Wait, Neza! Pit, she's run off again. Oh, Vesta curse me, I have not yet introduced myself! I am Reyna, the mayor of Solren."

"Pleased to make your acquaintance," Zeya replied with a bow.

"How was your journey here? Without much difficulty, I hope!" Reyna asked.

"Only minor trouble. We ran into brigands in the forest," Preza answered.

"Brigands in the Sol Forest? Dearest, Vesta! And they attacked the Selfa?"

"They did not realize that until later," Preza replied. "Upon seeing her signate, they threw down their weapons and fled."

"Pit! I imagine they did not pose much of a threat to you, but still, it is appalling that highwaywomen exist in this world. I am confident they did not come from our humble town, they must have come down from the north. Noorians, no doubt."

"They did not state from where they hailed," said Meleya.

"Well, it certainly was not from here! We are all respectable citizens of the Sisterhood in Solren! In any case, I imagine you desire rest after your long journey. I ensured the baths would be closed to the public in anticipation of your arrival. Or if you prefer to nap, our three best rooms have been made available to you. They are up the stairs and at the end of the landing. I will send someone to fetch you when the feast is fully prepared."

"A bath would be most pleasant," Zeya said.

"Excellent! The bathhouse is located just next door, and we have prepared it with the most exquisite perfumes and oils that coin can buy. I will arrange for your current apparel to be cleaned as well, and your armor oiled."

* * *

Zeya slowly lowered herself into the steaming water and immediately felt a large knot of tension she hadn't realized she was carrying melt away. She had no idea the hot bath would provide such instant relief, but she was grateful for it. The bath chamber was rather ornate. It consisted of smooth cerulean tiled walls that were embedded with precious gemstones and decorated with intricate carvings. The large heated pool had ample space for at least twenty women at once. Very different from what she had expected given the building's exterior appearance.

Meleya slid into the bath beside her and sighed audibly. "I am beginning to regret entering this pool."

"Why is that, Wombsister?"

"I fear I shall lack the willpower to leave!" she exclaimed and ducked her head under the water.

"How many more days till Rolier?" Zeya wondered aloud.

Preza entered the bath. "Vesta's tit! We have not yet reached the midpoint of our journey, and you are already thinking of the destination?"

"I know, I know. I just want to keep things in perspective," she replied. "Although, I am beginning to agree with Meleya, entering the water may have been a mistake."

"Give in to its warm embrace, Zeya!" Meleya teased. "I wonder what manner of feast the mayor will have prepared for us?"

"It matters not to me, just so long as they serve us mutton," declared Preza.

"The wolf loves her sheep!" Meleya replied. "I, for one, am most looking forward to getting a good night's rest on one of those long-fabled Solrennian beds. They say the mattresses are stuffed with goose feathers, fancy that!"

"Oh," Preza grinned, "and there had better be sisters who are... accommodating. Vesta knows, this will undoubtedly be my last opportunity to get licked for quite some time."

"Mutton and a companion for the evening, I will make sure to let the mayor know your demands," laughed Meleya. "What of you, Zeya? What are your desires?"

"Some peace and quiet would be nice. Maybe with a bit of mutton on the side."

"So, it seems you have finally learned to love the true food of the goddess," Preza goaded.

Zeya splashed water in Preza's face.

"If you intend to assault your enemy, you must make sure your first strike is effective enough to weaken her resolve," Preza stated in an instructional tone. She then shoved a large torrent of water at Zeya, drenching her.

"Preza! Are you attempting to drown me? I seem to recall the oath you made not so long ago, and you are very near breaking it, Woman!"

"Now, now!" Meleya interrupted in a mock chastising tone. "This is no manner for the saviors of the Sisterhood to behave! Keep this up, and Vesta will withdraw her blessing from you, forthwith!"

"Selfa Zeya? Please forgive the intrusion." Their amusements were interrupted by Neza who had entered the bathing chamber.

"Yes, what is it?" Zeya said, trying to shake off her embarrassment at being caught acting like a child.

"Mayor Reyna sent me with word that the feast in your honor will be fully prepared in an hour. She also sent me with attire for the evening. Do our esteemed guests prefer pants or a gown for the evening?"

"Pants!" the three exclaimed in unison.

"Very well, I will have them laid out for you."

The woman left, and the three begrudgingly got out of the bath and put on their robes. Meleya approached the table that held the oils and perfumes that had been prepared for them. There were more than thirty different bottles, more scents than any of them thought could even be contained within glass. Meleya looked over each carefully, until one bottle in particular caught her eye. She removed the stopper and gave it a gentle sniff.

"This is... interesting."

"What is it?" Zeya asked, walking over to the table.

"It is called Lover's Vengeance."

"Now *that* is a name for a fragrance!" Preza declared, joining them at the table. "I wonder why they don't give them all names like that? Why stick them with names like Lilac's Breath, Vesta's Aura, or Reigart's Seed?" She reached out her hand. "Let me try." Meleya handed her the bottle, and Preza took a deep sniff. "Ah, its name surely does it justice!" Preza poured a large amount onto her hand and rubbed it aggressively into her wrists, and neck.

"Preza! A scent is supposed to be delicately suggestive!" Meleya exclaimed. "You're drowning yourself with it!"

"Nonsense! If it smells good, it smells good."

Zeya coughed, after inhaling too much of Preza's new aroma. "At least now we know why they named it Lover's Vengeance. That scent will haunt us for the rest of our days."

* * *

At the feast, Zeya sat at the table of honor in the tavern hall. The mayor had insisted on announcing Zeya and her party before their appearance. Zeya, Meleya, and Preza were all against the pompous introductions, but their attempts to forgo the formality were in vain. Mayor Reyna was quite adamant and would not take no for an answer. Zeya eventually agreed, just wanting to be done with the whole affair. Still, she had to admit, the town had done an admirable job with the preparations. Large rectangular tables lined the tavern, and although every seat was filled, the hall was nothing like the congested havoc she had expected. An assortment of beverages and vittles were served, including the juiciest of mutton. Mayor Reyna insisted they filled their bellies with whatever they desired.

Besides Zeya, Meleya, and Preza, the mayor and a few other sisters also sat at the table of honor. Zeya did not much feel like socializing, but did her best to nod and reply whenever someone spoke to her.

The woman sitting across from Zeya had been talking nonstop throughout the entire meal. While the constant blathering was obnoxious to listen to, Zeya was somewhat thankful that the woman drew the attention of those at the table away from her.

"As to that, I wonder when the Hearth intends to tour with the buck? Or do you think they will keep him locked up in Vulna and expect us to make the journey ourselves?"

"Oh, Pruleila, do not concern yourself with that, I am sure they will begin touring as soon as the male has ripened, if he hasn't already," another sister replied.

"Maybe so, but my daughters have been starved for a man's seed for far too long! Why, by the time I was their age, I had already birthed five of them!"

"That is impressive, how many did you say you bore again?" Meleya asked.

"Oh, I stopped at twelve, but not for lack of trying. The Hearth just refused to grant me any more seed. They claimed I was too old to bear more. Too old! Pit! Why, I birthed the last three myself without requiring the aid of any midsisters!

"A word of advice, Selfa Zeya," the woman continued. "If you are wise, you will take the male's seed first chance you get, even before you return him to the Hearth. Vesta knows when you'll get another chance at him!"

"I would not dream of it, Sister," Zeya replied politely. "That is, of course, against the vow I took to the Sisterhood."

"Your friend then," she said, motioning to Preza. "What is your name, Daughter?"

"Preza."

"An Eza, eh? Well, you certainly don't have much time left before your womb sours! No doubt you'll be past your prime in a matter of years. I hope for your sake, the buck is already ripe! Of course, I'm assuming you already had a chance with the last male, I imagine you have a few little ones you left behind in Vulna? You Ezas were the lucky ones, at least compared to the poor Eyas. You younger sisters have yet to feel even a drop of the seed within you. Anyway, what village did you say you were going to again?"

"I did not," Zeya replied, not falling for the woman's ploy.

"Pruleila!" Reyna interjected. "You know better than to ask the Selfa of her destination! That is the business of the Hearth, and not for us to know."

"Of course, of course, but you can't blame an old hag for trying! I did hear that the Venery will take you through the Greenwood. Can you confirm that?"

"I can," Zeya replied.

"Vesta have mercy, for the Greishic surely will have none! I cannot imagine traveling in such close proximity to those wretched creatures. One of my daughters is posted in Haralda, and she has told me quite a few tales. Scouts have come back from the Greenwood raving mad, or with limbs missing. Terrible times we live in, terrible times. Those bastards will kill you, rape you, or eat you. Why, I've even heard they often partake in all three!"

"Pruleila, perhaps we should shift our conversation to a more cheerful topic," the mayor replied. "Now that the feast is dying down, it may be a good time for us to bring out the gifts we have prepared for the Selfa and her companions."

"Thank you for your sentiment, Sister, but we do not require any gifts," Meleya replied.

"Oh, do not be so quick to turn them down, dear Girl!" Pruleila exclaimed, beaming with pride.

The mayor rose and whispered something to Neza, and Zeya watched as the mayor's assistant walked to a side room and motioned for someone to come out. Slowly three beautiful women entered the tavern and made their way over to the table of honor.

"Now we're talking!" Preza blurted out.

"Selfa Zeya, Meleya, and Preza, may I present to you our three most renowned chamber companions." The mayor motioned toward the women. "I am afraid we were uncertain of your... tastes, but I assure you that they are more than capable of satiating your desires, whatever they may be."

Zeya stared in awe at the women. She could see, based solely on their looks, why they were well-renowned. They were some of the most beautiful women she had ever seen. Unfortunately, the overwhelmingness of the feast, both in food and company, left her feeling not incredibly sensuous. "I am afraid I must decline the offer. I have not rested well in many days, and intend to retire to bed as soon as possible," she stated. "With that said, the feast and company was grand, and both my companions and I, greatly appreciate your extraordinary hospitality.

"I too must politely decline," Meleya stated. "As the Selfa said, your hospitality has been worthy of Vesta herself, but I am afraid I filled my belly just a bit too much with the delectable meal."

"I certainly have no qualms," Preza stated, eyeing the women hungrily.

"Ah, I am glad one of you will take us up on our offer," the mayor replied. "I would not have wanted these wonderful sisters to feel slighted. Tell me, Preza. Do you have a preference?"

Preza took a moment to look each one over, weighing her options. "I regrettably seem unable to arrive at an answer to that question. Each one possesses the parts I like." She suddenly raised her eyebrows as an idea formed in her mind. "Mayor Reyna, would it be asking too much if I were to request all three?"

"Ha! A true woman, this one!" Pruleila howled.

The mayor considered the question. "I certainly have no issue with your request, so long as the chamber companions are agreeable. Sisters?"

The three women smiled and approached Preza confidently. Preza flashed a bright smile at Zeya as the chamber companions helped her from her seat and led her up the stairs.

"Well, she certainly is not regretting coming on this journey," Meleya scoffed.

* * *

The next morning, the mayor, Zeya, and Meleya stood waiting downstairs for Preza to join them.

"Very unlike Preza to be late," commented Zeya.

"Well, I am not at all surprised, considering the night she had," Meleya replied. "Mayor, I apologize for the delay. You do not need to stay. I am sure you have other matters to attend to."

"Nonsense, Meleya! What host would I be if I failed to see the Selfa and her retinue off? If word got out, I would be disgraced for the next ten generations! My portrait would be displayed in shame for all to see! 'Oh, that's that Mayor Reyna,' they would say. 'She tarnished our town's reputation by leaving the Selfa to depart on her own, what an awful mayor she was!' I can just hear their insults now."

An audible groan came from upstairs, followed by a loud thud and rapid footsteps. The door eventually opened, and Preza burst through, only partially dressed. She continued down the stairs attempting to finish buckling her armor.

"I trust our accommodations were satisfactory?" the mayor asked, smiling. "I am, of course, basing this off your tardiness, disheveled appearance, and the sounds the entire town was privy to last night."

Preza grinned widely. "Worry not. Your accommodations were most assuredly, satisfactory."

"Good. I hope our chamber companions lived up to their reputation."

"Their repute shall remain intact, as will that of Solren. I have every intention of visiting this town, and this establishment, again."

"Excellent. If you require nothing else from me, I had your horses brought from the stable. They are waiting for you outside, as are the fresh supplies the Hearth requested for you."

They followed the mayor out of the tavern hall, and Zeya's heart dropped as she saw a large crowd of sisters that had formed around their horses. They all stood very quietly as if waiting for something.

"I think this time they *are* expecting you to speak, Wombsister," Meleya whispered.

"Speak? And say what? I made no preparations for this!" she hissed back.

"Something inspiring?" suggested Preza.

"I can't."

"Just say a few words of hope, you know, something you have heard or read before," Meleya encouraged.

"Nothing is coming to my mind, nothing at all." Zeya began to feel panic rise up in her again. Her job was to find the male and bring him back to the Hearth. Being the face of hope for the entire Sisterhood was not in her oath as Selfa.

Meleya nodded with understanding. "Ok, I will speak, but mount your horse with me."

They climbed their mounts, and Zeya could see that even more sisters had joined the crowd.

"Sisters!" Meleya began in a loud voice. "We see the look of fear within you, but worry not, for even we have fear in our hearts! We fear not only the Greishic hordes breaking through our fortifications and spreading throughout our lands, but also for the downfall of the Sisterhood. The Sisterhood, the only life we have ever known, the sole order we can rely on in this turbulent world. But for every bit of fear within us, let it be eclipsed by hope! As the Venery moves onward, know that we will return, and when we return, we will have with us a man!" Meleya paused as cheering erupted from the crowd. "A man who will strengthen our numbers! A man who will plant the seeds of another great generation of women! Sisters, do not fear for us, for we have Vesta's protection. The Selfa has Vesta's Flame within her, and with it, her quest cannot fail."

An uproar burst from the crowd, and they began to chant. "Hail the Sisterhood! Hail the Selfa! Hail the Venery!"

Zeya leaned over to Meleya and spoke loudly into her ear, trying to be heard over the crowd's noise. "What should I do?"

"Just nod your head," she replied.

Zeya looked out at the crowd and gave a profound nod. The assembly broke their chant and cheered more fiercely than before. At that moment, Zeya began to understand. It did not matter how she felt, what mattered was that the Sisterhood held on to hope. Hopelessness would lead to dissent, chaos, and ultimately collapse. The fraction of hope she provided these women was enough to get them out of bed in the morning, enough for them to go about their daily routines and to sleep peacefully at night. While this realization did not wholly abate the burden of possible failure she carried, it lightened it significantly. Zeya stood up in her stirrups. "For the Venery!" She exclaimed with more fervor than she knew she held within her. She signaled her horse ahead, and the crowd, still cheering, parted and made a path for her and her companions.

IX

Mind and Body

Freila, Sieyna, and Gilza all sat around the council chamber waiting for Cereila to appear. The woman was very late. Not surprising, since her tardiness was a common occurrence, but this time she was far later than usual. While it was bothersome, it was usually excusable. Cereila had to climb the steps to the Aviary multiple times a day, and usually did so right before the Jurisa met to ensure all recent messages were available to the council. There were hundreds of steps leading to the Aviary, and a trip up the tower and back down could take as long as an hour.

After some time, footsteps could be heard running down the hall and toward the council chamber. Cereila entered, nearly bursting through the door and plopped down in her chair in a heap. Her face was red and the shine of sweat glistened on her face. She huffed audibly. "I am sorry, sisters, one of the divebirds refused to enter the Aviary. It remained fluttering outside and it took much coaxing to get it to settle in its cage. I ordinarily would have left it to the venaren to handle, but this one had a message."

"Was it from Memier? More news on the Greishic attacks?" Freila asked.

"That is what I assumed, which is another reason I waited for the bird to be brought in, but it was not. Still, good news. Apparently the Selfa has left Solren.

"She is on schedule, then?" Gilza asked.

"What did it say?" Freila asked.

"Apparently, they gave quite the speech," Cereila replied. She raised her spectacles and reread the message. "Mayor Reyna claims the town's spirits are still high from the address."

"A speech? That does not sound like Zeya," Freila commented.

"No. The mayor wrote it was her companion, Meleya, that got the crowd riled up."

Gilza nodded. "Stronger together. It would seem you raised them properly, Freila."

"I cannot take all the credit, my daughters are exceptional. I knew that from the moment I severed their cords."

"Let us hope their exceptionalism extends beyond flowery speeches," replied Gilza. "They have not yet reached the Greenwood, the most challenging portion of the Venery."

"They will make it through unscathed," Freila replied. "Having Preza with them will be a great boon, she has much experience fighting the Greishic."

"So did her mother, but she still fell to the creatures," commented Sieyna.

Freila stared at Sieyna with indignation and was about to respond, but the woman continued.

"Our foremothers should have quelled the Greishic ages ago when they had the chance," Sieyna stated. "But they were shortsighted and expected the beasts to die off on their own. They failed to eliminate them when they were weak, and now we are left to face the creatures at full strength."

"We cannot blame everything on our ancestors," Gilza replied. "The dire times we face now cannot wholly be attributed to the deeds of those that came before us. We must put our faith in Vesta, and in our fellow sisters."

"While you make a valid point, do not forget that it may very well be Vesta's will for us to perish," Sieyna replied. "Our punishment for generations of arrogance. Tell me, Cereila, what news of Selfa Delreza? She should be returning any day now, correct?"

"Yes," she replied. "Selfa Delreza has nearly returned from her Venery in Noor. She should be able to give a full report on the events that transpired there later in the week."

"Truly shameful the rumors from Noor turned out to be just that. It would have saved so much time and effort to have the male on this side of the Greenwood," commented Freila.

Gilza nodded. "Agreed. I am happy those responsible for spreading the false rumors have been dealt with. May their punishment serve as a message to any sisters who contemplate doing the same."

"Executing our own sisters, deserving or not, will not serve to increase our numbers," Cereila stated.

Gilza turned to Cereila. "The world is bad enough without added malcontent stirring throughout the land. We must eliminate these ideologies before they become rampant."

"Let us just pray to Vesta that the report from Rolier is genuine," Cereila replied.

"My dear sisters, we are at the point where we must investigate any whisper of a male, no matter the risk." Gilza continued, "It has simply been far too long since the last emergence. Assuming we have not lost favor in Vesta's eyes, someone must be hiding him."

"Freila, would you mind once more sharing what it was your agent reported? Did she actually *see* the male?" Sieyna asked.

"It is as I have stated hundreds of times, dear Sister. Feel free to consult the archives for my report if you would like to hear it again."

"Oh, I have read it many times, but there is one thing that just does not make sense to me, no matter how I try to fathom it."

"And what is that, Sieyna?"

"How is it that your agent discovered this male, and yet was unable to discern any details about him? His age, his precise location. Pit, even the color of his hair was absent from the report."

"Did you not hear what Gilza said, mere moments ago? A rumor of a male is all we need. I have instructed my agents to report to me *any* whisperings of a male."

"And yet, Freila, your agent in Noor had far more details regarding that supposed male, and the endeavor ended up being false."

"I cannot control if one of my agents interprets falsehoods as fact, nor can I control if they decide to spin their own. Believe me, for my own selfishness, I would have much preferred the male to have been in Noor, and thus save my daughters from the risk of crossing the Greenwood."

"As you say, dear Sister," Sieyna replied with a smirk.

"I do not much like your tone, Sister." Freila's anger grew as she met Sieyna's eyes. "If you have words for me, then by all means, speak them now."

"Apologies, Freila. At this time I have no words for you. I was merely agreeing with your sentiment."

"Next time you decide to *agree* with me, a simple nod will suffice. I find your malcontent with the transpiring events to be an affront to both me and my daughters."

"Enough!" Gilza exclaimed. "Your squawking has battered my ears long enough! Let us move on to the other matters at hand."

∗ ∗ ∗

Joreya had just finished cooking the remainder of ingredients from their food stores. She always hated cooking. It was a skill she never learned. The vegetables in the pan were noticeably burnt, but Joreya doubted her mother would even notice. The woman had been sick with worry after learning her daughters were not being summoned to take a man's seed but were being conscripted to defend Memier from the Greishic. There had been little word of her wombsisters in almost three days. It seemed the city required far more sisters to fight back the creatures than those already recruited. What little info Joreya had learned was that a great horde of Greishic had crossed the Reypar's eastern flow and had been trying to breach the Paling. The Regent had ordered all able-bodied sisters of a certain age to take up arms and help hold the line in protecting the Paling.

It was strange, being at home with just her mother. Surprisingly, the one positivity to come from all this was her mother had not struck her since everyone had left. Joreya took little cheer in it, however. She would prefer to face the beatings if it meant her wombsisters were safe at home. Joreya's mother had spent very little time outside of her bedchamber. There had been a knock at the door a day ago, and Joreya's mother had surprised her by rushing out of her room to answer it.

Unfortunately, it was not one of her daughters, nor was it even word of their wellbeing. It was a sister going door to door in search of steel or iron that could be donated to the city's defenses. It seemed Memier had resigned itself to melting down cookware to produce more arms. Joreya was far from knowledgeable in regard to military affairs, but even she knew such desperation was not a good sign. Her mother had been furious with the poor sister. She went to the kitchen, grabbed a heavy iron pan, and hurled it at the sister's face. Thankfully, her mother had missed, but the sister was barely able to retreat uninjured before her mother hurled another. Joreya wondered if Rueila would show half as much worry if she were out there on the battlefield. The thought made her laugh. Her mother, worried for *her*? No doubt she'd be delighted to be rid of her least favorite daughter, given the chance.

Joreya finished cooking her lunch and sat down to eat. The meal was overcooked and dry. She forced it down anyway. Joreya would have to visit the market later to get more food. She doubted her mother would give her any coin, but she could always take out some of what she had been saving from selling her carvings. The dream of selling her artwork to escape Memier seemed so distant now, but Joreya had not given up hope.

A muffled shout suddenly erupted outside, it almost sounded like her wombsister, Beya. Joreya got up and moved toward the door, but before she could reach it, her mother burst out and rushed forward, knocking Joreya to the ground in the process.

Rueila yanked open the door, and Joreya saw her wombsisters, Beya and Reya, standing outside. The twins were huddled against one another, filthy, and looked as if they had not slept in a week. Their mother quickly pulled them both against her in a secure embrace.

"Daughters, you have returned! Oh, Vesta be praised!"

Beya stared at her mother for a long while before answering. "We were sent home, Mother," Beya's voice sounded coarse as she spoke. "We managed to fight off the Greishic and preserve the city. For now."

Joreya looked at Reya, expecting her to respond, but her wombsister just stared blankly at their mother. Joreya had never seen such an empty look on her wombsister's face. Reya was usually energetic and full of life. The woman who stood at the door now seemed like a whole different person. Reya was filthy and disheveled in appearance, and Joreya couldn't be sure, but it seemed a large clump of her hair had been torn out.

"My daughters are heroes! Come in, quickly now! Mother's here." She guided them inside. "Joreya, fetch some water!"

Joreya nearly flinched in surprise at her mother using her given name. She could not remember the last time her mother did not refer to her as "little rat" or "useless girl." She quickly ran into their kitchen and began pumping water into a cup.

"What of Gureya and Eleza, daughters? Do you know if they are to return soon as well?"

"No, Mother," Beya replied, her voice wavering. "I haven't seen or heard anything regarding them since we were separated at the city square."

"Where is that water, little rat?" her mother demanded.

Oh well, it was nice while it lasted, Joreya thought. She quickly brought two cups over to them and attempted to hand them out, but her mother snatched the cups out of her hands, apparently wanting to provide such an offering herself.

"You must tell me all you have experienced the past few days. Leave nothing out," her mother said as she led them gently over to the table.

Beya helped Reya to a chair, then sat herself. She took a deep breath and began, "It was awful, Mother. Upon reaching the city square, we were offered a weapon, and a few of us were provided armor. When they ran out of proper iron and steel weapons, they began handing out hastily fastened spears that were little more than sticks. Most of the younger sisters were given the spears and tasked with staying back near the Paling. Those who were better equipped were sent to the front line to fight alongside the more experienced soldiers.

"On the first day, we mainly just stood around and received some very basic training. Although things were calm, we could all feel the tension in the air. On the night of the first day, we began to hear heavy thumping sounds coming from the Greenwood, followed by intense rustling. The watchtowers started shooting arrows lit with fire into the Greenwood. It seemed after every arrow was loosed, a Greishic cried out, whether from anger or pain, I could not tell. It was not long before the burning arrows provided enough light for us to see the dark shapes of the Greishic. I was standing atop the Paling and could see the entire battlefield. I had forgotten just how human they look. From where I stood, I may have mistaken them for sisters if not for their filth covered bodies and sharpened claws. Caked with dark mud, their bodies were well concealed on the dark night."

Beya paused for a long while, as if she was trying to remember something long forgotten. "The beasts came out of the Greenwood in vast numbers and began charging up the Eastern Slope. I heard a loud horn sound and turned to see Regent Vuleila on the rampart, signaling the sisters to take up a defensive position. I watched as arrow after arrow flew through the air. There seemed to be thousands of them, some flew from the watchtowers and others from the Paling wall. Most of the first wave of Greishic fell to the arrows, and those that made it through the barrage were swiftly cut down by our sisters in waiting. Very few of the creatures held weapons. Most attacked with their long sharpened claws. There were so many Greishic pouring out from the Greenwood, their numbers seemed endless.

"The second wave pushed forward, and this time many more reached the front line. I heard the clash of steel and flesh as the Greishic tried to drive through the line and break our sister's ranks. The Regent sounded the horn once more, signaling the next group of sisters to bolster the line. My group was called down from the Paling and sent through the gate. As I was on my way to the battlefield, I heard a sickening crack, followed by shouts off in the distance. I looked and saw one of the watchtowers topple and collapse to the ground, those inside screaming as it fell.

"The battle continued on. The hateful howls of the Greishic grew louder as they advanced toward the city. The next wave of the beasts came, this time with weapons in hand. Regent Vuleila's horn blasted again, and she too joined the battlefield. We all charged into the fray with her. I rushed forward, thrusting my wooden spear at anything that wasn't human. I'm not sure if I killed any Greishic, but I certainly stuck a few.

I heard my sisters' screams as many fell in battle. Others were screaming while being dragged by their hair toward the Greenwood. Sisters that had been standing alongside me mere moments before now lay dead upon the ground.

"Finally, after what felt like an eternity, the Greishic broke and began retreating to the Greenwood. In the fervor of battle, many sisters chased after them, myself included, but we were summoned back by Regent Vuleila's horn. She commanded us to search for any wounded sisters who still lived and help them get back into the city where they could be tended to. I looked around at the bodies that encircled me, I could barely tell the dead from the living. Hundreds of sisters lay upon the ground. Most had deep slashes carved into their flesh, others just lay with their bodies bent in unnatural positions.

Tears began dripping down Beya's cheeks. "But the worst..." She sniffed, trying to clear the sobs from her throat. "The worst part was the stillness of the battlefield once it was all over. The abnormal peace allowed us to clearly hear the sounds coming from the Greenwood. They were cries, cries of our sisters. Screams of torment echoed across the battleground. Some sisters cried out to their mothers in agony, others to Vesta. I also heard sisters yelling in provocation, cursing the Greishic before they were suddenly silenced. I cannot know for sure the fate that had befallen these sisters, but I am certain it was one worse than death.

"I just stood there, surrounded by my sisters and staring at the Greenwood. I heard someone near me speak, 'Our sisters fought bravely today, Child. They will soon be at peace and in the arms of Vesta's ever-burning Flame.' I turned and saw Regent Vuleila beside me. She too was covered in mud and blood, and gazed into the Greenwood just as I did. As she continued to stare, I noticed something in her eyes, something I never expected to see in the eyes of our heroic leader. I saw fear."

Joreya let out a breath she hadn't realized she was holding. She knew the Greischic were an ever-present threat, but until now, they always seemed so distant, so mythical. As long as they stayed behind the Paling, they were safe. At least that's what they had been told time and time again.

"We remained at the ready for another night, waiting for more attacks, but none came. Many of the younger sisters were sent home today, while the older ones remained on duty. On my way here, I ran into Reya who was wandering the streets in a daze, poor girl." Beya reached out and gently put her arm around her twin, who stiffened at the touch. "I am not certain what horrors she witnessed, but I fear they were worse than my own."

Joreya was startled to realize she had not heard Reya make a single utterance since she had returned home. "What is wrong with her?" Joreya asked.

Beya looked at Reya, with concern. "I don't know, she hasn't spoken since I found her. She screamed when I first touched her, but her cries calmed when she recognized me."

"Oh, my poor babies!" her mother exclaimed. "You have done your duty to the Sisterhood, Vesta bless you. I am proud of both of you and glad to have you back at home safe. Right now, you should get cleaned up and get to bed. I imagine after the long days you have had, some respite is much needed."

Beya nodded and slowly got up from the table, helping Reya up and guiding her to their bedchamber. Joreya's mother stared after them, her face fluctuating between relief and concern. She then began walking toward her own bedchamber, but before entering, she turned to Joreya.

"The next time there is a call to arms, you will join as well. I do not care what age they call for. The Sisterhood needs every sister they can find, even hopeless ones such as you."

* * *

The next morning there was a knock at their door. When Joreya's mother answered it, a soldier stood there, holding multiple parchments in her hand.

"Is this the residence of Rueila, mother of Gureya and Eleza?" she asked.

"It is, do you have word of them?" Rueila responded anxiously.

"Yes, Sister. Due to heavy casualties, your daughter, Eleza, has been posted to one of the watchtowers on the edge of the Greenwood. There is currently no estimate as to when she will be allowed to return home."

"And what of Gureya?"

The soldier hesitated for a moment. "I am sorry, Sister, but your daughter Gureya has not yet returned from the battlefield, and at this point, she is presumed to be either dead or captured."

Rueila stared at the soldier blankly.

"Sister?"

"I'm sorry, what did you say?" Rueila asked.

The soldier swallowed slowly. "Your daughter Gureya has not yet returned from the battlefield, and she is presumed to be either dead or captured."

Rueila's face slowly transformed to one of horror before she collapsed to her knees. "No... not my little Gur... Gureya... there must be... an error," she managed to sob out.

"I am sorry. While we cannot completely rule out the possibility of Gureya being found, it is unlikely that she survived the battle."

"Gureya! My daughter, Oh, little Gureya!" Rueila wailed.

The soldier bowed solemnly and left. Joreya felt pain fragment her heart, pain she had never experienced before. Her wombsister was dead, or worse, taken by the Greishic. She would never see her again. Tears welled up in her eyes and dripped down her cheeks. She took a step toward her mother. She wanted to embrace, wanted to cry with Rueila, but the thought filled Joreya with uncertainty. Would her mother want that? Beya and Reya remained asleep in their bedchamber, so they could provide no comfort. Joreya had never seen her mother like this. She decided to approach slowly.

"Don't you dare touch me!" her mother shouted. "It's *your* fault she's gone! You useless little rat!"

The tears streamed down Joreya's face. "No, Mother, I had nothing to do with it, I wasn't even there."

"Exactly! Had you been there, the Greishic would have gotten *you*, not my sweet Gureya! You took her away from me!" Her mother rose suddenly and grabbed a wooden plate off the nearby table. "You useless rat!" She swung the plate at Joreya, bashing her face with it. Joreya staggered back and fell to her knees, attempting to stay conscious as her vision began to blur. She raised her arms in preparation for another blow, but none came. Her mother had moved across the room and was rapidly searching through an old chest, raving like a madwoman. Old clothes came out of the trunk in a flurry, but her mother kept digging until she finally pulled out a little blue dress. Her mother stared at the dress before hugging it tightly to her chest as she slid to the floor.

Joreya recognized the dress instantly, for she knew it well. Gureya wore the blue dress when she was a little girl. Joreya remembered her wombsister wearing it proudly and spinning around the home, full of childish bliss as she danced to soundless music. Gureya dancing in that dress became a big part of their household until the day came when she outgrew both the dress and the dancing. It was a good memory.

Her mother continued clutching the dress and wailing. She held it to her face and breathed in its ghostly scent.

Joreya remembered Gureya offering her the dress once. She had said it would look cute on her, and since it didn't fit anymore, she had no reason to keep it. The gift filled Joreya's heart with joy. She had always loved the way the dress looked and had never before been given anything so lovely.

That was when her mother had burst into the room and yanked the dress away. Rueila even shouted at Gureya for attempting to give away the dress and screamed at Joreya for thinking that she, a useless little rat, would deserve anything so nice.

Joreya needed to get out. She needed to get away from her mother and to a place where she could properly mourn the loss of her wombsister. She decided she would carve a figure of Gureya wearing her beautiful dress, it would be her greatest masterpiece. She slowly got up and moved delicately past her mother, who was still on the floor and now petting the dress. Opening the door, Joreya ran down the steps to the street and went toward her hiding place. From the street, she could still hear her mother's cries. They were joined by a chorus of other wails that echoed throughout the city.

* * *

"A thousand of our sisters dead or taken," Regent Vuleila repeated to the others in the room. They all stood in the main chamber of the Regent's Keep, pouring over reports and attempting to recover from the recent battles.

"All with ripe wombs. It will take generations to replenish those numbers," Yelza commented.

"I am sure the Regent is aware of the full magnitude of the number," Nilza replied.

"Oh, dearest Treya," Vuleila murmured, her eyes staring at the wall. "She followed me everywhere without question, and I couldn't even follow her in death."

Nilza rested her hand gently on Vuleila's shoulder. "She died with honor and dignity, far more than we can say for many of the other sisters we lost."

"Better off than most, truly," replied Yelza, sadly.

Vuleila wiped her eyes and turned her gaze from the wall. "The time for mourning must come later. We barely survived that battle. Vesta help us if the Greishic still possess the numbers for another assault. I see no way we can survive it."

"The carpenters have inspected the damage to the Paling, and reported that any gashes appeared superficial and are no threat to the wall's structural integrity," Nilza replied.

"That is positive news, but I fear what will happen if the Greishic are left unchecked and free to strike our walls at will," stated Yelza. "We no longer have the numbers, nor the armaments to defend the whole Paling."

Vuleila nodded. "If the Greishic attack again, Memier will fall. I have no doubt of that. One breach, that is all it will take. One breach and a Greishic horde will flood through this city for the first time in history."

"Should we begin preparing citizens to fight the beasts within the city?" asked Nilza.

"Their numbers are far too great. It would be better to prepare them for evacuation," replied Yelza.

Nilza shook her head. "To where? Neither Rolier nor Coratch possess the means to take in refugees at this magnitude. It is also very likely the Greishic will run down our sisters on the road."

"Perhaps south. There may be enough riverboats in Wolenn to take many part way through the Greenwood," Yelza suggested.

"That faces the same challenge. Worse yet, leading a Greishic to one of the neighboring villages will only increase the speed of the Sisterhood's demise." Vuleila thought hard. There had to be some way. A way to save the city and its people. They had heard nothing of reinforcements from Haralda, and not a single divebird from the Hearth at all. It was possible more soldiers were on their way at that very moment, but they would not make it in time. Memier would have to continue to face this threat alone.

X

Rumors in a Small Town

Keila sat in Rolier's town hall and listened as one of her neighbors, Treila, droned on and on. "What I am saying is, I do not think the Hearth will be completely satisfied with the rate we are progressing. We are behind schedule on construction for the new riverboats. We should have had more than three of the barges completed days ago."

"I understand your concern, Treila, but the delay is not our doing," Mitilza, the mayor of Rolier, replied. "The delivery from Memier is late, and we cannot continue the project without the proper materials. We have the lumber, but very little else."

"Perhaps we should send a bird to Memier seeking information on the delay?"

"I have already sent one."

"Well, a messenger, then?"

"If you are volunteering, dear Sister, then, by all means, you are free to make the journey," the mayor answered.

Treila's face squinted up as she attempted to find a response to the mayor's words. "Well, I just hope it arrives soon. It'd be most regrettable to have our goods wasting away on the docks waiting for enough ships to deliver them."

"If I have not heard from Memier in another three days, I shall send another message. I imagine the Regent is rather busy at the moment, fending off the Greishic attacks," Mayor Mitilza replied.

"Have you more news of the attack, Mitilza?" another sister questioned.

"Yes, but before rumors get out of control, let me say, here and now, what information I know," Mayor Mitilza declared. "A few days ago, there was a massive assault on the Paling by the Greishic. And while our brave sisters were able to push them back to the Greenwood, many warriors were lost. However, do not be concerned. For as it stands, Memier is safe, as are we."

"But Mayor, what if some of the beasts managed to sneak around the city and are coming this way?" This question created a wave of panic and arguments in the town hall.

"Listen!" the mayor shouted, quelling the crowd. "The Paling was not built so that the Greishic could just *go around*. Our ancestors had more foresight than that!"

"But not enough foresight to extinguish the Greishic before their numbers were allowed to multiply?"

"I'm sure they had their reasons. Nevertheless, I repeat that we remain safe from the Greishic. Even in the unlikely event that Memier falls, the Hearth would surely send warriors to fight in defense of the other towns and villages on the Eastern Plateau. Have faith, sisters. Faith in the Hearth, and faith in Vesta."

Keila rolled her eyes at this. The Hearth would do nothing for them. Why would they send sisters of prime birthing age to protect remote villages that were made up mostly of gammers and hags? No, she knew the Jurisa would not think twice before letting them all die. Their traded goods made up a fraction of what the Hearth used in a month, they had nothing of actual value to offer the Hearth. Nothing except...

Keila cleared her throat. "What truth is there to the rumor that a selfa is crossing the Greenwood?"

The mayor hesitated for a moment. "There is authenticity to this rumor. I received word that Selfa Zeya will be coming to the Eastern Plateau, but I have no notion of where or when the Venery will reach its end."

This brought a new wave of emotion to the town hall, one of excitement.

"If the Selfa is coming east, then maybe the Hearth won't abandon us! Selfas are too rare to risk, especially in these times."

"Do you think she's coming here?"

"I bet the buck is in Memier! A city of that size must have plenty of places to keep one hidden."

"Sisters!" Mayor Mitilza once again shouted over the excited crowd. "Speculation at this point is of no use to us, but if the Selfa does come here, we will show her every bit of hospitality and respect that she deserves, agreed?"

"Agreed!" Most in the hall shouted in response. Keila did not. She had had her fill of the Hearth's self-seeking ways. That was why she had left Vulna in the first place. The Hearth only cared for the people when it benefited them.

The mayor adjourned the meeting, and as Keila was leaving the town hall, she noticed Heleila trying her best to make it inside. Her face turned downcast as the other villagers told her the meeting had ended. The woman noticed Keila and her face transformed with a smile. She hobbled over, relying heavily on her cane.

"Oh, Keila! I am so glad to see you! Were you at the meeting?"

"No, Sister, I just decided to stand outside, looking like a fool."

Heleila stared at her. It seemed she was not entirely cognizant of the sarcasm in Keila's words. Keila sighed internally and put on a smile. "I jest, Heleila! Yes, I was at the meeting."

"Oh, Vesta bless you, I cannot believe I missed it! I was on my way, planning to arrive early and get a good seat, but Aadeya had another one of her fits, and I had to tend to that. Poor thing, I really thought the new herbs were working! I wonder if I should take her to Memier to see a proper physician, but can you imagine? Me, making the trip to Memier with my leg? I haven't the coin for a wagon, and certainly wouldn't be able to get on a horse in this condition! And just imagine if my daughter were to have a fit on the journey? I'm not sure I'd be able to calm her down out on the road. No, I suppose my poor Aady will have to get better on her own. At least the frequency of her fits has been significantly reduced, why when she was a child she would sometimes have one or two a day! Imagine having to deal with that, oh, my blessed daughter, I should be grateful for the improvement. Vesta be praised."

Keila continued nodding through the woman's verboseness.

"But dear me, I do not wish to keep you. Say, would you, by chance, be heading home now? I would love to hear the news of the meeting!"

Keila considered lying and claiming she was going to do some shopping in town, but truthfully, she was tired and really did want to get home. "Yes, I am."

"Oh, good! I will walk with you. If you don't mind my slower pace, that is."

The pair began heading toward their huts on the outskirts of the village. Keila tried her best to tell Heleila what transpired at the meeting, but the woman's ramblings made concentrating a challenge.

"It would also appear that the rumors were true. A selfa will be crossing the Greenwood to the Eastern Plateau," Keila said.

"Truly? How grand! Is she coming here? Did the mayor say? Though I imagine she wouldn't have said, she may not even know. The Hearth is always so secretive! As if they think the person hiding the male will just up and disappear! Where do they think they'd take a male? The Selfa can sense him from very far away, so there's no place to hide from one, truly!"

"I am not so sure I share your enthusiasm, Heleila."

"No? What reason could you have for such sentiments?"

"I have seen plenty of selfa in my days living in Vulna, and while I have no first-hand experience with them, I can say one thing for certain. The Selfa are the arm of the Hearth, and the Hearth has but one goal. Facilitating the creation of the next generation of sisters. They will do whatever necessitates this, and they care not for what ruin it may bring to the rest of us."

"Well, that is certainly a dark outlook, Keila! Very dark, truly! But even so, just imagine if the Selfa did come to our humble village, I wager even you would wish to meet her!"

As the two women approached their huts, they bade their goodbyes. Keila entered her home and let out a notable sigh as she sat down at her table. It had been quite a day. Noticing her wrinkled bed, she got up, went to her kitchen area, and began mashing up some food in preparation for dinner.

XI

The Goddess' Braid

As the outpost of Haralda came into view, Zeya was glad to reach another milestone of the Venery. The feeling was bittersweet, however, as Haralda would be their last stop before the Greenwood. The outpost did not consist of much. Surrounded by wooden walls, there were a few buildings, including stables, guard towers, sleeping quarters, a mess hall, and training grounds.

"I thought it'd be... bigger," Meleya commented.

"It is as large as it needs to be," Preza replied. "The Greishic rarely make the journey up the cliff to enter the Western Plateau. Any that do are quickly felled by the sisters who watch over it."

"While that is good to hear, I now fear the Sisterhood is inadequately protected," Meleya replied. "Seeing how this tiny outpost is all that stands between a Greishic horde and us."

"There has not been a single Greishic to make it past Haralda in over a hundred years. I think we'll be safe. So long as we survive the Venery, that is."

"Guess we'll be having to leave our horses," Zeya remarked, stroking her mare gently.

"Yes, so make sure to give it one last big kiss, right on the lips," quipped Meleya.

"Gross!" Zeya laughed.

"Just please, no tongue, dear Wombsister!"

"But that's the best part!" Preza exclaimed.

"Ugh, you two really know how to take a joke too far," Zeya groaned.

They approached the guards at the gate who greeted them warmly. "Hail, Selfa Zeya, and welcome to Haralda. Captain Layna is expecting you. She can be found at the barracks. It's the large building just to the left."

As they entered the outpost, Zeya heard grunts and the clashing of steel coming from the training grounds. There were approximately thirty sisters, some of whom were currently engaged in a skirmish. They paid her absolutely no mind, and for that, she was grateful. The sisters of Haralda were disciplined. They had their duty, and they were respectful of it. There would be no gawking from them.

Someone from the barracks approached them with open arms. "Ah, the Selfa has graced us with her presence! Welcome, Selfa Zeya. I am Captain Layna."

Zeya bowed. "Greetings. These are my companions, Meleya and Preza."

"Preza? And a sister of such stature! I knew your mother well, and a greater fighter I have never known. Tell me, are you as skilled in battle as she?"

"They say that I am."

The captain nodded, then turned to Zeya. "With this one guarding your back, you will surely make it to the Slope unscathed."

"That is our hope," Zeya replied, then eyed Preza with renewed appreciation.

Captain Layna looked at the group, hesitantly.

"Yes, Captain, what is it?" Meleya asked.

"Forgive me, sisters, but I could not help but notice your hair."

"What of it, Captain?" Zeya asked.

"It's just… the two of you have longer locks than is suggested when facing the beasts."

Preza nodded. "I have told them this before, Captain." She turned to her companions. "Will you not cut your hair now?"

"My braid is short enough!" Meleya replied. "Besides, if a Greishic comes within striking distance of me, I plan on cutting it down."

Captain Layna looked between the Selfa and her wombsister cautiously.

"Speak freely, Captain," Zeya said. "We welcome your experience, and will not chastise you for your comments."

Captain Layna nodded. "Yes, of course. Forgive me, Selfa Zeya, but it would be wise to trim your hair shorter. The creatures have used our long hair to their advantage in the past. We on the borderlands know to keep it short to reduce the likelihood of such an attack."

Zeya ran a hand through her dark hair, then eyed her Wombsister's side braid. "What do you suggest?"

"Your companion, Preza, has a good length. The beasts will need to get in very close to get a handful of her hair."

Meleya shook her head. "I have always kept my hair in a side braid, is that not acceptable, Captain?"

Captain Layna hesitated again before speaking. "Acceptable, but not suggested, Sister. All Haraldans are required to keep their hair no longer than their shoulders. And while I do not doubt your capabilities to keep the Greishic at bay, I would strongly encourage you to keep shorter locks."

Zeya nodded. "Very well, I will cut mine." She turned to her wombsister. "Meleya?"

Meleya gripped her braid tightly. "I would prefer to keep it as is."

"As you say." Captain Layna replied. "Please, follow me to our barber, Selfa Zeya. She will get you trimmed up in no time.

The captain led them through the camp, and most Haraldan warriors continued to pay them no mind. Eventually, they reached a building with a line of women outside.

"New recruits," Preza commented.

"Aye," the captain replied. "We get fewer and fewer each year, but most are capable." The captain went to the front of the line. "Forgive me, sisters, but we have honored guests that are in greater need of a cut than you." Captain Layna motioned for Zeya to enter.

"Come in, please," a woman standing over a sister with a pair of scissors replied. She then looked up. "Oh, Selfa Zeya! What an honor! I am Lieutenant Grueza."

"Lieutenant, the Selfa has requested her hair be cut more to Haraldan standards," Captain Layna said.

"Trimming the hair of a selfa is not something I ever imagined having the pleasure of. Please, have a seat." The lieutenant motioned to a nearby empty chair. "I will be with you momentarily."

Zeya cautiously approached the chair before sitting. "She won't go too short, will she?"

Captain Layna smiled. "The lieutenant is more than capable of fulfilling your requests. I will wait for you outside."

"Thank you, Captain." Preza gave a slight bow as the woman left.

Lieutenant Grueza finished up with her current patron and moved over to Zeya. She ran her fingers through Zeya's hair, then pulled on it gently. "Most Haraldans choose to have it as short as possible, but it seems that is not your desire? How about I cut it to about here." The lieutenant held her fingers halfway up Zeya's neck.

"What's the longest you'd recommend?" Zeya asked nervously. "I've never had my hair short, Lieutenant, so forgive my hesitation."

"Understandable, my Selfa. It will be an adjustment, but I believe you will get used to it rather quickly. Most do. To your shoulders would be the longest I'd suggest."

Zeya ran her hands through her dark hair one final time. "Yes, let's do that."

"Excellent. Shall I begin?"

Zeya took a deep breath, then nodded.

The lieutenant got to work, and Zeya cringed with each cut. She convinced herself it would eventually grow back, but even that did little to calm her mind.

"You know, I normally don't even cut hair anymore," the lieutenant mused.

"Truly?" Zeya asked, thankful for the distracting conversation.

"Truly. The usual barber is in mandatory training. I'm not complaining, though. It's nice to get back to it."

"That explains a lot," Preza stated. "I wondered why a lieutenant was stuck with scissors instead of a proper blade."

"Aye. One of my first duties when I joined up. Sure beats my current ones, though."

"And what are those?" Zeya asked.

"Leading scouting parties down into the Greenwood."

"A rough duty, truly," Preza replied. "But I imagine you are good at it, considering you stand here now."

Lieutenant Grueza nodded. "I am. But it helps that luck has been on my side, at least for now." The lieutenant stopped cutting and turned to Preza. "But I know I don't need to tell you that, Sister."

Preza nodded solemnly.

After what felt like an eternity, the lieutenant set down her pair of scissors and stared at Zeya admiringly. "I hope you like it. Not my best work, but also not my worst. There's a looking glass in the corner of the room, if you'd like to see."

Zeya ran her hand through her hair. It felt strange. What her hand felt contradicted her expectations. She turned to Meleya and Preza. "How does it look?"

Preza nodded her appreciation. "Now you look like a warrior of the Sisterhood. Truly."

Zeya smiled. "And you, Wombsister? What are your thoughts?"

"It will take some getting used to. But you appear to be the same person."

"So you're next?" Zeya teased.

Meleya shook her head aggressively before gripping her braid. "Certainly not. I'm not saying I'll never cut my braid, but for now, I will keep it intact."

Zeya got up and went over to the looking glass. The sight startled her at first, but after a few moments, she found herself appreciating the cut. "I think I like it."

"I am glad to hear!" Lieutenant Grueza replied. "It has been an honor to cut your hair. I pray to the goddess that you and your companions will have a safe journey and that we will see you again before long."

Zeya bowed. "Thank you, Lieutenant. And you have my gratitude for taking the care that you did with my hair. Alé volás."

"Alé volás, my Selfa."

* * *

"Oh, Vesta! You look like a new sister!" Captain Layna exclaimed after they met her outside. "I hope it is to your liking?"

Zeya nodded. "Yes. Lieutenant Grueza did an excellent job."

"She always does." The captain smiled. "Sisters, I know you cannot stay long, but perchance, could you join us for a meal? It won't be much, but I can have it served with the utmost haste!"

"Regrettably, we cannot," Zeya replied. "We must reach the bottom of the Braid before nightfall."

The captain frowned. "I understand. Your horses will be well cared for until your return, I promise you that."

"Thank you, Captain," Zeya replied. "Both we and our horses appreciate it."

"How much Greishic activity have your scouts observed lately?" Preza asked.

"Not much, thank Vesta. Certainly less than usual, a few roving bands here and there. My guess is the recent assaults on Memier have thinned some of their numbers."

Preza looked surprised. "Assaults on Memier?"

"Aye, we received a bird a short while ago. The Greishic have been attacking the Paling, trying to breach the city. So far, the soldiers of Memier have been able to fight them back, though I expect they've been taking casualties."

"That's terrible," Meleya murmured.

"Indeed, it is. But we on the borderlands know our duty. May the captured break free, and the dead enter into Vesta's Embrace. Regent Vuleila is a skilled tactician and a formidable warrior. I'm sure she's been keeping the list of fallen sisters as low as could be."

The three remained silent.

"Fear not, sisters, for they were not taken from the Sisterhood in vain. The beasts will no doubt be recuperating from their defeat, which means you will have fewer roaming the Greenwood to face. Regent Vuleila has called for our aid, and I am only waiting on orders from the Hearth to charge into the Greenwood and draw the attention of the creatures. I expect a bird from the Hearth in a day or so. Once they get the message, they'll send us on in."

"It warms my heart to see that the Sisterhood's defense is in such capable hands," Zeya replied.

Captain Leyna smiled broadly. "Just doing my duty, my Selfa. It's you that's got the difficult path ahead."

Zeya nodded. "Well, if you will take us to the Braid, we should be on our way."

The captain led them across the outpost to the end of the cliff. Zeya looked over the edge and regarded the Greenwood below. The vast forest nearly filled her entire view. She was barely able to make out the other side of the massive canyon from their vantage point. Winding through the Greenwood was the Reypar River. Somewhere in the distance, its main flow rushed down from the northern mountains before splitting off into the four lesser distributary flows. The whole sight was daunting, and Zeya felt her stomach churn.

"Quite a view, is it not?" Captain Layna asked.

"That is putting it mildly. I have never before laid eyes on something so majestic, and yet, so ominous," Meleya replied. "I cannot believe we are to travel through *that*."

Zeya noticed a number of smoke trails scattered throughout the forest. "Are those—"

"Greishic camps, yes," Preza replied.

"There are so many!" exclaimed Meleya.

"Aye, every year the number of camps grows," replied the captain. "Thank Vesta, most of them are north of the route you will take. If I had it my way, I would send a detachment of sisters to aid you in the crossing, but the Hearth explicitly ordered me to do no such thing."

"The Hearth fears we will attract more Greishic with larger numbers," Zeya replied. "And they are probably right."

"They are. Still, I don't much like the Jurisa sending just the three of you through Greishic lands." Captain Layna paused, then cleared her throat. "In any case, the entrance to the Goddess' Braid lies just over there. It will take some time to descend to the forest floor. Additionally, I sent a few scouts down this morning to ensure you would not stumble into any beasts at the bottom. They returned shortly before your arrival and reported the way was clear. There were no fresh signs of Greishic activity in the immediate area."

"Thank you, Captain Layna. We appreciate your efforts to aid in the Venery," Preza said, bowing.

"I would do more if I could, sisters. If the Selfa fails to cross the Greenwood, the Sisterhood is finished. I have no doubt of that. Not immediately as the doomsayers shouting in the streets would have us believe, but within a matter of years, for certain."

The captain walked with them over to the entrance to the Goddess' Braid. Looking down, Zeya could see it was made up of a series of steep switchbacks. Comparatively, going down would be the easy part, while having to climb back up would be very strenuous. Far worse than ascending the stairs to the Hearth's Aviary. At least she would have the male on the return, and much of her burden would be lifted. *If* she found the male.

"Hail, Selfa Zeya!" Captain Layna abruptly shouted in a commanding tone.

Zeya turned and saw all the warriors of Haralda at the edge of the outpost watching them go.

"Hail, sisters! Hail, the Venery!" the women shouted in response.

Zeya looked at the captain and bowed deeply. She then faced the women of Haralda and did the same. Turning, she and her companions began their slow descent into the Greenwood.

* * *

When they were partway down the Goddess' Braid, Zeya began lagging back. Watching the care-free demeanor of her companions as they descended the Braid set something off inside her mind. Each step brought her closer to the end of the Venery and nearer to failure. She knew she would fail, somehow she would. Even if she did locate the male, there was no guarantee she could sufficiently protect him on the return. What if she found him, but he died when they were mere days away from Vulna? That thought had never occurred to her until now. Finding the male was the biggest hurdle, but getting him back alive was equally important, maybe even more so. If she found him and he didn't survive the journey, she surely would be seen as the worst selfa the Sisterhood has ever known. What kind of selfa fails to protect the most precious phenomenon in the entire world? She would be hated, maybe even banished. How could she live her life then? How could she survive? By preying on the weak as the brigands did? As the burden on her mind grew, her breaths became ragged and irregular.

What if they were returning through the Sol Forest and those same brigands attacked once more and killed him? There was so much that could go wrong, why didn't the Hearth send more sisters with her? Contrary to what the leaf on her breast signified, she knew she was not destined for greatness, she was just an ordinary woman! Why was it she who was tasked with being the only one to protect—

"Zeya, what's wrong?"

Meleya jarred her from her thoughts. She hadn't realized, but she had completely stopped walking and stood gazing blankly at the forest below. She looked at Meleya and slowly shook her head.

"What is it?" Preza asked.

"I... I can't."

"Can't what?" questioned Preza.

"Can't... this!" Zeya shouted, throwing her arms up in resignation.

"Zeya, we are with you and will see you safely through the Greenwood. We will do it together," Meleya stated.

"No, not the Greenwood, the Venery! It's too much, we don't know for certain that there even is a male in Rolier! Even if there is,

I'm not sure I will be able to find him. What if Vesta has taken her gift from me and I am unable to sense him? Or worse, what if I never had it to begin with? What if I imagined it all? A fever dream of a silly girl who fantasized about being more important than she was!"

"Calm yourself!" Preza hissed, approaching her. "Your hysterics echo off the cliffs and will attract the beasts."

"The Greishic? Let them come! I'd rather be taken by the beasts than face the Sisterhood as a failure!"

Preza turned red with anger and punched Zeya in the face. Zeya collapsed to the ground under the force of the blow and stayed there in shock. Meleya dropped to one knee, making sure her wombsister wasn't too injured. Zeya slowly raised her head and stared at Preza, her face frozen with confusion and disbelief as a welt began to form.

"Don't you *ever* speak lightly of the Greishic! I would choose to kill you myself than let them take you. There is nothing worse in this world than being taken by them. Nothing! Being captured means you will face endless rape and torture that only abates once they have impregnated you with their unholy seed. Only then will you find some peace, but only for a time. They would leave you be as their abominable offspring grows inside you, but any respite would be short-lived. The rotten creature in your womb would continue to develop until it was strong enough to force itself out, tearing your insides as it went. You would experience more pain at that moment than *all* the torture, *all* the rape, combined. If you are fortunate, you will lose consciousness from the pain and finally be resigned to peace as your body is left to bleed out, and you slip into oblivion. I have seen it happen, I have seen sisters begging for death, pleading with Vesta to take away their pain. I have seen those close to me go through this fate, so don't you ever speak such words again! Do you understand?"

Zeya and Meleya stared at Preza in astonishment. They had never before heard her speak of the Greishic in this manner.

"Do you understand, Zeya?"

"Yes, I understand," she replied, weakly. Her head drooped, and she began to let out deep sobs. "I'm... sorry. I am just so overwhelmed by this burden. There has been so much doubt building in my heart since we left Vulna. I don't see the Venery ending successfully, there are too many things that can go wrong."

"This is not your burden alone, Wombsister," Meleya said gently, caressing Zeya's hair. "The three of us were tasked with the Venery, and just because it is our duty to protect you, that does not mean we are not going to help you find the male. Even without Vesta's Blessing, we will do whatever we can to help you find him."

"You may not realize it, Zeya, but we too feel the weight of failure pulling down on our hearts," Preza replied. "But I did not swear myself to be your protector out of blood-bound duty. I did it because I believe in you."

Meleya nodded. "If we are unable to protect you or you do not find the male, we too will return to the Sisterhood as failures, never forget that. You are not the only one with this burden."

"How do you carry it?" Zeya asked weakly.

"Like anything else that weighs me down. With all the strength and determination that I have within me." Meleya smiled. "And of course, with the aid of my sisters,"

Zeya nodded and slowly rose from the ground. Preza reached out her arm, helping her up, then pulled Zeya in for a firm hug. Tears began to stream down the big woman's face.

"Don't worry, Girl. We are with you now and always will be," Preza whispered.

Meleya joined the hug.

"Thank you, sisters. I know I would have no chance of completing this journey without the two of you." Zeya pulled away from the embrace, wiped the tears from her eyes and took a deep breath. "OK. Let us continue the Venery."

* * *

At nightfall, the party reached the bottom of the Goddess' Braid and made camp. The forest floor of the Greenwood was deceptively tranquil, even at dusk. Sounds from birds and other wildlife could be heard, along with a light breeze that rustled through the trees. It was hard to imagine that both danger and death could be lurking just out of sight. It would take them three days to cross the forest, and their path was far from a direct one. They would need to ford all four of the Reypar's distributary flows, and between the third and fourth lay the heart of Greishic territory. The sun would rise late in the canyon and set early. In the denser parts of the Greenwood, it was easy to lose all sense of bearing. Not to mention the ever-present risk of running into any Greishic hunting parties wandering throughout the forest, or worse, stumbling into a Greishic camp.

"I really wish we could have a fire," Meleya complained after climbing into her bedroll. "It's so cold."

"You would risk bringing the Greishic down on us for a bit of warmth?" Preza questioned.

"Obviously not, otherwise we'd all be around a roaring fire! Wombsister, come here and keep me warm!"

"I would prefer to keep my distance from your frigid feet."

"Pit! You're not very helpful. Heyfic, come warm my feet!"

The bird stared at her blankly before cocking its head.

"Have it your way, silly bird. I'll just freeze to death in the night and you'll be stuck guarding my grave." She rolled over in a huff. A moment later, she began laughing.

"What is so funny?" Zeya asked.

"Oh, I was just reminded of the time Preza demanded we help her sneak sweetcakes from the kitchen!"

"I made no such demand, I merely offered you a share of the spoils if you aided me," Preza replied sternly.

Zeya smiled, remembering the incident. "We were so close to perfectly pulling off our heist, but thanks to Meleya's clumsiness..."

"My feet were numb! I was barefoot, and that floor was like walking on a frozen lake in the midst of winter."

"You knocked over a stack of serving trays!" Preza exclaimed. "What does that have to do with your cold feet?"

"My body wasn't responding properly."

"I just remember stuffing sweetcakes down our pants in a frenzy as we heard the cook approaching," Zeya giggled.

"It was so hard to run with those sweetcakes, wasn't it!" Meleya continued. "Remember when the cook caught us, then called for Mother? I thought we were going to be in so much trouble, but Mother just sent the cook away, claiming that she'd deal with us on her own."

"She sure dealt with us," Preza said, smiling. "She took half our sweetcakes for herself as punishment for getting caught, then encouraged us to eat any remaining evidence!"

The three sisters burst out laughing before remembering where they were and quickly stifled their mirth.

"You two get some rest. I'll take the first watch," declared Preza.

Zeya climbed into her bedroll and slept deeply and peacefully for the first time in a long time.

* * *

The next morning, Zeya awoke to Preza, gently shaking her.

"It's time to continue our journey," she said.

Zeya yawned and winced from the pain where Preza had struck her. She looked around, disoriented from her slumber. "Why didn't anyone wake me for my watch?"

"Meleya and I both agreed it was best to let you sleep. You appeared so peaceful and surely needed a full night's rest."

"Thank you, Preza."

Heyfic flew into their camp and dropped something in front of Meleya. She bent down and picked up a small rabbit. "Look, Heyfic brought us breakfast!"

"Is it safe for a fire?" Zeya asked.

"A small one should be fine in daylight, just keep the smoke to a minimum," Preza replied.

As Meleya began preparing the rabbit, Zeya and Preza got the fire going. Zeya was pleased to have freshly cooked meat for breakfast, even if there wasn't much of it. She wondered if the Greenwood would not be as bad as she had been led to believe.

"Does anyone remember how far it is to the first river crossing?" Meleya asked.

"About a half day's journey from the foot of the Braid to the Reypar's western flow," Preza answered. "Assuming we don't run into any beasts. Though, that is unlikely since the bulk of their numbers tend to stay further east or north."

"Good, it's been too long since I've had a proper bath!" Meleya exclaimed.

"We noticed, dear Wombsister," Zeya said with a smirk.

"Oh! Betrayed by my own blood!" Meleya replied, feigning hurt. "Though I must point out that I also have to put up with your most formidable stench, Wombsister!"

Preza grunted. "Cease your petty bickering, sisters. For the combination of both your foul scents is near more than I can handle."

XII

Suspicions

"The Selfa and her companions should have descended the Goddess' Braid into the Greenwood by now," Cereila reported to the other members of the Jurisa. "They were on schedule, when we last received the update from Solren."

"May the goddess guide their path," Gilza murmured. "Let us pray that they will not be slowed by the beasts when traveling through those Vesta-forsaken lands."

"Has Memier been kept up to date on the Venery's progress? Considering the recent attacks, they may not be as organized as we would like," Freila stated.

"I have received no birds from Memier in a few days, but Regent Vuleila is a dutiful sister. She will be prepared for the Selfa's arrival."

"And are we certain Rolier is unaware that they are the destination?" asked Sieyna.

Freila nodded. "Unless someone in this room revealed that information, there is no way they could know."

Cereila nodded. "The correspondences I sent to each village were vague at best in regard to the emergence. But, rumors do have the tendency to fly."

"I just hope whoever has the male will choose to keep him hidden rather than flee when the Selfa arrives," stated Sieyna. "If the traitor were to escape to the mountains, or worse, attempt to take him down the Yeren River, the male would surely be lost to us for good."

"My daughter will find him," said Freila. "Even if the one harboring the male flees, she will still find him."

"I hope so, for your sake, Freila," Sieyna replied, threateningly. "Not only is it your daughter on the Venery, but also a report from one of *your* agents that led us to establish it in the first place."

"My agent in Rolier is trustworthy. If she says there is a male in the village, there is a male."

"And did you not also trust your agent in Noor?" retorted Sieyna.

"I must admit that I did not have the same level of confidence that I do now. There is far less risk involved in sending a selfa a few days north to Noor than there is in sending one to Rolier. As I said before, I would not have wanted my daughters to travel across the Greenwood unless I was all but certain there was a male on the other side."

"And your daughters' loyalty to the Hearth, is that something we should be concerned with?"

Freila stood and shouted in anger. "From what dark corner of your mind do you conjure these questions? I take great offense at your attempt to sow the seeds of doubt regarding the loyalty of the Selfa in front of this council. Why in Vesta's name are you questioning her loyalty now?"

"It was merely an innocent question, Freila. Why it would elicit such an aggressive response from you is beyond me."

"Enough!" Gilza interrupted. "We must investigate any rumor of the male. It does not matter how dangerous the journey may be. While the loss of a selfa on a Venery would be tragic, it would be far more so if we let the last male slip through our grasp."

"Agreed," Freila replied, looking at Sieyna darkly.

Gilza continued, "Cereila, do you have any other reports to share with the council?"

"No, Sister. That was all for today."

"Very well, let us adjourn this meeting, then," Gilza proclaimed.

Freila left the council room and was heading back to her chamber when someone called to her from behind. "Might I have a word with you, Sister?"

It was Sieyna.

Freila hesitated, suspicious of the woman's intent. She really doubted Sieyna wanted to apologize. The woman had taken every opportunity to attack her in front of the council as of late. "As you wish, Sister. I was just on my way to my chambers. Would you care to join me there?"

"That will do."

Freila opened the door to her chambers and motioned for Sieyna to enter. The woman gave her a wolfish smile as she stepped in and helped herself to one of the cushioned chairs in the room.

"I recently received a message from Selfa Delreza, who, as you know, will soon be returning from Noor. She had some fascinating information to share with me."

"To share with you? Why was this information not in her official report to the council? Just because you once took Delreza under your wing does not mean she reports to you. As a selfa of the Sisterhood, she is to communicate any and all pertinent information to the council as a whole."

"Do not quote Sisterhood Law to me, Freila," Sieyna replied, anger seeping into her voice.

"Then once more, I must ask, why was everything not reported to the Jurisa?"

"Oh, don't worry, her full account will be told. Once she returns and I can verify the information she provides, the council will know the truth."

"The truth of what? I am failing to comprehend the purpose of this conversation."

"Call it, common courtesy, my dear Sister. I wouldn't want you to be taken by surprise by any veiled information."

"And yet you have not spoken of the details that are veiled."

Sieyna smiled wickedly. "I must say, I always found the timing interesting."

"And just what timing are you referring to?"

"Oh, you know." Sieyna leaned forward in her chair. "Selfa Delreza just happened to be away in Noor on a fool's errand the moment you received your report from Rolier."

"I cannot control the timing my agents adhere to, dear Sister," Freila replied coldly.

"Perhaps not, but you must admit it will be of great fortune to you and your daughter if she locates the male in Rolier."

Freila locked eyes with Sieyna. "And you implicate me in this... what? This conspiracy? Tell me, Sieyna, what would I gain from my daughter successfully finding the male that the Sisterhood would not? Congratulations and cheers from the Sisterhood for raising such a fine child? Oh yes, you have discovered my secret! Vanity! I am so vain that I would risk my position, and possibly even my life in the manipulation of the Sisterhood!"

"I do not purport to know your intent. Perhaps you would sacrifice yourself for your daughter's glory? So that she will be praised and elevated above all others in the Sisterhood?"

"You have known me for years, Sieyna. Have I ever struck you as the vainglorious type? Do you think that is a quality I wish to instill in my daughters? Your baseless accusation is just that. Now, I will politely ask you to depart from my chambers. I have much to attend to, and you have far overstayed your welcome."

Sieyna rose from the chair and bowed mockingly. "As you wish." She began walking toward the exit but then turned to face Freila, a wicked smile still on her face. "Until next time, *dear Sister.*"

Freila quickly shut the door and collapsed into her chair. *Who does that fool think she is?* she thought. *Sieyna has no concept as to what she's dealing with! She deems I would risk the lives of my daughters over something as trivial as glory? The cow's meddling means I will have to act with further haste.* Freila would not let her plans fall to shambles because of the jealous suspicions of one self-important woman. This was beyond Sieyna, beyond the Jurisa, beyond even Freila herself.

* * *

Freila moved through the streets of Vulna, noting all the carefree citizens. They were lucky not to carry the burden of knowledge that she possessed. The Greishic, the Sisterhood's demise, it was all merely a distant thought to them. The younger sisters in particular wandered about as if they hadn't a care in the world.

Younger. Pit, Freila thought. *The youngest generation grows older with each passing day. They may all be nothing but child-less hags in a matter of years.*

As she approached her destination, she stared up at it admiringly. Vesta's Temple was one of the few buildings in the city that rivaled the Hearth in its majesty. Although it was not nearly the height of the Aviary, it still towered over the nearby buildings. The Temple held hundreds of glazed windows, set with a red hue, each with a flame burning within. The Temple servants dutifully kept aflame these torches both day and night. It was a rare event to see a torch gone out. Freila approached the massive doors. They always stood open, an invitation for all to enter, devout or otherwise. She entered into the vestibule and walked past cut stone pillars and archways until she reached the main chamber. One of the Temple servants took notice of her and approached.

"Greetings, Freila of the Jurisa, how may I assist you on this Vesta-blessed day?"

"Good evening, Sister. Excuse the discourtesy, but might Sister Yeleila be available? I am afraid she is not expecting me, but the matter is urgent and I must speak with her, forthwith."

The servant hesitated for a moment. "Apologies, Freila of the Jurisa, but Sister Yeleila is currently meeting with another of Vesta's faithful."

"And for how long do you anticipate she will be unavailable?"

"I cannot say with certainty, but you are welcome to wait if you like. Would you like me to lead you to her chambers?"

"Thank you, Sister, but that will not be necessary. I know the way."

The Temple servant gave a gracious bow and Freila moved down the hall toward Yeleila's chambers. She climbed the stone steps up three levels and sat on the bench outside the room. Muffled voices could be heard from inside, and Freila was just able to make them out.

"Oh, Sister, do not let your heart be weighed down by fear. Let it be a vessel unto Vesta and she will fill it with hope and joy." Yeleila's soothing voice seeped through the gaps in the chamber door.

"But Sister Yeleila, I haven't much time left! My good years have come and gone with no male in sight. Am I not a failure to the Sisterhood and to Vesta for bearing no child? Will I even be welcomed into her Embrace when I pass from this world?"

"Sister, do not let your mind be troubled. It is not Vesta's desire for you to bear children, only that you live your life the way she intended. How is it any fault of yours that you were given no seed with which to grow a child?"

"But the teachings of the Sisterhood say—"

"The teachings of the Sisterhood are for us while we live, Child. They bind us together and allow us to exist with amity. Do not mistake Sisterhood Law for the will of the goddess. We all have a role to play in this world, and none of it the same as our neighbor. Only Vesta knows what our business truly is while we live, not the Hearth, and not those around you. Do you understand, Child?"

Freila heard the sister exhale loudly, as if a great burden had been lifted.

"Yes, I understand. Thank you, Sister Yeleila. I was fearful I would face chastisement by you as well," she replied, gratefully.

"And who gave you such an idea?"

"Something I heard, I suppose."

Yeleila chuckled. "Oh, Child, it seems I must scold you after all. Perhaps you should form your concerns by spending time in Vesta's Temple listening to her teachings rather than from rumors on the streets. In fact, if that is the word around Vulna, maybe all of its citizens should spend more time in the Temple."

"Perhaps you're right, Sister Yeleila."

"Is there anything more you wish to discuss, Child?"

"No, that is all. I appreciate you taking the time to meet with me."

"Feel free to come as you like. You may even find that the teachings will fill your heart with wisdom, even when you think you are in no need of guidance."

"Yes, I will surely return for your next benediction."

"I look forward to it. Have a Vesta-blessed day.

The door creaked open and Freila quickly jerked her head back, not realizing how near her ear was to the chamber door. The sister exited with what appeared to be a spring in her step and made her way down the stairs. Yeleila leaned out from her office and watched the woman go.

Freila smiled at Heleila and rose from the bench. "It seems you may soon have a new dutiful servant."

"Doubtful. They rarely come back once they get the answers they sought." Yeleila sighed. "I'd get so much more done if they'd only listened to the true teachings of Vesta instead of absorbing rumors and falsities." Yeleila finally looked at Freila. "And I was unaware one of the duties of the Jurisa was to eavesdrop at my door. Tell me, Freila, will guards soon come to my chambers to take me away for speaking so negatively about Sisterhood Law?"

Freila frowned, suddenly remembering why she was there. "I am afraid your words may not be as far from the truth as you think. May we confer, privately?"

"Yes, of course, Freila of the Jurisa is always welcome here. Please, come in."

Freila entered the chamber and took a seat at Yeleila's writing desk. It sat directly in front of one of the Temple's many lit braziers that shown through the nearby red-glazed window. Yeleila took a moment to peek out into the hallway, then quickly closed the door. Finally, she pulled heavy curtains across the door.

"A precaution. This door leaks worse than a basket filled with water, as you well know." Yeleila walked over and sat across the desk from Freila and cleared her throat. "So Freila, why have you graced my presence on this Vesta-blessed day?"

"It would seem some things are coming to light that should have remained in shadow. I was recently accosted by Sieyna who questioned me in-depth over my agent in Noor. She feels I planned for Selfa Delreza to be away on a fool's errand so that my daughter would be sent on the true Venery."

"And what evidence does she have? I imagine she must have something if she told you of her knowledge."

"The shrew claimed to have it soon."

"Any idea as to its nature?"

"No. But If I were to guess, it'll be something Selfa Delreza brings back from Noor. She's due at the Hearth any day now. I suspect it may be something she retrieved from my agent, Yureza. I had my doubts on her trustworthiness, but we were left with few options and the woman seemed agreeable."

Yeleila frowned, then rose and stared deeply into the nearby brazier. After a time she turned her gaze out the window. "This cycle is destroying us and they can't even see it. 'All's fine, the Sisterhood will protect us!' I heard someone exclaim that today with honest certainty. How is it the goddess has made them all so blind? They follow the doctrine of the Sisterhood which praises Vesta and tells us all to follow her teachings, and yet they ignore one of her most basic commands."

"The desire for power mixed with religious beliefs certainly has a way of muddying up the message. Throw in fear and you get what we have now. Blind followers of the goddess that the Sisterhood teaches and not Vesta herself," Freila replied.

"That sister who was just here was the ninth this week! It will only get worse as time continues on. The Sisterhood is picking and choosing the parts of Vesta's teachings that further their agenda. Women fearing they will be rejected from Vesta's Embrace for never bearing children, madness! I thought having a friend on the council would help reverse this, Freila."

"I too thought I could help steer the Sisterhood once again down the right path, but there is simply not enough dissent among the council. Gilza is far too set in tradition to see what repercussions her actions may have, and Sieyna's lust for power has contorted her mind into an unrecognizable heap of rot. Cereila is too fearful to go against either of them, she has essentially been reduced to little more than a parchment-pushing doter."

"And you, Freila? Have you resigned yourself to the existing state of affairs?"

"Not yet. Though I must admit, I regrettably do not speak against the other members of the council as often as I once did over the fear of being labeled an antagonist. I suppose that no longer matters. I will be labeled much worse when our scheme is discovered."

Yeleila sighed, then returned to her seat. "Are you still able to say with confidence that Zeya will succeed in her quest?"

"I have complete faith that she will find the male and see him safely to his destination. What becomes of him after that is impossible to say. I have begun to write the letter. While I am confident my daughters will do the right thing, I still feel great unease in my heart. There is always the possibility they do not all go along with my plans."

"And you intend to reveal everything in this letter?"

"I have yet to decide. I am not certain what Zeya will do if she discovers the whole truth. Though, Vesta forgive me if my final correspondence to my daughters is wrought with lies and manipulation."

"May Vesta forgive us both. While I too feel that this is the right course of action, it is hard to be certain. I long for what was written in the days of old. When Vesta's voice would echo like thunder from the clouds, commanding us on how to proceed with such burdensome tasks."

"Divine guidance would certainly help turn the Sisterhood to our cause," commented Freila.

Yeleila shook her head. "There are many in the Sisterhood too blinded by their own beliefs. They would not heed the goddess' words even if she appeared burning flame in hand and outright commanded them. I pray that it will get better."

"It will. I doubt the two of us will live to see it, but it will." Freila stood. "Thank you, Friend. I was somewhat shaken by the events of today, but your company, as always, is a boon to my heart."

"You are welcome here any time, Freila." Yeleila stood and walked Freila to the door. "Given Sieyna's words, it is possible we may need to accelerate all our plans."

Freila nodded. "I have already considered it. I plan on getting the message to Rolier as soon as I am able. The rest is up to you. I will see you in a few days for our scheduled meeting. Farewell."

"Goodbye, dear Sister."

XIII

Alé Volás

Zeya slipped into the cool stream that was the Reypar River's western flow. The water moved gently here. It was a pity they couldn't linger for too long. This part of the river was an excellent spot to wash away the dirt and grime her body had accumulated over the past few days. She ducked her head underwater and felt her entire body relax as she listened to the river's gentle rumbling flow around her. After coming up for a breath, she dreamily looked toward her companions and saw that they too were enjoying the break as much as she. Zeya rolled onto her back, floating peacefully, and stared up at the sky. The trees obscured most of her view, but she managed to make out some soft clouds drifting above her. The serenity was deceiving. They were in the thick of it now. So far, they had been lucky not to cross paths with any Greishic. She hoped to Vesta that luck would hold for the entirety of the journey.

Zeya heard someone swimming over to her, but she was so relaxed that she didn't bother to look.

"Meleya? Is that you?" Zeya asked dreamily as the splashing grew closer. Suddenly, strong arms grabbed and flipped her over, forcing her to sink to the bottom of the river. Snapped from her tranquility, she kicked herself up to the surface and wiped the water from her eyes. She saw her wombsister laughing while swimming circles around her.

"You ruined my meditation!"

"I did, dear Wombsister, but I had a good reason! You seemed in such a deep trance that I feared you would drift out to sea long before you awoke from it!"

"I never interrupt your daydreams!"

"That is because I do not daydream. I save my fantasies for the moonlight," Meleya replied suggestively.

"Oh, really?" Zeya dove underwater and gripped her wombsister's leg, then pulled, throwing her off balance.

"Hey!" Meleya yelped as she splashed into the water.

"That'll teach her," Zeya murmured to herself. She swam over to Preza, who had finished bathing and was getting dressed.

"Clean already, Preza?"

"You should know I'm never clean. Freshly washed, though."

Zeya laughed. "Thank Vesta, we have three more of the Reypar's flows to cross. I imagine the sisters of Memier will be amazed by our cleanliness upon our arrival." She climbed onto the bank and began pulling on her clothes.

"I'm not ready yet!" Meleya called out from the river. "I've barely had any time to wash, much less relax!"

"You've had long enough," Preza shouted back. "Get your pretty backside out of the water and back into your clothes!"

Meleya grinned. "Preza, I never knew you took notice of my backside!"

Preza grunted.

"I'm going to visit the thicket." Zeya moved away from the river.

"You should have just pissed in the river," replied Preza.

"In the river? We were bathing in that!"

"I imagine there's enough animal piss in there, yours would not have made that much difference. But do as you please."

Zeya spotted a tree that was to her liking and made her way over to it. She unbuckled her pants and was about to squat when she spotted something, it looked like...

"Ahh!" she shouted, reeling in surprise.

Preza came running over, axe in hand, and ready to take on whatever threatened the Selfa. She relaxed slightly when she saw Zeya standing over the decomposing body of a dead sister, which lay partially covered in the brush.

"What? What is it?" asked Meleya, who arrived shortly after with sword in hand and only half-dressed.

"A fallen sister," Zeya replied sadly.

Meleya bent down and examined the body somberly. "Alé volás, Sister."

"What do you think happened to her?" Zeya asked.

"Greishic got her, no doubt. A scout from Haralda would not have been taken down by wolves, and even if she was, there would be fewer remains," answered Preza.

"But the beasts didn't eat her?" asked Meleya.

"They don't always devour our flesh. They kill for the pleasure but eat for the need. The Greishic that killed her may just not have been very hungry."

"Preza, should we burn her remains?" asked Zeya.

"I wish we could, but if she was killed by a Greishic, they may be nearer than Captain Layna thought. A pyre large enough would draw too much attention."

Preza bent down and gently lifted the body of the fallen sister. She carefully carried her to the stream and released the sister into the water.

"May the flow of the Reypar take you gently into the next world," Preza said softly.

Zeya and Meleya nodded solemnly, and the three shared a moment of silence for their fallen comrade.

"It breaks my heart to see one of us dead," Meleya remarked. "Every fallen sister brings us closer to extinction."

Zeya watched the body float downstream. For a moment, she wondered if the sister's family still held on to hope that she would one day return safely. Or if her companions back in Haralda were waiting to welcome her back with open arms. Zeya doubted it. Sisters went into the Greenwood and never returned. It was the way of it. She was sure the sisters of Haralda were used to death by now.

* * *

Joreya woke to a quiet home. Her wombsisters Beya and Reya were still asleep beside her, and she stared at them thoughtfully. Joreya could not imagine the horrors they had experienced for it to be necessary to sleep this long. She herself had suffered nightmares thanks to her wombsister's recount of the battle but she knew the retelling paled in comparison to the actual events. Joreya had never seen a Greishic up close, but Beya's description would haunt her all the same. Reya never uttered a single word and had tossed and turned all night in a restless slumber.

Joreya climbed out of bed, taking care not to disturb her wombsisters, and dressed. Her face was still tender from where her mother had struck her with the dinner plate, but thankfully, the swelling had diminished. Leaving the bedchamber as quietly as she could, she was surprised to discover her mother was not yet awake. It was just as well, for today was the day she would finally sell her next batch of carvings at the market. She fantasized she would sell the remainder of her inventory in a single day. That would give her plenty of coin to leave both Memier and her mother behind. She did feel bad about abandoning her wombsisters, especially in such a state, but they would understand. They knew what their mother was.

Joreya descended the stairs outside her home and began making her way to her hidden workshop. The streets were far emptier than expected. A few sisters were milling about, but nowhere near the amount there should have been on a market day. A small family walked past her, seemingly carrying the entirety of their belongings on their backs. *They have so little faith in the Paling*, she thought. *So little trust in their fellow sisters and the leadership of Regent Vuleila. I wonder if they're headed to Coratch or Wolenn?* She considered for a moment trying to join them in their flight but then thought better of it. She'd be helpless in whatever village or town she ended up in without more coin, and she doubted the smaller villages would have as much interest in her artwork.

Joreya reached the entrance to her workshop and moved the grate aside. Before entering, she paused. Did she hear a horn? It was faint and far off in the distance, but it certainly sounded like a horn. Joreya didn't hear it again, so she figured it had just been her imagination.

No doubt brought on from her wombsister's recount of the battle. Disregarding the phantom horn, she entered the drain, retrieved her small chest of carvings, and began carrying it to the market.

When Joreya reached the market, she nearly dropped the chest in shock. There were hardly any vendors selling their wares, and worse, there were only a handful of sisters buying. Her heart sank as she realized she was unlikely to sell even a single carving today. She would have to postpone her escape from her mother even longer. She tried to tell herself it was only temporary. Once the Greishic retreated back into the Greenwood, things would go back to normal. The market would be flooded with sisters looking to make a good bargain, and she'd be right there with her art, ready to sell. Unfortunately, her hope did little to lift her spirit.

Dejected, she left the market and began making the trek back to the grate with nothing but her thoughts. *I'll be stuck in this city forever. Stuck with her. Vesta has surely cursed me.* Joreya eventually fought back her descent into despair and decided that she would just have to try again on the next market day. And if things were the same, she would try the next, and then the next. No matter how long it took, she would escape.

As she reached the grate, Joreya heard a horn again. There was no doubt this time, it was a horn. It blasted louder than before, or maybe it was just closer. She could hear something else too. It was like a hammering, a pounding that echoed throughout the entire city. She was unable to dwell on the sound, however, as it was quickly drowned out by the clanging of the city bells.

* * *

"Call to arms! All sisters, take up what you can in defense of the city! The Greishic are breaching the Paling!" Regent Vuleila shouted out across the city. She hoped many would hear and spread her word. "Brace the walls! Brace them for Vesta's sake!"

They had no warning. No warning of their imminent doom. A massive Greishic horde poured out of the Greenwood, breaking through their remaining defenses with what seemed like renewed strength. Many held weapons, axes and swords, and were using them to try and tear through the Paling. *It's like the beasts waited to attack until we let our guard down, but that's not possible, is it?* Vuleila barely had time to order a retreat behind the Paling before the beasts descended upon them. Not everyone made it, and she could still hear the screams of those left behind over the sounds of battle.

"Regent, citizens are arriving with make-shift weapons, asking what we need."

Vuleila turned to see one of her guards looking at her with hope in her eyes. "Feyna, send any and all citizens to the Paling! Instruct them to gouge anything that breaches the wall. Tell any who possess experience with a bow to join me on the parapet. We will rain down on them like thunder from above."

"Yes, Regent!" The guard ran toward a group of gathering citizens with the orders.

It was heartening, seeing the city come together, putting aside their petty differences and bickering in order to defend their home. Vuleila hoped they held enough vigor to survive the battle. She climbed onto the parapet, grabbed a bow and loosed arrows as quickly as she could. There were thousands of Greishic, all fighting to break through the Paling.

"Regent! The Greishic are attacking the gate!"

"Stay your ground, soldier! The gate will hold! Keep them off the wall!" Vuleila continued firing at the beasts, but they did not yield. The bodies were piling up on the field and... Regent Vuleila stopped firing as she noticed one Greishic in particular. It was standing there and seemingly looking directly at her. But that was her imagination, wasn't it? The creature appeared to summon a pack of the beasts over to it and then proceeded to point directly at her. She didn't care if she imagined the exchange or not, she quickly began firing arrows at the anomaly until it was struck and fell down dead. "Oh, Vesta, let that have been an invention of my mind," she murmured.

The sound of splintering wood reached her ears, then was followed by growls and human screams. The Greishic had broken through the Paling.

"Sisters! Any, and all! Seal the breach! Seal it for the Sisterhood and the lives of your future daughters!"

She watched as a small group of women carrying naught but sticks and stones rushed toward the hole and began beating down any Greishic that dared enter. Yelza, along with a group of women rushed forth with timber and rubble and managed to close the breach before more Greishic made it inside. The victory was short lived, more wood cracked as another rift in the Paling tore open. Yelza moved her group toward it, but this one was larger and the Greishic flooded in, unchecked. Vuleila saw Yelza fall, slashed in the throat by one of the beast's sharpened claws. Another sound of the Paling being torn apart reached her ears. They were quickly becoming overwhelmed and losing the battle.

"Captain Veneya, with me! To the Keep! We must get word to the villages and the Hearth on what fate has befallen us this day!"

"Aye, Regent, but I'd rather not leave the battle!" Captain Veneya turned to those standing beside her. "You four, see the Regent safely to the Keep and bolster its defenses until she gets done what needs doing!" The captain faced Vuleila and gave a respectful bow. "May the goddess guide your path, Regent."

Regent Vuleila nodded to her captain graciously. "And yours. Alé volás, Sister."

* * *

"Mother! We must go and defend the Paling now!" Beya shouted at Rueila who stood looking out the window of their home. "The city is under attack and they have called for everyone to help defend it!"

Rueila looked indignantly at her daughter. She had no right to speak to her in such a way! Rueila was no soldier and never had been, and she was past her prime too, so why did her daughter expect her to join the battle to defend the city?

"Do not take that tone with me, Child!" Rueila stated, angrily. "Leave it to the City Guard. My children have served this city enough, do you want to end up like Gureya? My sweet Gureya."

"But Memier needs us! All of us! The Greishic are breaking through!"

"I will hear no more of it!"

Beya stared at her mother. "Mother, will you at least take Reya and flee the city? Head for the eastern gate, that will be your best chance."

"Flee and go where? No, Daughter, I will not leave my home. I have faith in the soldiers and you should too. This is why they exist."

Beya let out a sigh. "Mother, I am going to help. I pray that I will see you and Reya again when this is all over. Please, I beg of you, take Reya and flee!" She then turned and ran out the door.

Rueila quickly moved to the door and shouted after her. "Beya! Come back! This is not your concern! I command you to return to me at once! Beya!"

When it was clear her daughter had no intention of coming back, Rueila angrily slammed and bolted the door. *Why do my daughters continue to disobey me? No doubt the little rat has put defiance in their hearts. Where is that little rat anyway? If anyone should go and fight, it's her.* Rueila began moving toward her daughters' bedchamber, but stopped when she heard shouts outside, followed by a loud thud that shook her home. She went to her window and peeked outside.

Three women were running down the street, screaming incoherently in panic. As the women got closer Rueila released a surprised shout. It was not three women, it was one. The other two were those beasts! The woman noticed Rueila watching from the window and shouted to her.

"Help! Please, help!"

Rueila quickly ducked back inside and away from her window.

"Sister! Please hel—" The woman's cries were cut off and replaced with a rough sounding howl.

Get out, I have to get out! Rueila thought in a panic. *Reya and Joreya, I must wake them, we must flee!* Something loud and heavy slammed into her door. She whirled, staring in fear as the sound came again. The beasts had seen her. She heard scratching and howls as the Greishic tried to get in. "Reya! Joreya! Come and help!" she shouted. "They're getting in!"

Another slam, this time she heard wood splintering from the impact.

"*Sha, Cundi!*" one of the creatures shouted through the door. The cry was followed by another strong impact, then a crash. The creatures had broken through.

Rueila screamed in terror and ran to her kitchen, looking for anything she could use as a weapon. She grabbed a knife and retreated to her daughters' bedchamber, slamming the door behind her.

"*Sha gur, Cundi,*" one of the creatures taunted.

"Reya! Joreya, wake up! They are here!" Rueila went to the bed and was surprised to only find Reya sleeping there. Joreya was nowhere to be found. She violently shook Reya, until she awoke. "Daughter! Get up, the Greishic are here!"

Reya's eyes widened in fear. She sprang out of bed to stand at her mother's side.

They both screamed as the creatures forced their way into the bedchamber and approached them slowly. Three creatures entered, the one in front stood tall looking down on them with a filth-covered, disfigured face. Its lips curled into a smile and it revealed sharpened teeth.

"*Noge cah, cundi,*" it said.

"*Do coondris guya mai clah,*" one of the others replied, gesturing toward Reya.

"Get out of my home!" Rueila shouted and brought her knife up threateningly.

The creature made a sickly laughing sound as it continued to approach her. "*Cundi lita das kiya.*"

The creature lunged, and Rueila screamed, swinging wildly with the knife. A loud, angry howl erupted from the beast as Rueila's knife met its flesh.

"You will not take my daughter!" Rueila shouted defiantly, pushing a shivering Reya further behind her.

"*Mai guya tali coondris!*" The three Greishic moved forward, undeterred by Rueila's swinging blade.

"Reya, I am sorry."

In a flash, Rueila turned and slashed her daughter across the throat. Reya clutched her throat and failed to gasp as blood poured out of her and she collapsed to the ground. The Greishic moved in and grabbed at Rueila who stood screaming in anguish over what she had just done. She suddenly felt immense pain as one of the Greishic managed to grab her hair and yank her to the floor. It pulled, dragging her away from her slain daughter and into the other room. "Joreya! Joreya, help me!" Rueila cried out in vain.

"*Cundi mas klia gen!*"

One of the creatures stomped on her arm, breaking the bone, then pulled with all its strength. The last thing Rueila saw before succumbing to darkness was the creature proudly holding her arm over its head.

XIV

The Prize

"Back again? I'm always surprised by how much fruit you eat," the shopkeeper commented.

"It is good for a woman of my age," Keila replied.

"Indeed, and also for a woman of any age! I'm just glad you always choose to buy from me. You're almost single-handedly keeping me in business, Keila!"

"I find that hard to believe, I do not buy *that* much."

"True, it is an exaggeration, but I am always happy to see you at my stand, Sister." The merchant smiled warmly. "What will it be today? The usual?"

"Yes, dear Sister."

"Very well, berries, pyrus fruit, and apple of paradise. The berries are most fresh, picked them this morning. Anything else?"

"No, that will be all."

Keila handed her basket to the fruit merchant, who carefully placed each one inside. The merchant gave her a bow of thanks before turning to the next customer in line.

Keila strolled through Rolier, browsing through the other merchants and their wares. She came across Breyna's stand and rolled her eyes. The woman was selling her poorly-made and incredibly garish furnishings. Breyna was certainly no artisan. Her furniture was painted in a displeasing manner with bright colors. No doubt this was to hide her lack of carpentry talents. Keila examined one of the side tables that was for sale. It was shoddy work, to say the least.

"Hello Keila, finally come to make a purchase?" the carpenter asked.

"Afraid not, Breyna. I am in the market for something of sturdier construction. I doubt these pieces would last more than a few years."

"Oh, I assure you, they will last far longer than that. If you would only give one a chance, I am certain you will be pleasantly surprised."

"I think not. Why, when I was a woodworker in Vulna I made—"

"Made sure every piece would last five generations. Yes, you have told me this many times before."

"Five generations. Do you have anything here that will last even half that?"

"No way to know. They may, but I won't be around to see it. I must point out that there is also no way for you to substantiate your guarantee. Unless you intend to live longer than any sister born of this world, you'll be in Vesta's Embrace long before your claim reaches its expiration."

Keila stared at Breyna darkly. "You can feel it when you make it. Sense it in the wood, in the joints. At least a true craftswoman can. Your pieces are better put to use as kindling than used as decor in a home."

"Then why did you cease selling your majestic pieces? Afraid of the competition? How many pieces have you sold in this village? I have sold over a hundred with little difficulty."

"Sold to other tasteless villagers, no doubt. You should be overjoyed that I left my business behind in Vulna. If this village knew what true craft was, you'd be without patrons in less than a fortnight."

Breyna laughed. "Words are easy. Actions much less so. Now, if you have no intent to make a purchase, I am afraid I must ask you to leave me in peace. You are keeping me from my, as you say, tasteless patrons."

"I was just about to be on my way, I am afraid I cannot bear this unpleasant sight any longer. Farewell, *Sister*." Keila spoke the final word with disdain and left.

As she was nearing her home, she heard shouting coming from Heleila's hut.

"We've been over this many times before, Aady! You won't be able to leave until things change!" Heleila exclaimed.

"I am tired of waiting, Mother! I can make the journey on my own, there's no need to wait any longer!" Aadeya shouted back.

Keila had never seen Aadeya angry before. The poor girl always seemed so docile at home and rarely left the hut. The fits were a terrible illness to suffer from, Keila knew this first hand. She had a friend back in Vulna who eventually succumbed to such a malady.

"Just a little longer, I promise. You will have the strength needed in the days to come, once they arrive from Memier."

"Mother, I can make it on my own, I do not need any help! I have gotten through this long with my condition, I know I can make it further!"

"No, Aady! You mustn't try, you will die and my heart could never bear that, please..."

Their voices softened, and she was no longer able to make out the words. Keila couldn't blame Heleila for keeping her daughter locked up in the hut. As the girl's mother, she knew what was best for her daughter, fully grown or not. Besides, it wasn't like there was much to see in this village. One hut was as good as the next. Keila wondered if Aadeya was thinking of permanently leaving the village. She had spoken of a journey, but there's no way she would be able to travel far with her convulsions.

Keila entered her hut and put the fruit basket in the kitchen. She pulled out one of the pyrus fruits and began her usual routine of mashing it up, singing to herself as she did. "Mashing, mashing, mashing. I must make sure it's soft and smooth, no chunks, no chunks at all." Satisfied with the results, she took the plate of fruit and set it on the table. Before sitting down, she walked to her window and drew the curtains tightly. She paused, listening intently for the sound of any interlopers.

Satisfied that there were none, she turned to her bed and took a moment to admire the intricate pattern she had carved into the wood. *Quality furnishings are carved and stained, not painted. Breyna will never understand such a basic fact.* She bent down and lifted the bed. It swung up with ease as its well-oiled hinges performed their duty admirably. Locking the bed frame into place, she grabbed the plate of mashed fruit off the table and slowly opened a trap door that lay hidden and peered inside at the wonderful gift Vesta had bestowed upon her.

"Still sleeping?" she cooed. "Don't worry, when you awake, I'll feed you, my child. My beautiful baby boy."

XV

Between the Flows

Zeya looked across the second stream of the Reypar River. The flow was far deeper and more swift than the crossing they had faced the day before, and she doubted they'd be able to ford it with as much ease. Fortunately, once they made it to the other side, they'd be halfway through the Greenwood.

"See anywhere to cross?" she asked her companions.

"We may have to travel further downriver," Preza answered. "Meleya? What are you doing?"

Meleya was halfway up the trunk of a tall tree that hung partially over the river. "Just trying to get a better look."

"See anything?" Zeya asked.

"No. Appears worse downstream. At least as far as I can tell." She turned to look the other way. "Wait, I think..." she trailed off, staring upriver.

"Well, spit it out, Woman! What do you see?" Preza demanded.

"I think it's a shoal. If the current isn't strong, we could cross there, though it might be hard to see from the ground."

"Good enough for me," replied Preza. "How far?"

"About a hundred paces past those boulders." She gestured to an outcropping a fair distance away.

"Zeya and I will check it out. Tell us when we are near to it."

Meleya remained in the tree, directing the other two as they made their way past the boulders to the alleged shoal. It was much further and took them longer to find than Zeya thought it would. Once Meleya confirmed they were in the right spot, she began climbing down from the tree.

"Is it crossable, Preza?" Zeya asked.

"Looks better than anything else in the area. We could spend some more time searching, but this is likely as good as it will get this time of year."

"Then I feel we should try and cross. If we keep searching—"

"Help!"

The two whirled and saw Meleya struggling with someone. No, not someone. Something.

"Greishic!" Preza shouted and they both took off running toward Meleya.

The beast swung at Meleya, striking her with enough force to knock her to the ground. It quickly jumped on her, pinning her down. She tried to draw her sword but could not pull it from the scabbard while the full weight of the beast was on her. The creature snarled, its fetid breath causing Meleya to wince. It slashed at her with its filthy elongated nails, but she managed to grip its wrists before the jagged claws met her flesh. Dried mud flaked off the creature's muscular body as it roared again. It broke free from her grasp and began striking her repeatedly with its fists. Meleya brought her hands up in defense, trying to block the blows, but many made it through. She reached, again attempting to pull her sword from its scabbard, but was unable to free it. Trying to fend off the creature with one hand, she reached for the dagger at her boot. The beast bared its teeth and moved in to bite her flesh.

Zeya sped past Preza and pulled a dagger, ready to throw. "We're coming!" she shouted, but her wombsister did not seem to hear. She raised her dagger to throw.

"No! You might hit her!" Preza shouted at her.

"But it's going to kill her!"

A loud screech suddenly sounded from overhead, and Zeya's heart leapt as Heyfic swooped down from the heavens toward the beast.

The hawk slashed the creature with his razor-sharp talons, and the Greishic roared in pain, diverting its attention to the new threat. Heyfic continued to thrash the Greishic, and the beast swiped angrily at the bird. The creature landed a blow and struck Heyfic hard, causing the hawk to shriek as the impact drove him to the ground.

"Heyfic!" Meleya cried. Partially free from the beast, she managed to pull the dagger from her boot and shoved it toward the creature's chest. It turned in surprise as her blade entered its flesh and the creature let out an agonizing cry. The Greishic fell off Meleya as blood poured from the wound, mixing with its mud-encrusted skin. Meleya leapt to her feet as it tried to attack once more, but its wound had made it weak and slow and she was able to easily avoid its claws. She drew her sword, ignoring the creature as it shouted in its harsh tongue. Her blade came up, ready to end its wretched life. She brought her weapon down with a battlecry and her sword cleaved the Greishic's head from its bloodied chest, sending it to the ground in a heap.

Meleya stood there, breathing heavily and staring at her attacker's headless body in a daze.

"Meleya! I thought it had you!" Zeya exclaimed when she finally reached her wombsister.

"Are you injured?" asked Preza, looking at Meleya's mud and blood-spattered face.

"Not... my blood." Meleya gasped as she continued to stare at the body, then snapped out of her trance. "Heyfic!"

She began searching frantically for her fallen companion. "Heyfic? Heyfic!" She spotted the hawk and knelt beside him. "Oh, Heyfic," she whispered, tears welling up in her eyes.

Zeya bent down and put an arm around her wombsister, expecting the worst.

Heyfic was lying on the ground, his wings spread, but he appeared to still be breathing.

"Is he OK?" Zeya asked, hopefully.

"Yes, thank Vesta. He seems intact, only stunned."

"Do you think he'll recover?"

"I think so, but it will take some time." Meleya wiped a tear from her filth covered cheek as she watched Heyfic with concern. "He saved me." She gently folded his wings back toward his body and stroked her friend's head.

"He did. We all owe him our gratitude," replied Preza. "I am sorry we didn't reach you in time."

"Don't dwell. Your duty is to protect the Selfa, not me."

"I may be duty-bound to Zeya, but my promise to your mother was to see you both through the Greenwood safely."

"Some great warrior I turned out to be," Meleya scoffed. "I couldn't even handle one of the wretched beasts on my own."

Zeya stood and studied the body that lay twisted in an unnatural position a few paces away. "It's been a long time since I have seen a Greishic this close. I had forgotten how human they look."

Preza glanced at the body and spat. "Even if their figure shares some resemblance to our own, do not forget their minds are no greater than that of a rabid dog. We were lucky it was female. The males are far more vicious than their counterparts. Do not be hard on yourself, Meleya, the creature took you by surprise. Had you been aware of its presence before the attack, events would have gone much differently."

"Dead is dead, caught-off guard or not. I nearly got Heyfic killed."

"Indeed, but there is little use in lamenting over it. You both survived, and I doubt it will be the final Greishic we face on this journey. You will be given the opportunity to redeem yourself."

Meleya smiled weakly at Preza's words, but Zeya noticed the confidence that typically adorned her wombsister's face was no longer present.

"We should get moving. The sounds of battle will have attracted other nearby beasts," Preza stated. "What of Heyfic?"

"I will carry him." Meleya pulled a cloth from her pack and tenderly lifted the hawk and laid him in the center of it. Carefully, she tied the corners and fashioned it into a bundle that she could carry. Standing with Heyfic in hand, she nodded to Zeya and Preza, signaling that she was ready to continue.

* * *

The three crossed the river's flow with no issue. Now midway through the Greenwood, they were approaching the heart of Greishic territory. This is where there was the highest concentration of camps and activity. Not all the creatures roamed throughout the Greenwood, many stayed within the confines of the camps, only leaving when hunger or bloodlust dictated it.

"Listen," Zeya hissed, as she noticed movement in the brush a short way from where they stood.

They froze and heard the crunch of fallen leaves that could only be from footsteps. Preza signaled for them to seek cover, and the three ducked behind a fallen log covered with thick undergrowth.

They watched as a group of Greishic entered into sight. There were seven of them in total, and two carried weapons, one an axe and another a sword. The weapons had seen better days. The sword's blade was chipped and covered in rust. The axe's edge was in better condition, but the wood of the handle appeared weakened by rot.

As the Greishic approached, their stench overwhelmed Zeya. It reminded her of putrid meat mixed with rotten milk. She slowly drew her daggers, careful not to make a sound. Her sisters did likewise. Meleya cautiously set the bundle holding a stunned Heyfic down in preparation for a fight.

Zeya gestured to Preza, questioningly, *Attack?*

Wait. Be ready, Preza signaled in reply.

The Greishic hunting party walked right past them, and Zeya had to resist the urge to gag as the smell grew more potent. Her heart raced. She was fairly certain they could take on the beasts if they kept the element of surprise, but what if more were nearby? Their fight would attract the creatures, and they could easily be overwhelmed.

One of the male Greishic stopped only a few feet from their hiding place and sniffed the air deeply.

It can't smell us, can it? Zeya thought. *How can it smell anything over its own foul stench?* Out of the corner of her eye, she saw Meleya grip her sword tightly in both hands, ready to leap out and attack.

Three other creatures stopped with the male, and they held what sounded like a conversation in their gruff language.

"*Erea cule cah?*"

"*Noge dulack sitre coondris.*"

"*Kai cundi. Noge dulack leh?*" The male motioned in Zeya's direction, then it began to move toward her. The creature peered forward, sniffing deeply once more.

That was when one of Zeya's daggers flew through the air and stuck it in the face. It collapsed to the ground, and the other three Greishic howled in alarm as Preza and Meleya leapt from cover, weapons swinging. Preza cleaved one Greishic nearly in half with her battle axe, its blood spraying on the ground as it fell. Meleya screamed with fury as she ran another through with her sword.

The third Greishic lunged at Zeya with its axe, but she dodged, letting the creature fly past her. She brought up one of her daggers, and stabbed multiple times at the creature's exposed back. As it fell, Meleya leapt over it and charged at two of the remaining foes. One held the rusted sword and swung at Meleya wildly. She easily evaded the attack and countered with a slash of her own. Her finely honed blade met the rusted one, breaking it in two. Her swing continued forward until it met with the Greishic's chest.

"*Coh curi gular coondris, mazak!*" the creature cursed loudly as Meleya brought her sword back around and cut it down.

Zeya had just finished dispatching the sixth Greishic and turned to see Preza struggling with the final one, another large male. It managed to avoid her first axe swing and slashed Preza's arm with its long nails. She grunted in pain, spun her axe over her head, and brought it down. The Greishic dodged again and grabbed Preza, baring its teeth as it moved in to bite her. She slammed her head into the beast, knocking it back. It staggered, and she took the opportunity to kick it in the groin. Yelping in pain, the Greishic tried to remain standing, but the endeavor was short-lived as Preza brought her axe down on its skull, splitting it open.

Zeya and Preza took a moment to catch their breaths while Meleya quickly ran over to where she had left Heyfic. She was relieved that he was safe and undisturbed.

"I told you... you'd have the chance... to redeem yourself, Meleya," Preza said, gasping for air.

Meleya smirked. "You did, but there is no way you could have known it would be so soon."

"Maybe I did. How is your level of confidence now?"

"Better. I expected the Greishic to be much more of a challenge."

"Don't forget, the Greishic's—"

"Strength is in their numbers," Meleya finished. "I feel I've heard that somewhere before."

Zeya pulled her dagger from one of the fallen beasts, wiped the blade, and sheathed it. She stared for a moment at the bodies littering the ground. "At least they're not very good with weapons." She said, kicking the broken sword.

"Thank Vesta for that," Meleya agreed.

XVI

Messengers

Freila lay awake in bed, listening intently. She had not heard a single sound outside her chambers for some time. Everyone must be asleep. Finally.

Freila slowly got out of bed and moved noiselessly to the door, listening. Feeling satisfied that no one was in the hall, she cracked open her door and peeked outside. All was clear. She went to her table and picked up a sealed, tightly rolled letter that lay there. Freila had completed it as soon as she returned from meeting with Yeleila. She knew what would happen if her deeds were brought to light, and she had no desire for everything to fall to ruin now. The Sisterhood would know the truth. One way or another, they would know, but she needed to assure their salvation.

Gripping the letter in both hands, Freila stared at it. *So much to explain, and yet so little time remains to address it,* she thought. *This will have to do for now. If I'm somehow not found out, I will send another. I will explain everything. I will tell the whole truth.* She tucked the letter into her robe and tied her sash tightly.

Freila carefully opened the door to her chambers, wanting to avoid any creaking, and slipped out into the hallway. The stone passageway was calm. Even the brazier's glowing embers burned in reticence. There was a strong possibility Sieyna was having her watched and expected her to send some sort of warning to alter her plans. Sending a mysterious letter in the dark of night would surely bring the suspicion of the Jurisa down on her. If she was caught and the message opened, much would fall to ruin.

There was no telling how much information Selfa Delreza had on her plot. It would not take much for Sieyna to turn the Jurisa against her, and she would never get a message out imprisoned in a cage.

Sieyna thinks she knows my plans, does she? Sieyna would— No, the whole Sisterhood would quake in fear if they knew half of what my ends were. When all is said and done, they will thank me. Thank me for the risk I took on their behalf. Or at the very least, all will fail, and none will be around to remember my transgressions.

She was approaching Gilza's bedchamber door, and for once, she was glad the old gammer snored so loudly. It would mask any noise Freila might make. The entrance to the Aviary came into view, and she hurried over to it.

"Are you in need of something, Mother Freila?"

Freila froze.

"Mother Freila?"

She turned to see a guard looking at her curiously. "Evening, Sister. No, I was just looking to get some fresh night air."

The guard's expression did not change, but she nodded. "Strange hour, for a walk, but I know these are stressful times for us all."

"Truly, Sister." Freila had to stop herself from gripping the letter in her robe. "How are you managing?"

The guard smiled warmly. "Well enough, Mother Freila. I have hope in my heart that we are near a turning point. One for the better, that is."

Freila smiled. "As do I, Sister. I can't wait for the days when the male is returned to the Hearth and the joyful cries of children once again fill these halls."

"I pray to Vesta every night for just that," the guard replied. "I fear it won't be long before I am unable to bear children. An honor I've always looked forward to."

Freila knew this conversation was taking too long. She should cordially bid the guard a good night and continue on, but her heart was moved by the woman's words. She approached the guard and reached her hand out, resting it gently on the woman's shoulder. "What is your name, dear Sister?"

"Saneza, Mother Freila."

"Well, Saneza, without going into restricted details, I can tell you that I am doing everything to ensure you the chance of having a child."

"I know, Mother Freila. I have complete faith in you and the rest of the council, but I know some things are just out of your control. If Vesta has cursed us, not much anyone can do about that."

Freila's warm smile did not falter.

Saneza flashed red with embarrassment. "I am sorry, Mother Freila. I should not have spoken in such a manner."

"Think nothing of it, Child. Frustration is completely normal, and warranted in these times."

The guard nodded. "Well, I suppose I have kept you long enough from your walk. Thank you for taking the time to speak with me."

"And you for speaking with me, Saneza."

Saneza smiled and walked away, and Freila immediately felt for the letter inside her robe. Relief filled her as she touched it.

She continued to the end of the hallway and began climbing the spiral staircase to the Aviary. It had been many years since she last made the trek up these stairs. She usually relied on the venaren to send any missives for her, but this one was too important for anyone else to carry.

The winding steps seemed to go on forever, and this high in the tower, the torches weren't even lit. Thankfully, the nearly full moon shining through the windows guided her path. Breathing laboriously from the effort of ascent, she reminisced about making the climb to the Aviary first with Meleya, and then with Zeya. Somehow the journey seemed much easier back then. *My daughters,* she thought, *I am sorry for misleading you. I pray that you will hold no ill-will toward me and will find it within your hearts not only to forgive me but also to accomplish what needs to be done.*

After some time, she reached the top of the stairs and quietly entered the Aviary. She was very careful not to disturb the divebirds. Even Gilza's snoring could not mask the racket they would unleash, and it would surely wake the whole Hearth. She made her way over to the cage she sought and gently lifted the cloth that covered the wooden enclosure. There were several divebirds, all sleeping peacefully. Opening the cage, she paused as its hinges let out an audible creak, but the sound did not seem to disturb any of the animals, thank Vesta.

Reaching inside, she carefully pulled out one of the birds, its iridescent neck glimmered in the moonlight as she attached her message to its leg. After closing the cage and rolling the cover back down, she carried the bird over to the window and held it out.

"May Vesta see this letter carried swiftly and safely to its destination," she prayed. Freila released the divebird, and its wings beat audibly as it flew off into the moonlit night.

XVII

Heart of a Sister

Zeya stood up from her watch and yawned. There was still an hour left before day broke over the Greenwood, but they should be on the move. She shook Preza awake, then roused Meleya. They were now between the third and fourth of the Reypar's distributaries and just outside the heart of Greishic territory. Thankfully, they had not crossed paths with very many more since their last skirmish. What few they did come across were easily avoided as the creatures seemed distracted and in a hurry.

The party would reach Memier before nightfall. Finally, they'd be able to let their guard down and enjoy a hot meal. The thought of a nice hunk of roasted meat slipping right off the bone and into her mouth filled Zeya's heart with merriment and her stomach with longing.

Meleya offered Zeya a piece of bread, which she accepted graciously. She knew it had gone stale, but was happy to put something in her belly. Taking a bite of the dried bread made her long for some succulent meat all the more.

Zeya looked over at Heyfic who seemed much better after being struck. The day before, he had been able to fly short distances when encouraged, but he still was not yet back to full strength.

"How is he?" Zeya asked.

"Vesta willing, he will be his old self before much longer. He took quite a hit. I've never heard of a fowl being dazed for so long."

"He's a fighter," Preza replied respectfully. "I wouldn't be surprised if he outlives us all."

"He better outlive me," Meleya stated.

"Why's that?" asked Zeya.

"I don't think I could withstand losing him."

"Given our path today, there is a great chance he *will* outlive us," Preza replied. "From here on out, we should remain as quiet as possible. Not only with our words but also with our steps. We are entering the heart of the creatures' territory. We could stumble upon, or be swarmed by a pack of them at any time. Keep to hand signals whenever possible."

"Always the cheery one, Preza," jabbed Meleya.

"I am serious. I know we've had our moments of cheerful banter, but none today. Not until we reach Memier."

Zeya and Meleya nodded their understanding. There would be plenty of time for merriment and mirth once they cleared the Greenwood and were secure behind the Paling wall. They gathered their belongings and continued on their journey.

* * *

A loud scream rang out. One that sounded human. Zeya had never heard anyone scream like that before. The sound made her stomach flip and her blood turn to ice. The cry of agony came once more.

They all moved toward the sound as quickly as stealth would allow, stopping only when the source of the scream came into view. It was a sister. Naked below the waist, she lay bound upon the ground. What little clothing she did wear had been reduced to filth covered tatters. Her body was covered in cuts and bruises, and one of her eyes was completely swollen shut. Over her stood a pair of Greishic who were letting out a sickly sound that resembled laughter.

"*Gurete nuc sha lita, cundi! Cua cua cua!*" one of the Greishic bellowed as it kicked the sister, the claws of its feet digging into her flesh.

She let out another scream.

"*Coondris lita! Kai lita guash!*"

Zeya could take it no longer, she wanted to charge at the beasts and kill them where they stood, all of them! She wanted to show them a fraction of the pain they were inflicting on her sister! She managed to resist the urge, but only just. Turning to Preza and Meleya to formulate a plan, she was startled as Preza leapt past her, shouting a battle cry full of passionate hatred.

On instinct, she, too, leapt out and charged forward with Meleya right behind. The two Greishic shouted in surprise as Preza barreled down on them, swinging her axe. One of the creatures released a yelp as the axe made contact, causing its innards to slide from its body.

"*Coondris! Coondris cula!*" the other managed to shout as it backed away from Preza's axe. "*Coond—*" Its speech was cut short by Meleya's sword.

Greishic began emerging from the trees, some held weapons, others armed only with their sharpened nails. Three, then seven, then Zeya lost count as the beasts swiftly descended upon them.

"You fetid, chickenshit, bastards! See how you do against one of us unbound!" Preza taunted.

This drew the attention of the first three Greishic. Zeya saw an opening and took it. Sliding behind the group, she slashed two of them behind their knees with her daggers, causing them to stumble to the ground. Preza's axe came down hard on the third Greishic left standing before her, nearly cleaving it in half. She then brought her axe around to finish off the two Zeya had wounded.

Meleya slashed, spun, then slashed again. She narrowly managed to elude a claw aimed at her throat before leaping forward and plunging her sword into the Greishic's heart.

Zeya threw a dagger into the back of a Greishic that stood nearby, and it fell in a heap. Turning to take on the next opponent, she noticed something strange. Directly outside the field of battle, a single Greishic stood watching the fight. It was not attempting to come to its ilk's aid. It just held on the edge, motionless.

Zeya's focus was quickly drawn away from the abnormality when she heard Preza cry out. She whirled and saw that a Greishic had gotten behind Preza and slashed her with its claws. Preza grunted and kicked backward at the beast, knocking it toward a tree. It smashed into the tree with a loud crack, from bark, or bone, or both.

"*Cundi, sha leh guash!*" one of the creatures shouted in its guttural tongue as it sped toward Zeya. She charged at it, wanting to meet it head-on, but it dodged at the last moment, knocking her off balance. It grabbed a broken spear that lay upon the ground and hurled it at Zeya, who struggled to stay on her feet. The spear shot through the air, but the creature's aim was poor, and the spear drifted wildly from its target.

"*Sha vi va logua, Cundi!*" The Greishic roared in anger as it once again rushed at Zeya. The charge was short-lived as the tip of Meleya's blade ruptured out of its chest.

Zeya nodded to her wombsister, then turned to face any remaining Greishic. She was surprised that no more were left standing, but she did manage to catch a glimpse of one fleeing into the forest. She had never heard of the Greishic fleeing from battle in this manner. They usually fought to their dying breath.

"What happened to the bound sister?" Preza asked, covered in Greishic blood and breathing heavily. "Where is she?" Her voice grew more desperate.

Zeya felt horror as she realized the fleeing Greishic had fled with their sister while they were distracted with the fighting. She took off, running after it at full speed. She knew if she was fast enough, she could catch it and save her sister. She sprinted through the forest, trailing the sound of crashing footsteps ahead of her until she reached a clearing and saw the beast had stopped.

"Let her go!"

The Greishic stared at Zeya, its eyes full of hatred. It dropped the sister on the ground and stood tall, stepping forward to face her. Slowly it pulled a sword from a scabbard she had not noticed before, and took up a stance, holding the weapon threateningly. Much to her astonishment, the sword was not rusted or broken. The blade's keen edge appeared spotless and well cared for.

"*Sha vin gur mai clah?*" the creature growled, then charged.

She dodged the attack and attempted to counter, but the creature deflected her strike with ease. Zeya was surprised once more as she realized this Greishic knew how to fight with a sword. It quickly jabbed its weapon toward her, and she barely managed to parry the thrust with her daggers. It continued its assault with unrelenting strikes. She was entirely on the defensive and began to feel her strength wane as she struggled more and more to dodge or block each blow. The creature managed to knock one of her daggers from her hand, sending it flying. Zeya misstepped from the strike and tripped to the ground. She was barely able to roll out of the way as the creature brought its weapon down.

"Greishic!" Meleya, her wombsister, stood weapon drawn, and eyes filled with fire as she stared at the creature.

It turned to Meleya, now seeing her as the more significant threat, and confidently approached her, sword at the ready.

"Careful, Meleya! It's skilled with a blade!" Zeya called out as she pushed herself up from the ground.

Meleya slowly circled the Greishic, waiting for it to make the first move. It lunged at her with its blade, but she easily deflected the attack. It retreated slightly, then swung its sword, but she again blocked it. It almost seemed to be testing her defenses, but that was madness, wasn't it? The creature eyed Meleya with intrigue and gave her a wicked smile before licking its lips.

"If I didn't know any better, I'd say you were about to ask me to the tavern," Meleya joked, but Zeya could hear unsteadiness in her wombsister's voice. "Sorry, but I don't let miserably ugly creatures court me.

"*Sha vi guya mai clah, cundi.*"

"You will die today, beast."

Meleya charged at the Greishic, attempting to catch it off guard. The creature raised its sword, and they met with a clash of steel. It pushed her back with its superior strength and jabbed. She twisted, narrowly avoiding the thrust, and returned with one of her own. The Greishic caught her blade with its own and knocked it back. The beast began striking her with merciless speed and power.

Zeya watched, waiting for an opportunity to aid her wombsister. She finally saw an opening and launched her last dagger at the creature's chest. The blade flew through the air, dead on target, but the Greishic brought up its sword and deflected it before it could strike flesh. She looked around desperately, trying to locate one of her lost daggers. She spotted one near where the captured sister lay, but the Greishic was between her and the dagger.

The creature shifted back to Meleya, who had taken the opportunity to take up the offensive. She fought the beast with the edge and point of her blade, trying her hardest to spill its blood.

Preza entered the clearing, breathing heavily and ready to join the fray, but before she could assist, the sound of more Greishic approaching drew her attention. Preza spun to face the new threats, battle axe in hand.

Meleya cried out as the Greishic succeeded in cutting her, but the wound was superficial, and she fought on.

Zeya then heard another shout, this one from the captured sister. Fearing she was being carried off again, Zeya turned to provide what help she could but was stunned to witness the captive sister unbound and sprinting at full speed toward Meleya's foe with Zeya's dagger in hand.

"You bastard!" the sister shouted.

The Greishic turned in surprise, unable to mount a defense before the sister plunged the dagger deep into its chest.

"You bastard! You bastard! Aghhh! You bastard!"

The Greishic stumbled back, blood pouring from its wound. It reached out weakly toward the sister, trying to grab her, but its strength gave way, and it collapsed to its knees. Meleya stepped in and quickly finished the Greishic off. It fell backward, lifeless eyes staring up at its former captive.

"Aghhhhh!" The sister let out another guttural scream. She grabbed the knife embedded in the creature's chest and plunged the blade into the beast over and over. "You bastard! You bastard! You... bas... tard..." She collapsed, sobbing and wailing.

Zeya looked around the clearing, and saw Preza, covered in blood and mud, standing over multiple Greishic corpses and gazing sorrowfully at the sister. Zeya shifted her gaze to Meleya, who also stood staring at the woman sadly. In a haze, Zeya approached Meleya, wanting to ensure she was not wounded, but when she drew near, her wombsister grabbed her in an embrace, holding her tightly. They released each other and looked down at the sister, who still sobbed violently on the ground.

Preza knelt down beside the woman. "What is your name, Sister?"

There was no response.

"You are in danger no longer, Sister."

The sister's sobs began to ease slightly.

"What is your name?"

"My... name is... Eleza," she managed between sobs.

"And where do you hail from?"

"Memier. I was defending it from the..." She looked at the dead beast. "Defending it from the Greishic. They attacked with vast numbers a few days ago. They overpowered the watchtowers and dragged many of us into the Greenwood.

"You are free from them now," Preza said, gently gripping Eleza's shoulder. "We will see you safely back home to Memier."

Eleza began shaking her head vehemently. "No, no, no!" She started crying hysterically again. "No, no, no, no. Not Memier. No, no, no. Not home. Not home, not home!"

Preza kept her hand on Eleza's shoulder, waiting patiently for her to calm down.

"Please, I don't want to go back."

Preza slowly nodded with understanding.

"I can't go back, not now, not ever. I can't go back there, not to my home, not to my mother, not to my wombsisters. When the Greishic took me, when *that thing* took me, it raped me. Again and again, it raped me. I heard stories of what the Greishic do, I knew, but it was so much worse. It wouldn't let the others touch me. I belonged to *it*. I don't want the memories, I don't want to remember! I can't... I can't relive it."

Zeya felt her heart sink. Seeing the panic and the hurt on Eleza's face devastated her, she could not even imagine what such trauma was like. As the woman said, they all knew the stories, but to actually experience it. She could think of no words that could provide this woman with comfort.

"I know he impregnated me with his unholy seed. I can feel it. I can feel it growing inside me. I don't want that thing's foul offspring tearing apart my insides, I don't want to be responsible for bringing another one of them into this world." She looked at Preza, then Meleya and Zeya. "Please. I want to die."

Preza slowly bowed her head, then looked up at her companions.

Zeya stared at Preza in disbelief. She wanted to shout at her. This was madness! There was no way this woman could know the beast had impregnated her! Time heals all wounds! This sister could live to fight another day. She could go on to be a great warrior, a protector of the Sisterhood! Eleza needed to live! They would need every able-bodied sister to fight the Greishic before the end. She wanted to shout at the sister to be strong, to survive.

But Zeya didn't. The look on Eleza's swollen and bruised face was that of absolute defeat. She would not come back from this. Zeya resigned her thoughts and weakly nodded her head, agreeing with Eleza's last wish.

Meleya stepped forward, slowly raising her sword.

"Wait," Eleza whispered softly.

Maybe she will fight on, Zeya thought, hope creeping into her.

"I would be honored if the Selfa would do it."

Zeya's heart descended even lower than she thought possible. Kill Eleza? Her? She didn't want to, but she knew she had to. How could she disregard the dying wish of her dear sister, Eleza?

Nodding, Zeya bent down and pulled the dagger sticking out of the dead Greishic. She took her time, wiping the blade, ensuring that it was not tainted with a single drop of the creature's blood. She stared at the dagger and felt her mind slip into a haze. The dagger's polished silver leaf on the pommel glistened in the sunlight that reached the clearing. The day had turned so peaceful. Zeya knelt down beside Eleza and firmly put her hand on the woman's shoulder, squeezing it slightly. She looked at Eleza, questioningly. Was she sure this is what she wanted?

Eleza looked back, tranquility in her unswollen eye, and nodded gently in affirmation. "Hail, Selfa."

"Alé volás, Eleza."

Zeya drove her blade into Eleza's heart, holding it there until she felt her sister fade. She withdrew the dagger, fell back, and wept.

After some time, Meleya pulled Zeya to her feet.

"It was what she wanted, Zeya," Meleya said, her cheeks stained with tears.

"I know, and I saw peace in her eyes until she felt Vesta's Embrace, but still..."

"You did well, Zeya," Preza replied. "Eleza would have laid awake at night, living in constant fear that she would once again be taken by the Greishic. In her mind, she would relive the violation of her body night after night. Many sisters are unable to recover from such trauma. I know I barely did."

Zeya and Meleya both stared at Preza in shock.

"Are you saying that... you were...? That they...?" Zeya was unable to finish her question.

"Yes."

"Why did you never tell us this?" asked Meleya.

"For many reasons. Some things are better left unspoken."

"But if you survived, then she—"

"No, Zeya. Not everyone possesses the strength of will to surmount the trauma such an experience has on the mind." Preza paused, lowering her head. "I myself nearly succumbed to madness or death. It took love and support from those around me, and even then, I barely made it through. It is something I still carry with me, and will, for the rest of my life."

"Preza, I am so sorry," Zeya replied softly.

"I do not wish to discuss it any longer. Maybe someday I will, but not today. We should be moving on with the Venery."

"This Greishic, have you ever seen one like it before?" asked Meleya, looking down at the creature's body.

Preza moved and bent over the partially mutilated corpse. "I have not. I have never seen or heard of anything even resembling its prowess with a blade."

"It was more intelligent than any others we have come across," Zeya stated. "It watched us while we fought, then upon realizing it couldn't defeat the three of us at once, it took Eleza and fled."

"It doesn't look much different from the others." Meleya nudged the corpse with her boot. "Its body is still covered with filth, its teeth are still sharp, and its nails are still— wait, no. Its nails are cut short, not grown into claws like the others."

"With a blade, it probably doesn't need them," Zeya replied.

"Maybe. Its skill with a sword was beyond anything a Greishic should possess, but..." Meleya trailed off as the creature's sword caught her eye. She picked it up and examined it carefully.

"Is it one of ours?" asked Zeya.

"Yes, thank Vesta. It was crafted by the Sisterhood. Likely in Memier, but the markings are difficult to make out."

"Good to know the beasts haven't begun using forges," stated Preza.

"I hope it was a fluke, a mistake of nature," Zeya added.

"As do I, but regardless, Memier must be warned, and the Hearth must be notified," Preza replied.

"What of Eleza's body?" asked Meleya. "We have neither the time nor the means to give her the proper observances."

"We do not." Preza looked down at Eleza's body. "We could at least hide her body under some brush to keep the Greishic from eating her. May not keep the animals away, though."

The three moved Eleza's body out of the clearing and into some deep underbrush, making sure she was as concealed as possible.

"May your mind find peace in Vesta's arms, dearest Eleza," Preza spoke the words softly, then walked away.

* * *

They continued moving through the Greenwood until the sound of the Reypar River's easternmost flow reached their ears. The final crossing. Once they forded the stream, they'd be out of Greishic territory and nearly out of the Greenwood. From there, they'd face a leisurely climb up the Eastern Slope and right through the gates of Memier.

Zeya could abide being in the Greenwood no longer. She desired to be free of this horrid forest filled only with danger and death. She wanted out.

A loud scream erupted from nearby, breaking Zeya from her thoughts.

"Another sister in danger!" hissed Meleya.

"I'm not sure if we can—" Zeya was interrupted by another loud cry, this time from a different sister. "A second?"

Suddenly multiple shouts of suffering were heard coming from various locations around them. It was as if they were surrounded by screaming sisters.

"Preza, what should we do?" asked Meleya.

"I... I don't know. Can the two of you handle another fight?"

"I think I can," replied Zeya. "But that would depend on the number of creatures."

"There are too many captives! Listen, a sister, another sister, and another! There is no way we could save them all! The risk would be too great," lamented Meleya.

"But perhaps we could save a few?"

"No, Zeya. Meleya is right. We cannot risk the Venery to save our fallen sisters. When we reach Memier, we will inform Regent Vuleila and let her decide if a rescue is likely to succeed."

Another scream sounded, this one was very near.

"That one was close, let us at least go in for a closer look," suggested Zeya.

"I don't—" Preza stopped as the nearby cry rang out again, more intense than before. "All right, let's have a look."

They approached the direction of the cry cautiously until a Greishic camp came into view. This was no temporary campsite. There were permanent looking huts along with a large fire pit located at the center. Twenty, maybe thirty Greishic were moving about the camp.

"No, please, noooo!" A sister's screams were heard coming from one of the huts. It was followed by a sickly sound of flesh tearing from bone. "Aghhhh..." The sister's anguished shout started strong before fading into silence. A moment later, a Greishic exited the hut carrying a severed arm in its hands.

"Oh, Vesta," Meleya whispered.

The Greishic took the arm to the fire pit and began roasting it. Zeya had to hold back a gag as the scent of cooking human flesh reached her nose. She nearly vomited as she realized they could do nothing for this sister, nor for any of them. The other nearby screams were too close. Any disturbance would see them facing every Greishic within earshot. Sisters were being tortured, being raped, being eaten, and they could do nothing.

"We should go," Zeya whispered dejectedly. "I wish we hadn't come here, hadn't *seen*."

"All the more reason to find the male and produce another generation of warriors," Preza replied, then spat on the ground. "We will train them to kill every last one of these animals, I'll see to it, even if I have to teach them myself."

The three slowly backed away from the camp and headed toward the river. Zeya turned and looked back as she heard one final scream.

XVIII

Unmasked

"Yes?" Freila responded to the knock at her door. It was the middle of the night, far too late an hour for someone to be disturbing her without valid cause.

"I apologize for the disturbance, Mother Freila, but an emergency meeting of the Jurisa has been called," came a voice through the door.

"Very well, I will be there shortly."

An emergency meeting at this hour could only mean bad news. Either she had been found out, or worse, her daughters had fallen. What else could it be? No doubt Selfa Delreza had returned by now and Sieyna had gotten whatever evidence she had. Likely enough to reveal Freila's conspiracy and have her executed. But her daughters, could they have fallen? No, they should still be in the Greenwood, or perhaps just recently made it to Memier. Word of their fate would not have come this soon.

She pulled on her cloak and went to the door, hesitating before opening it. *I could run,* she thought. *I could flee this city and live in exile.* Freila knew of places that were outside the Sisterhood's reach. If she fled to one of them, she could probably live out her remaining years in peace. After debating this for a while, she sighed and opened the door.

Freila was surprised to see no one outside her room. No guards, no Sieyna wearing a wicked smile, just an empty corridor. As she made her way toward the chamber of the Jurisa, Freila began to relax. If they had discovered what she had done, surely they wouldn't allow her to walk the halls so freely. Freila glanced over her shoulder, ensuring no one was following her, but all she saw was more emptiness.

When she got to the meeting room, she saw only the two guards who were normally stationed outside the door.

"Evening, Mother Freila," one of the guards said with a warm and respectful smile.

"Greetings, sisters. I hope the night is treating you well," she replied.

"As well as usual, but I suppose that could change. I hope this urgent meeting does not bear dark news."

"As do I." Freila nodded solemnly to the guard before entering the council chamber. Inside, the other three were already seated and waiting for her. Freila stiffened when their eyes shifted toward her.

"Apologies for calling this meeting so late, but we have an important matter to discuss." Cereila's voice shook a little as she spoke.

Freila took her seat, and smiled warmly at the others.

Gilza cleared her throat. "I do hereby call this meeting of the Jurisa to order. We have been summoned at this late hour by Cereila who has just received an important message from Memier."

Freila felt a weight lift from her heart. It seemed she would not be thrown in a dungeon today. She prayed there was no devastating news of her daughters.

"Yes, thank you, Gilza," Cereila replied. "Sisters, I have received multiple messages from Memier, and it seems the city is in dire need of aid."

"The Greishic?" Sieyna asked.

"Yes, the creatures have been assaulting the city day and night. Regent Vuleila does not think they will be able to last much longer. She sent three messages, all requesting immediate aid." Cereila looked at one of the messages again. "The Regent also thinks the beasts will breach the Paling before long. There have been multiple attempts by the creatures to weaken the wall."

"What of Zeya? Has there been word?" Freila asked, concern entering her voice.

"No, I am afraid there have been no updates as to the location of Selfa Zeya," Cereila replied. "The message from Memier mentioned nothing of the Selfa, so perhaps she has not yet made it through the Greenwood. Then again, the message is a few days old. Regent Vuleila did mention something most peculiar, however." Cereila hesitated, as if trying to decide whether to continue.

"Well, out with it, woman!" Sieyna exclaimed.

"It would seem that both the Regent and her soldiers have noticed... have noticed a change in the behavior of some of the beasts. As Vuleila stated in her previous message, she felt the attacks on the Paling were more coordinated than usual. In this message, she reinforces that belief, claiming to have seen, with her own eyes, the Greishic using tactics during their assault." Cereila moved her spectacles closer to her face. "In her words, 'Not the typical small beasts following the larger into battle. There is a sense of organization that I have never before seen. I recognize the absurdity of this statement, but in all my years living on the border, I have never before witnessed anything like it. I believe we are facing a new evolution of the Greishic, and it is one that will not easily be defeated.' She continues to state that if it had only been her who noticed this behavior, she would have deemed it a result of lack of sleep or delusion, but many of her trusted warriors also have reported similar observations."

"I find it hard to believe that this new threat could suddenly appear without our previous knowledge," Gilza replied. "The Greishic have always been dumber than the soil they walk upon. They live only on instinct. They kill, they eat, they multiply. They are animals. If her observations are valid, we surely would have noticed such behavior before now."

"The Regent also wrote that their behavior implies increased intelligence. The beasts were demonstrating a comprehension of military strategy. What's more, it seems the Greishic were taking far more of our sisters prisoner than normal."

Gilza shook her head. "An intelligent Greishic is as likely as male triplets being born here in the Hearth! Perhaps you were right, Sieyna, maybe Vuleila *is* losing her prowess. We may want to begin looking for candidates to replace her."

"I do not think we should so quickly discount her observations," Freila countered. "She said in her previous message that the Greishic had never attacked the Paling with such ferocity. These may very well be the signs of the end of days. I do not think intelligent Greishic are as unlikely as you believe, Gilza. But I pray that you are right."

"As do I," Gilza replied. "Regardless, there is nothing we can do. We haven't the numbers to fight dull-witted Greishic, much less ones displaying a modicum of intelligence."

"Perhaps Vesta has turned her favor from us in favor of the Greishic," Cereila said.

"No, Vesta would never show favor to those wicked beasts," Gilza replied.

"How long would it take us to mobilize a force large enough to be of help?" asked Freila.

Gilza waved her hand, dismissively. "Why are you so eager to send daughters of prime child-bearing age off to die, Freila?"

Freila looked at Gilza in surprise. "What do you mean? There are thousands of sisters in Memier who could bear children. Should they not be saved? If the Greishic breach the Paling, Memier will fall. If the city falls, there is nothing to stop the creatures from spreading east and razing the other towns on the Eastern Plateau."

Gilza nodded her head. "I do not deny that it would be devastating if the Greishic breached the Paling. However, the Hearth, as well as the majority of the Sisterhood's population, lies in the west. If the beasts wish to go east, then let them."

"But losing all sisters to the east would ravage the Sisterhood's already thinning numbers!" exclaimed Cereila.

"Gilza, surely you aren't willing to sacrifice our sisters to distract the beasts from us!" Sieyna shouted in surprise.

"Calm down, sisters! Allow me to make my case without interruption. Your claims may not necessarily be valid. Regent Vuleila has already reported that a large number of ripened sisters have fallen or been captured by the Greishic. That would leave much fewer sisters able to bear children than you think. Additionally, excluding

Memier and Coratch, most of the sisters on the Eastern Plateau are old with dried-up wombs and would serve no more use in furthering the Sisterhood. I am not saying they should be abandoned entirely. We should send a warning to all the eastern towns and villages, make them aware that there is a possibility the Greishic may break through the Paling. We should tell them to send all daughters of childbearing age to Rolier or Wolenn so they can take the Yeren River west."

"The Yeren will only get them to the southern Greenwood," Freila replied. "Though perhaps we could send soldiers to help protect them the rest of the way."

"No," answered Gilza, shaking her head. "We should not endanger the lives of any more sisters. If refugees from the east make it through, then Vesta be praised, but if they do not, so be it."

"Gilza! What of the Selfa? What of the male? Are they to be abandoned as well? I don't understand the logic in your judgment!" exclaimed Freila.

"Our plans for the Selfa and the male will be unaffected. I am confident she will pass through Memier before it falls, assuming it falls at all. Do not forget that the Paling has stood for generations. It has withstood countless Greishic attacks in the past. I am not convinced that it will fall now. But assuming they do breach the city and flood onto the Eastern Plateau, the male should be safely riding down the Yeren toward us, by the time the creatures reach Rolier."

"And do you still intend to send soldiers to protect the male once they disembark from the Yeren River?" asked Cereila.

"Naturally. I already stated that our plans in that regard will be unchanged. If Vesta should will it and the Selfa reaches the end of the Yeren at the same time as the refugees, then all shall have an escort to safety. But I will not risk more sisters' lives to save what is sure to be a paltry number of ripened from the east."

"I cannot abide this," Freila stated.

"Good thing you won't have to," Gilza said, eyeing Freila harshly.

"What do you mean?"

"This brings us to the next item that requires our consideration. It has been brought to the Jurisa's attention that it was you, Freila, who suffused the rumor that a male had emerged in Noor."

Freila looked at Gilza in surprise, then turned her head and glared at Sieyna, who wore her wicked smile. "I assume this claim comes from Sieyna's forked tongue? Tell me, Gilza, did she provide any evidence for such a baseless accusation? Sieyna accosted me in my chamber not yet a full day ago, threatening me with the ramblings of a madwoman. Yet when I asked her for proof, she was unable to provide any."

"It was you, Freila, who encouraged the sending of Selfa Delreza to Noor to hunt for him," Gilza continued, unphased by Freila's protests. "It was you, Freila, who received word from one of *your* agents that there was a male in Rolier. It was you, Freila, that urged this council to send your daughter on the Venery to Rolier. The opportune timing of these events cannot be denied."

"Sieyna has had it out for me for years. Any report coming from her or her pupil, Delreza, would undoubtedly be filled with falsity and exaggeration."

"Oh, I'm sorry," Sieyna replied, her smile growing broader. "I neglected to mention something when last we spoke. Selfa Delreza left out one minor piece of information from the report she sent from Noor. You see, dearest Freila, Delreza has returned from Noor with a prisoner, a prisoner that you would be interested to know has implicated you in this plot. She stated that you not only encouraged her to spread the rumor of a male emergence in Noor but, in fact, paid her most handsomely to do so."

Freila felt her heart skip. She knew she took a considerable risk in trusting Yureza, but she had been low on options and running out of time.

"Surely any testimony brought forth against me from this prisoner was beaten out by Selfa Delreza and does not hold up to the standards of the Jurisa."

Gilza nodded. "You speak true, Freila. The accusations of one sister, especially those made under duress, would not be enough to lend credence to this matter. However, your agent also gave up all correspondence she had received from you. Thanks to the actions of Selfa Delreza, your surreptitious exchange was recovered and is enough to implicate you in this conspiracy. That combined with the woman's word has all but sealed your fate."

Freila held Gilza's gaze. The emotionless expression on the older woman's face was impossible to read. She looked at Sieyna, whose eyes glistened with delight, the wicked smile remaining on her face. Freila then looked at Cereila, who looked back at her regretfully. Freila knew she was trapped. She had been caught. *Thank Vesta I sent that message last night— No, not Vesta,* she thought. *Vesta could have prevented all of this to begin with.*

"Do you wish to say anything in your defense?" asked Gilza.

Freila looked at the woman defiantly. "Know this. What I did, I did not do for glory. Not for the glory of myself, nor for the glory of my daughter. What I did, I did for the slight possibility of the Sisterhood surviving. For the even more minute possibility of the Sisterhood *thriving*."

Gilza looked at Freila curiously. "Please expound on your defense, Freila. It may bring you leniency when your punishment is decided."

"No. I will say no more. You would not understand, nor would you agree."

"Are you certain, Freila? We are not as closed-minded as you believe." Cereila looked at her hopefully.

"I am certain."

Gilza nodded. "Very well."

"Guards!" Sieyna shouted.

The two guards quickly entered the room with weapons drawn, ready to face a threat. They appeared confused when they saw none.

"Take Freila to the dungeon where she will await her execution," Sieyna commanded.

The guards hesitated and looked at Gilza, who nodded her head in affirmation. They sheathed their swords and approached Freila who rose, offering no resistance, and let herself be led out of the room.

* * *

"Cereila."

"Yes, Gilza?" Cereila asked nervously.

"Send word to Regent Vuleila. Tell her it is imperative that she send her most-trusted sisters to Rolier with the Selfa. Once Selfa Zeya locates the male, they are to take him from her using any means necessary and return him to the Hearth, posthaste. Be sure to emphasize that Selfa Zeya is to know nothing of this plan."

"I will send it out as soon as this meeting adjourns. What am I to write regarding her call for aid?"

"Write nothing. She will assume we sent this missive before receiving hers."

Cereila stared at Gilza in disbelief before nodding.

"Regarding the male," Sieyna began, "perhaps we should also send Selfa Delreza to the Eastern Plateau to intercept and guide him safely back to the Hearth. Vesta only knows if Selfa Zeya had her mind twisted by her mother and will attempt her own treachery."

"Do you feel Selfa Delreza would be able to make the journey after having just returned from Noor?"

"I do. She will do her duty, whatever it is. Resupply and fresh horses should be all that is required."

"Very well. Give the order."

XIX

A Night in Memier

Zeya breathed a sigh of relief as the Eastern Slope came into view. The incline that led up to Memier was a welcome sight. The city was not yet visible from where they stood, but Zeya was able to just make out the tip of the Paling wall.

As they exited the forest, Zeya noticed the twin watchtowers that ordinarily stood overlooking the Slope, lay in ruins upon the ground. Broken wood beams lay in disorder, some of which still smoldered from the attack. There were a number of bodies littering the terrain, some Greishic and some human.

"The creatures must have hit hard to have taken down the towers," commented Preza. "The legs of the towers are thicker than the Paling itself, and the Greishic have historically ignored them. They usually attempt to sprint past the defenses and evade the arrows our sisters fire down upon them. My heart aches for those who were posted here."

"How many occupied each tower?" Meleya asked, looking around at the bodies.

"About twenty, from what I remember. But it was not uncommon during times of battle for that number to double."

"So many sisters," Zeya murmured sadly.

Preza nodded. "Let us hope most of them made it safely back behind the Paling before the towers came down."

"Memier fought well," Meleya remarked, focusing on the Greishic bodies strewn about. "I'm glad its warriors took so many of the beasts down with them."

They continued the trek up the Slope, passing hundreds of bodies as they went. Overhead, a fully-healed Heyfic flapped solemnly through the air. *I'm glad I don't have his view*, Zeya thought. She had never before seen the results of a battlefield. She tried to think of each fallen sister as a unique individual, someone with a family, a mother, maybe even daughters, but she could not. Her mind kept grouping them together as mere casualties of war. Zeya felt solace in knowing these dead sisters were far better off than the captured ones. At least these were now at peace.

The companions reached the top of the Slope, then collectively gasped in horror.

"Oh, Vesta, no," Meleya whispered in disbelief.

They stood staring across the field, which held the remnants of a great battle. An immeasurable number of Greishic and sisters lay strewn across the battleground. Beyond the field, the city of Memier, once safe and protected by the Paling wall, lay in ruin. Smoke from still-smoldering ashes reached for the sky with its tendriled fingers.

The damage to the Paling wall was clearly visible from where they stood. Countless rough-hewn cuts marked gashes large enough for enemies to infiltrate the city. The spectacle was made even eerier by its noiseless sonancy. Not a sound reached Zeya's ears, and the dead silence of the battle since passed sent chills down her spine.

"Do you... do you think any remain alive?" Meleya asked, breaking the stillness.

Preza slowly shook her head. "Any survivors would have fled the city en masse, and the rest..." she trailed off. "Though it is a possibility that some may still be in hiding."

"Does this mean the Greishic are already spreading across the Eastern Plateau?" Zeya asked.

"Maybe. If they are, it will make our journey far more difficult. With luck, the beasts may have retreated back into the Greenwood, anxious to torment their captives— Oh, Vesta. I can't believe I spoke those words."

"It's all right, Preza. We know what you meant," consoled Zeya.

They reached the Paling, and Zeya stood staring up at the massive logs that once made up Memier's defenses. Each piece of timber was placed so tightly against the other that there was little view of the city's interior. As they made their way toward the nearest breach, Preza peered inside and exhaled audibly.

"What? What is it?" Meleya demanded.

Preza pulled her head out. "More bodies. More dead sisters."

"Any sign of Greishic?" Zeya asked.

"No, but I couldn't see very deep into the city."

"Should we enter? Or perhaps find a gap further to the edge of the Paling and keep to the city's outskirts?" Meleya asked.

"The city is quiet," commented Zeya. "I would think we would hear evidence of the creatures if a horde resided inside. Preza, what do you think?"

"The Greishic have never been known for stealth or for laying traps. I think it's safe to enter. We should search for any survivors who may have gone to ground."

Preza climbed through the breach, with Zeya and Meleya following behind. Inside, the deserted city was even more disturbing. There was a mixture of burned out buildings, along with many that remained completely intact, untouched by the battle. More bodies littered the streets, nearly all were sisters. Most lay with makeshift weapons, primarily heavy tools, hastily-fastened spears, or blood-stained stones at their side. One woman lay dead with a bloodied iron pan still in her hand.

"They fought for their city," Preza murmured. "They took up what arms they could and challenged the ill-begotten beasts to the very end. They were true sisters."

"Why did the Greishic leave so many bodies behind? Why not take more to eat?" questioned Meleya.

"Too much to eat. The bodies would rot before the Greishic got to them all. Though, I am sure those bastards filched their fill."

Zeya stood frozen, overcome by grief. "When did this happen? Why did the Hearth not send aid?" Her words quickened as tears streamed down her cheeks. "A regiment of sisters from Haralda could have rushed through the Greenwood far faster than we did. They could have helped them! Did they care? Did the Hearth even care?"

Meleya put her hand on Zeya's shoulder. "We don't know how events transpired. I doubt Mother and the Hearth would have just left an entire city to die."

Zeya nodded slowly and wiped her tear-stained cheeks.

Preza grunted. "We should search further into the city."

They progressed closer to the center of Memier, and while the number of bodies lessened, they found no one alive.

"What's that building?" Zeya asked, pointing to a large, rather ornate stone structure.

"The Regent's Keep. The seat of her power and living quarters," Preza responded, hope creeping into her voice. "If there are any survivors, they surely would have sought shelter there! It's well fortified and easy to defend."

They approached the Keep, but their hope dwindled as they saw one of its large wooden doors had been torn open. Moving quietly with weapons drawn, the three women entered.

The entrance hall of the Regent's Keep was a mess. Banners of the Sisterhood, soaked with blood, lay strewn upon the ground. Splintered wood, broken make-shift weapons, and more bodies completed the display. It was apparent that the Greishic forced their way into the building, in an attempt to reach every last woman alive.

"The final stand of Memier," whispered Meleya.

"Let's hope not," Preza replied. "The Keep contains many chambers, so there may yet be sisters who survived. I believe the Regent's throne room is just through there. That would be a good place for us to begin our search."

The three moved across the hall to the doorway Preza had indicated. Two large red doors with gold accented carvings stood partially open. Slowly opening one of the doors further, Meleya peeked inside.

"More dead."

"The Regent? Is she in—"

Preza suddenly cut off as the three sisters heard the unmistakable growl of a Greishic from within the throne room. They raised their weapons as Meleya pulled the heavy door wide open and they stepped into the room, ready to face their foe.

Inside, no creatures charged at them, and Zeya saw nothing but more bodies. She was surprised how little the throne room was damaged. If not for the bodies, Zeya would not have known a fight had even taken place. Banners containing the Red Flame still hung pristinely around the room, along with other untouched furnishings. A handful of fallen sisters lay mixed with the bodies of the Greishic but far less than she would have expected. They saw no immediate threat and began exploring the room further.

"Not many dead sisters, here," Zeya remarked.

"There may have only been a few left," Preza replied.

"Is one of them the Regent, Preza?" asked Zeya.

"Aye, Vuleila lies over there, at her desk. Her wound looks... self-inflicted."

Zeya looked at the Regent, whose face was nothing but serene in death. She sat behind her desk as if sleeping, cradling a horn in her lap. If not for the blood-covered parchments spread across the desk, Zeya may have tried to wake the dead woman.

"This one was self-inflicted too," Meleya stated, looking down at the body of a sister, still clutching a blade to her bloodied-throat.

"Alé volás, sisters," lamented Preza.

A growl sounded again, and the three raised their weapons, looking around and ready for the attack.

"I see it, it's wounded!" Meleya pointed to the origin of the growl. A Greishic lay with a deep slash across its face.

"Left for dead, huh?" Preza chided as she walked over to the beast. "Your little friends leave you behind all alone?"

"*Sha... cund*—ack!" The Greishics attempt at speech was interrupted by a gargled cough.

"I'm sorry, what was that, beast?"

"*Sha cundi... logua!*" It managed between coughs.

"Good riddance." Preza brought her axe down on the Greishic, silencing it for good. She turned to the others. "Let us leave this Vesta-forsaken crypt behind."

They exited the Regent's Keep, and Zeya was surprised to discover night had fallen over the city. Another day had passed. No doubt they would have been feasting by now, hearing the gossip of the city and fending off questions about their destination. As much as she hated the attention, Zeya would have gladly taken the looks of adoration from the sisters of Memier over the dull-eyed stares they now wore on their pallid faces.

"Do you think it's safe to camp in the city for the night, Preza?" Meleya asked.

"Should be. We haven't seen signs of any recent Greishic activity. My guess is they either fled back into the Greenwood or are spreading across the Eastern Plateau as we speak."

"Let us hope they retreated," stated Meleya.

Preza grunted. "Hope. We've been hoping for so long. Hoping to survive, hoping to find the male, hoping to save the Sisterhood. I'm sure everyone in this city *hoped* reinforcements would arrive in time to save them. *Hoped* the Paling would hold. *Hoped* they would be spared, and *hoped* the beasts wouldn't find them. Look where hope got them. Dead. Hoping, hoping, hoping. I'm done with hope."

"Mind your words, dear Sister," Meleya replied. " Hope is the only thing keeping the Sisterhood going. Should we just lie down and give up? Let the Greishic take us to their huts and torment us until our deaths?"

Preza's head drooped, and she began sobbing loudly. The large woman's body trembled violently as she let the tears flow free. "This world is not worth living in. We are on a fool's quest. Travel across the land, through the Greenwood, to a remote village and *hope* we find the only male born in more than fifty years? How idiotic does that sound? What duty-bound belief would see us on this mad quest?"

"Your duty to me." Zeya stared at Preza with burning eyes. "You swore an oath that your blood would spill before my own. You swore to guide me on the Venery, you swore, not only to be my companion but also to be my shield. Preza the Oath-Breaker is not a title that becomes you, nor is Preza the Defeated. It was not long ago you struck me in an attempt to bring me to my senses. Must I be the one to strike you now?

"We are not on the Venery due to irrational faith. We have strong evidence to support the Venery, evidence from *our* mother. Have you ever known her to act rashly? I have not. She has always been nothing but logical and calculative. If she thinks there is a man at the end of this road, then there is a man at the end of this road. What say you, Preza?"

Preza remained silent.

"What say you, Preza? My protector. My sister?"

Preza slowly raised her head and gazed into Zeya's burning eyes with her dampened ones. Eventually, her lips curled into a weak smile. "I say we get a good night's rest and continue this journey until hope becomes truth."

* * *

On her watch, Zeya stared out the window at a lifeless street. The full moon overhead illuminated the bodies on the ground, while the pools of blood surrounding them glistened in its pale light. They had appropriated someone's home and set up camp for the night. She looked at her sleeping sisters. Not a hint of the day's experiences showed on their serene faces. She prayed they had peaceful dreams. Heyfic, who was awake and perched near Meleya, looked back at Zeya with curiosity in his eyes.

Alone with her thoughts, Zeya's mind turned to her mother. She remembered how proud her mother had been when she became a selfa.

I knew you were the one from the moment I set my eyes upon you, my daughter. You will be praised above all other selfas who have ever lived. You will find the male, and you will save all of humankind. Zeya had believed those words with all her heart. She was so young, and her mother spoke with such confidence. She had trained hard with both Preza and Meleya, trying to become the capable warrior that was expected of a selfa of the Sisterhood. Her days not spent preparing her body were spent preparing her mind. All for the Venery. She had been so nervous when they departed Vulna, but she had felt ready. How naive she was. No amount of training could prepare her for this. Reading reports and historical tomes about the savage Greishic was one thing, but actually witnessing her sisters being raped, eaten, or torn apart was something no words could ever describe. Far worse, seeing such a fate befall an entire city was beyond compare.

Preza's loss of confidence earlier that day had hit her hard. She knew this journey was taxing on her companions, but she never thought it would affect Preza. The woman was a stone. If her sisters broke, what would keep her going? She hadn't entirely believed in the words of reprimand she had used to scold Preza. Zeya actually agreed with many of her sister's sentiments, but succumbing to such feelings would do them no good, especially not at this point in the journey.

A loud crash echoed across the city, jerking her from her thoughts. She stuck her head out the window and looked around. The streets remained quiet, and there was no movement to be seen. Zeya debated waking her sisters, but decided against it. The crash had not disturbed their peaceful slumber, and it was best to let them rest. Drawing one of her daggers from its scabbard, she slipped out the door and into the night.

Zeya wandered in the direction of the crash until she heard the sound of someone, or something, struggling. She approached the grunting with caution, but could not clearly make out its source. Climbing atop a nearby building, she slowly moved forward, trying to get a better view and stay out of this possible foe's sight. Peering over the edge of the roof, she saw a large stone drain that was grated with iron bars. A sizable piece of broken stone lay against the grate, obstructing her view of what was making the sound.

An ensnared Greishic? Zeya thought. *It looks like it's trapped securely. I should leave it to starve. There may be more in there, and a swift death is far more than these creatures deserve.*

Figuring whatever was in there could wait until morning, she climbed down from the roof and began making her way back to camp. She suddenly stiffened as the sound of sobbing reached her ears. Human sobs. At least she assumed so. The cries were faint and hard to make out, but she had never heard tell of a crying Greishic. Then again, she had never heard of a sword-adept beast either. Zeya approached the drain. The sobs had become grunts once more, and she was almost close enough to see. Her stomach flipped as she saw what appeared to be *human* hands sticking through the grate. The hands were attempting to move the large broken stone, but were not strong enough to do so. Zeya ran the rest of the way to the drain.

"Sister?"

The grunting stopped, and the hands swiftly retreated back through the grate, but there was no response.

"Are you a sister?"

Still no response.

"Speak! Or I will leave you to your prison."

After a few moments, she heard a low, weak voice. "I am. I am Joreya of Memier, daughter of... daughter of Rueila."

"How did you come to your cage, Joreya?"

"I was trapped when the Greishic broke through the Paling. This large stone fell, blocking my exit."

"Are there any other sisters in there?"

"No, it's just me."

"Very well, let me see if I can help free you."

Zeya placed her hands on the large stone and attempted to push it. It did not budge.

"Try and move it with me, Joreya."

She tried again, this time with Joreya's aid, but the stone would not yield. Trying once more, she pushed with all her might, but to no avail.

"I am unable to free you myself," Zeya spoke into the darkness of the drain. "But I have two companions, one is very strong, I'm sure together we will be able to free you."

"No. Please, don't leave me!"

"I will be right back, Sister. Do not worry."

"Please, no!" Joreya's voice became panicked and grew louder and louder with each word. "I have seen nothing that wasn't Greishic in days! Please, don't leave me alone, not again. You will forget about me, you will, I know it! I will die in here!"

"Silence, Woman!" hissed Zeya. "Your hysterics will bring every remaining Greishic in the city down on us!"

Joreya ceased her pleas.

"On my honor, I will return with help, and we *will* free you. Do you understand?"

Joreya was once again silent.

"On my honor," Zeya repeated, then left the drain.

Back at camp, she gently roused her sisters and told them of Joreya.

"A survivor?" Meleya asked incredulously.

"Yes, a young one, she is trapped by a large stone. I tried moving it myself, but my strength was not enough to free her."

"And... where is this drain?" Preza asked, failing to stifle a yawn.

"Not far."

"Very well, let us go and rescue the last citizen of Memier."

As the party approached the drain, Zeya called out to Joreya in a whisper. "I am back, Sister. And I have brought help."

"That is a big rock," Meleya remarked. "You think we'll be able to move it?"

"I'm sure the three of us will manage," Zeya replied.

"Four," came a mousy voice from within the drain. "I can help. I won't be useless."

"Four then," Zeya agreed.

The three companions attempted to heave the stone with all their might, Joreya doing what she could through the grate, and it slowly began to tilt.

"Keep... pushing! Almost... there!" Preza managed between grunts. "Use... those legs... of yours, ladies."

The large stone continued to move, then suddenly jerked and toppled to the ground with a deafening crash. All four women froze, expecting to hear the sounds of an alerted Greishic horde charging at them.

After several moments of silence, they relaxed, and Zeya let out a breath. "I hope that means the beasts are no longer in the city," she stated.

"Or only the deaf ones remain," Meleya smirked.

Joreya climbed out of the drain and stepped into the moonlight. Her eyes looked around at the others, appearing fearful until her gaze settled on Zeya's silver leaf.

"You're the Selfa? Selfa Zeya!" she exclaimed.

"I am."

"I was rescued by the Selfa! My wombsisters are never going to believe this!"

"What can you tell us about the attack, Joreya?" Zeya asked.

"Not much, I'm afraid. What I do know I heard from my wombsisters. They fought, defending the Paling from the Greishic. Two were sent home a few days ago, once Regent Vuleila deemed the risk had lessened. They helped push the Greishic back, but the creatures must have returned. I was inside the drain when I heard the sounds of nearby battle. I..." Joreya paused, looking embarrassed.

"You what, Sister? Speak freely, you will receive no judgment from us," encouraged Meleya.

"I wanted to help, I really did. But I had no weapon and had never been allowed to have even the most basic of training. My mother, she wouldn't agree to it. So I hid. I stayed in the drain and cowered, covering my ears in an attempt to silence the screams that echoed around me."

"I doubt you would have turned the tide of battle, Sister," Meleya replied.

"Still, I could have tried. After the cries faded, I came to the entrance and saw the grate had been blocked. That is all I know. I am sure another sister could tell you more."

The three companions glanced at one another.

"What? What is it?"

Zeya finally spoke. "Joreya. We found no other survivors. You are our first, and probably the only in the entire city."

Joreya looked at Zeya in disbelief. "No, that can't be. Surely there are more in hiding? Memier is home to many sisters. They must be somewhere."

Preza gently shook her head.

"The Regent's Keep! Yes, that's where they must be. I remember my wombsister, Eleza telling me it was the strongest place in the city. All the survivors are likely there as we speak, just waiting to be rescued."

"Joreya," Meleya began in a calm voice, "we searched the Keep. We found nothing but fallen sisters and Greishic bodies."

"No. That cannot be! No, no! My wombsisters! They can't be dead!" Joreya suddenly darted past Preza and began running down the street.

"Joreya! Wait!" Meleya called out, as the three ran to follow her.

They chased her until she climbed a set of stairs and entered a home. A moment later, they heard her scream in horror. Zeya drew her daggers and rushed in, ready to face the threat, but she stopped when she saw a woman lying on the floor with multiple limbs missing and a look of horror frozen on her face.

"My... mother."

Meleya stepped forward and gently put her hand on Joreya's shoulder.

"I hated her, I really did. I hated her for how she treated me. As if I was not even human. She would treat dogs better than me, but... but she—" Joreya burst out crying. "Oh, Vesta, she didn't deserve this. I don't care how much I hated her, no one deserves to die like this."

"They do not. One day the Greishic will be defeated, and all our fallen mothers, sisters, and daughters will be avenged," Preza stated solemnly.

"Were there really no other survivors?"

"None that we saw," Meleya replied softly. "But I am sure some sisters escaped through the eastern gate. They would have had time to flee the city before the Greishic swarmed it."

Joreya walked slowly to her mother's body. She stared into her mother's lifeless eyes for a long time.

"Goodbye, Mother." She turned to the others. "I have one favor to ask. If it's not too much trouble."

"You may ask it," responded Zeya.

"The last I saw of two of my wombsisters, they were... they were in the bedchamber, that one." She pointed to a doorway that appeared to have been torn open. "I don't think I could take seeing their bodies too. Could... could one of you look for me, please? I must know."

"I will check for you, dear Sister," Zeya replied. She walked across the room and entered the bedchamber. It was dark, but Zeya could just make out the figure of a body lying on the floor in a pool of blood.

She moved to the bedside and gently pulled one of the blankets over the sister before returning to the main room.

"Nothing?" Joreya asked, hopefully.

"Nothing. The room was empty."

Relief flooded Joreya's face. "Oh, thank Vesta. I pray they got out safely. Maybe they're already headed to one of the nearby villages." Joreya hesitated. "What will happen to me now?"

Meleya and Preza both looked at Zeya expectantly.

"We are leaving the city at daybreak. You are welcome to travel with us until we reach the next town."

Joreya nodded graciously. "Oh, thank you! Thank you! I promise I will help. However I can."

* * *

The next morning, the four companions finished gathering their belongings and stood ready to continue their journey. The next stop would be Rolier. Their destination and the end of the Venery. The weight of the end once again began to weigh heavily on Zeya's mind. Would the male be there? Would she find him? *One step at a time*, she thought. *We need to make it to Rolier first.* Encountering roving bands of Greishic out in the open would be dangerous. It would be far more difficult to avoid them with no cover to conceal themselves. And although being able to detect the creatures from a distance could work in their favor, the beasts would also be able to spot them.

"Are you sure you wish to join us, Joreya?" Meleya asked. "It may be safer for you to travel south to Wolenn and catch a riverboat to the west."

"I don't think I'd make it to Wolenn alone. Besides, I am looking forward to seeing the male!"

"Aren't we all," Preza smirked.

"How long is it to Rolier from here?" Joreya asked.

"We should be there in a couple of days, assuming we face no delays," Preza answered. "And we won't know the risk of that until we reach the gate."

They made their way through the city toward the eastern gate. More bodies lay upon the ground, though far fewer than in the central part of the city. Zeya hoped that meant that very few, if any, of the beasts made their way this far into the city.

As the eastern gate slowly came into view, Zeya felt her stomach twist. The gate had been very nearly torn down. One side lay in ruin, its massive hinges barely able to keep it up. The other, while intact, was embedded with deep cuts. It seemed the fleeing residents of Memier had attempted to barricade it from the outside in the hopes that it would stop the creatures' pursuit. It hadn't worked. Worse, it was likely their makeshift barricade served only to prevent any additional sisters from fleeing the city. Piles of bodies, very few Greishic, lay against the gate and near the walls.

"Oh, Vesta," Joreya whispered.

Everyone stood staring at the spectacle for some time before Preza finally spoke. "Let us move on from this forsaken city."

"So the Greishic are roaming the Eastern Plateau then," Zeya murmured.

"They sure as Pit didn't turn around once the gate was torn down." Preza released a deep sigh. "The stables are just outside the city, we should check them. If the goddess really is on our side, she better have left us some mounts."

They were surprised to find that the stables appeared to be untouched by the creatures. While most of the stalls lay empty, a few horses had been left behind. They took three and set the rest free. Joreya had never been on a horse before, so she rode with Meleya. As they rode, Zeya was surprised to see joy on Joreya's face. She had the look of a caged animal that had just been freed.

"Joreya, have you never been out of the city before?" Meleya asked.

"Never. Mother wouldn't allow it. There was also little reason to leave Memier. Everything we needed was within the Paling walls."

"Everything but open space," Preza replied.

Joreya laughed. "That's true! I never thought the wind in my hair would feel so good!"

"Joreya, this is but a light breeze! If you want wind, then hold on tight." Meleya pushed their horse into a full gallop.

Zeya smiled as Joreya's laughter grew more distant. "Glad she can still laugh after all she's been through."

"New experiences make the old ones easy to forget. For a time."

"She has a lot to forget." Zeya hesitated. "Preza, I did find one of her wombsisters dead in their home, but I couldn't bring myself to tell her."

"I suspected as much. You seemed more shaken when you came out of that room."

"Joreya also mentioned having a wombsister named Eleza. I hope that was not the same one we... the one we freed."

"I caught that as well." Preza thought for a moment. "Probably best not to bring any of this up. Let her hold tightly onto whatever fragment of hope remains within her."

Zeya smiled. "I'm glad you're giving hope a second chance, Sister."

XX

Forward unto the End

"More tracks. These turn and head north," Preza declared after studying the ground.

"How many?" asked Zeya.

"Enough to cause trouble, especially for the smaller villages. But it is fortunate for us that they broke off from the main road. That means less we may have to face."

The four women had been following Greishic tracks since leaving Memier. Thankfully, they found no other sign of the beasts. No mutilated bodies of fallen sisters met their sight, and no captives screaming in agony reached their ears. The four companions were a day's journey closer to Rolier and to the end of the Venery.

"And what about that?" Joreya pointed to a distant cloud of dust rising from the ground.

"Refugees or Greishic," Preza replied. "Though I pray they're refugees. The cloud is heading straight for Wolenn."

"I wish we could warn them," Meleya murmured.

Preza nodded in agreement. "We find the male swiftly enough and there will be time to. The river will see us to Wolenn faster than our horses will."

If we find the male, Zeya thought. The burden on her heart only grew as they approached Rolier, and her sisters' words of urgency only served to weigh her down all the more. She felt enough pressure having to find the male and make it back. Now they had Greishic to worry about as well. *Oh Vesta, let him be there, let me find him.*

They continued onward until Preza abruptly halted. She sat on her horse listening, with her hand raised, signaling them to remain silent.

Enemy ahead, Preza gestured.

Close? Zeya signed in return.

Yes.

Preza motioned for them to dismount and came right up against Zeya's ear to whisper. "I heard them. Definitely Greishic. Not sure how many, but we'll be noticed if we try and go around."

Zeya turned her lips toward Preza's ear. "We can easily outrun them on horseback."

"I don't like the idea of leaving any of the creatures alive to hunt our sisters. Send Meleya to scout. If it's a few, we can handle them."

Zeya nodded and turned to her wombsister to relay the plan.

"*Coondris! Coondris Noge!*" A cry erupted nearby and the companions whirled to see a single Greishic standing on the road pointing at them. "*Coondris!*"

"Joreya, stay behind us and hold the horses!" Meleya shouted, pressing the reins into her hand and pushing her back.

The Greishic that had spotted them charged forward as three others came from around a small hill.

"Stay together, keep them away from Joreya and the horses!" Preza ordered.

Zeya pulled two daggers from her belt and launched one at the leading beast. Her blade missed, and the creature continued its charge. She threw another, striking the creature in the arm, but it barrelled forward, undeterred.

"Save your blades!" Preza roared.

The first Greishic leapt forward, slashing at the three sisters, but the creature's reach fell short as Meleya thrust her sword through its chest. The remaining beasts reached them and the three sisters separated to take them on.

Zeya rolled to dodge her foe's attack, then swept the creature's leg, knocking the beast to the ground. Before it could get up, she rolled sideways toward it and plunged her dagger into its chest.

"Meleya, watch out!" Joreya called as two more beasts entered the fight.

Meleya quickly dispatched her first foe and turned to face the others. They split, and one headed straight for Meleya while the other went toward Joreya.

"Zeya, protect Joreya!"

"I've got her," Preza shouted and the sound of her axe sinking into flesh followed.

Joreya wanted to drop the reins and flee as the creature charged right at her, but she mustered what courage she could and remained facing the Greishic. The beast got within reach of her and swiped with sharpened claws. Joreya leapt backward, managing to dodge the attack, but the creature readied for another. The horses reared in fear, and yanked Joreya to the ground, but she managed to hold onto the reins.

Zeya rushed past Preza and dove dagger first toward the final creature, knocking it to the ground. She thrust her blade deeper into its flesh and waited until its struggling ceased.

"You good, Joreya?" Meleya asked after she had dispatched her remaining foe.

"Yes, I... I'm good."

"You stood your ground. I'm impressed," Preza remarked.

"But I wanted to run, I wanted to drop the reins and run all the way back to Memier."

Preza smiled. "True bravery is wanting to flee and holding your ground. We may make a warrior out of you yet."

* * *

Freila lay awake in her cell, staring at the stone ceiling above her. She missed her bed. The stiff board she lay on now just lacked a certain comfort she had grown accustomed to. She wondered if people really slept on beds like this. Freila knew she was privileged. Being a council member and living at the Hearth certainly had its perks, but this bed was absurd. Would it kill the Dungeon Keeper to provide at least a straw filled mattress? Though perhaps the poking of the straw would cause her more discomfort? *Enough distraction*, she thought, *there are more pressing issues that need a solution.* She turned her focus to the decision she would soon have to make.

Freila knew she would be brought before the Jurisa soon, and she needed to decide whether she should come clean and confess to them everything she knew. Her plan for the male, the Sisterhood, all of it. Cereila may understand. She had always shown a keen sense of logic, but the woman had lost her passion for change. And besides, it would take more than one councilwoman to overlook her transgressions.

Gilza would never accept Freila's plan. The old woman was too set in the ways of the Sisterhood. Any ideas that were contrary to her beliefs would be deemed both blasphemous and treasonous. That's what pained Freila the most. She was trying to *help* the Sisterhood. She was trying to *save* them, all of them. Freila didn't even consider trying to convince Sieyna. It seemed the woman had had it out for her from the moment she was accepted to the Jurisa. Sieyna would not be satisfied until Freila dangled from the gallows.

Freila's mind went back to the day Zeya had discovered she was a selfa. It was startling how blue her child's eyes glowed, and yet, it served as a sign to Freila. Witnessing the blue flame burning inside her daughter confirmed her belief that she was doing the right thing. She had known at that moment that all her previous scheming and manipulation had been for the greater good. Freila had waited far too long for the right selfa to come along, one that she could mold to her purpose. Zeya would break the cycle. Zeya would save all of humankind.

The door to her cell creaked open, and two guards entered.

"Mother—" the guard cleared her throat. "Freila, you are hereby summoned to the Council of the Jurisa to stand trial for your crimes against the Sisterhood."

"Very well. Let's get on with it." Freila stood and held out her hands.

The guards fastened shackles tightly to her wrists and pushed her out of the cell. She was led through the Hearth and up to the council chamber. No one did so much as glance in her general direction. *It seems word has already spread*, she thought, *and that means my fate has already been sealed.*

The door to the council chamber opened, and Freila was guided inside. Gilza eyed her with disdain as she was brought before the Council of the Jurisa. Sieyna watched with nothing but pleasure in her eyes.

Gilza cleared her throat. "Sister Freila, after much deliberation, and with the evidence presented to us, the Jurisa has found you guilty of conspiring against the will of the Sisterhood. Using your position on this council to manipulate not only the Sisterhood but also the Venery bears one punishment. Death. Do you have anything to say in your defense that may lessen the charges and your punishment?"

So they wish for me to grovel at their feet and beg for their mercy, she thought.

"Freila? Are we to take your silence as an admittance of your guilt?" questioned Gilza.

Freila met Gilza's eyes defiantly. "What purpose would me defending my actions have? You have already made up your minds. Do not forget, I am one of you, I know how this council functions."

"You *were* one of us," Sieyna replied snidely. "You are no longer a member of the Jurisa, you are now a prisoner, and you will treat us, your superiors, with respect."

"Superiors? Oh, dear Sieyna, how quickly you have forgotten your duty to the Sisterhood. The Jurisa is to humble itself before the people, not elevate itself above them."

Sieyna rose sharply from her chair. "Don't lecture me, you barren bitch. You manipulated the Sisterhood for your own gain. Explain to me how that is humbling yourself before it?"

"Enough! Sieyna, be seated," Gilza commanded. "Freila, you have served the Sisterhood faithfully for many years, so I will ask you once more. Do you have anything to say in your defense that may lessen your punishment?"

"I have nothing more to say."

"Very well. In order to spare both you and this council any further embarrassment, we will forego a public execution and allow you to take poison. Is this agreeable?"

They wish for me to slip quietly into Vesta's warm Embrace? To go calmly out of their lives without a fight?

"No, it is not."

The three council members stared at her incredulously.

"In accordance with that which was constituted by the Sisterhood, by our foremothers, I accept the prescribed punishment of a public hanging, to be held not more than a week from my sentencing. Failure to comply with this would see me freed from prison and exiled from the city." She looked at Gilza. "Is *that* agreeable, Sister?"

"Freila! Surely, you do not wish to face such a public humiliation?" Cereila demanded, speaking up for the first time. "You were an esteemed member of this council! What changed in you, I do not know, but we are allowing you to maintain any respect you may have in the eyes of the public."

"Let it be known that I have chosen my fate. I have chosen my punishment. Either prepare the knot or release me."

"As you wish, Freila," Gilza replied. "Guards! Return the prisoner to her cell!"

The guards stepped forward and, gripping Freila by her arms, began dragging her out of the room. Before they cleared the door, Sieyna called out. "Oh, Freila! You should know that your plan, whatever it was, has failed. We sent word to Regent Vuleila, ordering her to apprehend your daughter along with her companions once the male has been found. Your schemes have all been for nothing."

Freila stared directly into Sieyna's eyes. "If you think that worries me, you are gravely misguided. My daughters *will* succeed, and my daughters *will* receive all the glory that is due to them. They are, after all, *my* daughters. All three of them." She then turned and walked gracefully from the room, the guards following behind her.

XXI

A Letter from the Fallen

Keila stared at her baby adoringly. She thanked Vesta every day for the gift she had been blessed with. The thought that it was her chosen above all other women always brought a smile to her face. Still, she worried about the Selfa coming to the Eastern Plateau. Did the Hearth know? How could they? She was always so careful. If someone had seen her beautiful boy, she imagined there would have already been an uproar. No need to bring a selfa all the way from the Hearth when a nosy neighbor would do. But what were the odds that there was another male on this side of the Reypar? It was highly unlikely that such an event would take place. With sadness, she knew within her heart that the Selfa was coming to Rolier for her beautiful baby boy.

It wasn't that she had renounced the ways of the Sisterhood. She did intend on announcing him to the Hearth, to the whole world, just not right away. She only wanted to have time with the boy, just wanted dearly to have a chance to raise him on her own. Keila knew the Hearth would rip him from her, take him back to Vulna and never let her lay eyes upon him again. She merely wanted a few years with her baby boy! He was no good to the Sisterhood until he ripened anyway, and no one could care for a child like his mother. Could they not understand that?

There was a knock at the door, and Keila nearly yelped in surprise. She quickly regained her composure and lowered her bed on its hinges, once again concealing her beloved child.

"Shhh, little one. I will return shortly. Just rest now. Rest, my son."

After smoothing her pillow and bed covers, she snuck a look out her window. To no surprise, Heleila stood outside. Keila debated pretending not to be home, but her neighbor appeared distraught.

"Yes, Heleila? Is everything all right?" she asked, unlatching the door.

"No, no, it's not, I'm afraid. Terrible news, just terrible! Have you not heard?"

"I have not heard any news. I've been in my home all day."

"Oh, it's awful, just awful! Memier has fallen! The whole city, all those lives, all those sisters, dead."

"Fallen? To the Greishic?"

"Yes, at least that's what they're saying!"

"So, it could only be a rumor?" Keila asked with hope in her voice.

"I doubt it. Mayor Mitilza called for an unscheduled town meeting, that's the true reason I came. It's set to start soon. I wasn't sure if you were aware."

"Do you... Do you think the Selfa was in Memier when it fell?"

"Oh Vesta, I hope not! If she was taken or killed, then truly all is lost. I pray she was only passing through and not searching for the male inside the city. Or maybe she found him and they got out of the city before the attack? Oh, what if the male was killed by a beast? Then we'd truly be left with no more hope."

"We can only hope she had already found the male and they escaped."

"Will you be attending the meeting, Sister?" Heleila asked.

Keila hesitated and glanced over at her bed. Did she really want to hear such grim tidings? Unscheduled meetings weren't called for good news. Either the Greishic were coming here, or the Selfa was. Either way, her life was about to become far more complicated.

"I will, but I have some matters to attend to first. I will meet you there. Please save me a seat if you can."

"I will try, dear Sister!"

* * *

It seemed the whole village was in attendance at the meeting. Even Heleila's daughter made it out. She hadn't been this near to Aadeya in a very long time. The woman certainly didn't look sick, but then again, the fits were not the sort of illness one wore on their face. The town hall was loud with chatter. Keila could tell the village all assumed the worst from listening to their conversations.

"I heard everyone in the city was taken captive by the Greishic!"

"So the Selfa was among those taken?"

"Yes, I heard that too! Taken while trying to protect the male."

"Was the male taken too, then?"

"No doubt he was. The Sisterhood is finished! Vesta has doomed us all!"

"Please, sisters! Don't be so quick to accept falsehoods as fact! I heard the Hearth started the rumor of a male in Memier just to get the Greishic to attack it!"

"Why would the Hearth do such a thing? And what would the beasts want with a male? Don't they have their own?"

"The beasts knew we could easily defeat them with our next generation, that's why."

Keila had to stifle a laugh when she heard that last bit of conversation. She had seen the Greishic up close, and they surely were not the type to show such forethought.

The hall grew silent when the mayor climbed onto the platform and took a deep breath. "Sisters. I am sure you have all heard by now that Memier has fallen to the Greishic. I have brought you all together to share what information I have. I am afraid it is not much, but you all deserve to know. First and foremost, yes, I can confirm that the Greishic breached the Paling and took the city."

Panicked shouts erupted from the crowd. Many bombarded the mayor with questions.

"Sisters, please! Remain calm until I finish telling you all I know. Now, I have in my possession a letter received this morning via divebird. It came from Memier and was written by Regent Vuleila herself. I am going to read it aloud so that we all have the same information. Please wait until I finish reading before asking any further questions." Mayor Mitilza unrolled the letter and began to read it aloud.

"To the residents of Rolier, it is with great sorrow and regret that I, Regent Vuleila, must inform you that the city of Memier has fallen to the Greishic. They came in vast numbers. They came with what seemed like strategy. They came in wave after wave until they broke our ranks and besieged our walls. The Paling held them back for a long time, and our sisters fired arrow after arrow, but the number of creatures seemed limitless and we could not keep them all back.

"Eventually, they breached the Paling and flooded into the city. Know and feel pride in your hearts that the citizens of Memier, your sisters, fought them with all the fury of true women. I stood side by side with sisters who were far from their prime as we met the creatures in battle. Few of these women held weapons, and many had no training, but still, they fought. They fought hard to defend not only their homes, but also yours. Even now, as I write this letter, I hear them fighting the beasts outside my very door.

"I sent multiple messages to the Hearth requesting they send aid, but never received a reply. I am beginning to wonder if they have abandoned us. I pray that is not the case. I pray that they have sent sisters into the Greenwood to fight the Greishic scourge and keep them from spreading toward you. But my faith in the Sisterhood has wavered, and I am uncertain if they even care for those of us on this side of the Reypar anymore.

"I wish I had hope to offer you, but I do not. I would suggest that if you have not heard from the Hearth within three days of receiving this message, you abandon your homes. Head north to the mountains, or take the Yeren River west and try to cross into the Western Plateau.

"Please spread this message among all sisters of the Eastern Plateau. I know my time left on this earth is at an end, and I may be unable to get a letter out to every village before I fall. Even now, I hear the Greishic attempting to breach my door. Please do not forget the bravery of your sisters who were lost on this day. They fought for the survival of us all.

"Alé volás, sisters. Regent Vuleila."

Silence filled the hall for several moments before it exploded once more with shouts.

"Dead! We're all dead! Oh, Vesta, save us!"

"The Hearth has abandoned us! They have left us to die!"

"My daughter was visiting Memier! What news of survivors? Please! Did she say anything about survivors?"

"Sisters! Order! There must be order!" the mayor shouted, trying to calm the crowd.

"We should flee! Forget waiting three days, let's get out of here now!"

"And go where? There is nowhere to hide from a Greishic horde!"

"We should send word to Wolenn, Coratch, and the other villages. They deserve to know."

"Curse Regent Vuleila, how could the Hearth put such an incompetent leader in charge of Memier's defenses? This is all her fault!"

"And you could have done better?"

"I might have. I wouldn't have let the city fall, that's for sure."

"Then go! Go and take back the Paling yourself!"

Keila listened to the women drone on and on. The village was falling apart. If the Hearth had truly abandoned them, they were better for it. If the Selfa had died in Memier, they were better for it. She could sneak off into the mountains and take her boy with her. She would raise him as she was destined to. Only... Only the Regent's letter had mentioned nothing about the Selfa. What could that mean? Was she being secretive, or had the Selfa simply not reached the city?

"Sisters! I will adjourn this meeting immediately if we do not have silence!" Mayor Mitilza's voice rang out above the rabble of the crowd. It finally got them to quiet. "Now, I want you all to know, my reason for sharing the letter from the Regent was not to instill panic. It was not to cause an uproar and have the women of this village flee in droves. My reason for sharing the letter, word for word, was to stop any erroneous rumors from spreading and to prevent falsehoods from being mistaken for facts. It is my belief that we should heed Regent Vuleila's wisdom. Not only was she a formidable warrior, but she was also a skilled tactician. If she felt we should wait, I am inclined to believe her. It is highly likely that a bird is on its way from the Hearth as we speak. They may provide guidance on how best to handle the situation at hand."

"But they abandoned Memier! The Hearth cares nothing for us!" a woman near the front row shouted.

The mayor raised her hand, quieting the murmurs of agreement that spread throughout the hall. "While I agree with you that the Hearth did not act swiftly enough to preserve Memier, we cannot take that to mean they abandoned the city, or any of us. It takes time to send a divebird to and from the Hearth, and it is possible any correspondence simply did not reach Memier in time. Do not forget that the Hearth has sent a selfa to the Eastern Plateau. They think a male exists on this side of the Reypar. I find it hard to believe they would abandon what is likely the Sisterhood's final hope at survival."

"Have you heard anything regarding the Selfa?" Heleila spoke up.

"I have not. I shared all I knew at our last meeting. I am unsure whether the absence of her mention in the Regent's letter is cause for concern. My guess is she either passed through Memier before the attack or had yet to reach the city before it fell."

"I do not intend to wait three days before acting!" someone shouted. "The writing is on the broken Paling wall. I plan on gathering my belongings and leaving today. Why should we not take a three-day head start against the Greishic when one has been presented to us?"

Many echoes of agreement emanated from the crowd.

"I will not try and prevent you from leaving. But know that if you leave before the three days have passed, anything left behind will be forfeited to the greater good of the Sisterhood. Your homes, your belongings, anything you cannot take will no longer be yours. If we receive any refugees from Memier, I will see that they are housed in any vacant huts. You may not be allowed to return to the homes you once knew."

"That's not fair! You cannot take my home! I built it with my own hands!"

"If you care so much, then why are you so quick to abandon it? As I said. Flee now if you must, but it may have repercussions."

"I still wish to leave!"

"Me too!"

"What of the riverboats? Will they be available to take us west?"

"I will authorize a single barge to disembark and take the Yeren River west. However, that authorization comes with one requirement. You *must* dock in Wolenn and share this message with them. Like she said in her letter, I am not certain if the Regent managed to send out multiple birds before the city fell. It is possible not every village and township knows of our new plight."

Keila turned to Heleila. "Will you leave the village?"

"Not immediately. I will wait a few more days. Imagine if we left and gave up our homes only to have reinforcements arrive from the Hearth! It would be devastating to my daughter and I, simply devastating."

"Agreed. I will probably stay a little longer, as well. We don't even know if the Greishic are headed this way."

"I am glad to have your company, Sister," Heleila said, patting Keila on her shoulder. "Plus, I am holding out hope for the Selfa arriving, won't it be grand? It will be such a light to us in these dark times, would it not?"

"Truly." *Darkness, more like*, Keila thought. While she did not wish for the Selfa to have perished in Memier, she did hope the village would not be graced with her presence. Keila took great care in the planning and execution of keeping her son hidden. Still, she was not entirely sure of the accuracy of the Selfa's gift. Rumors of the Selfa being able to detect the heartbeat of a male from more than a day's journey away swirled in her mind, but that was all just religious aggrandizement, wasn't it? The best she could hope for was that the Selfa had been forced to turn back upon reaching the Greishic-infested city of Memier. Forced to abandon the Venery until the Sisterhood could take back the city. Something that would no doubt take years. That would give Keila enough time to raise her son without the Hearth stealing him away.

"If you change your mind, you be sure to knock on my door before you flee the village!" Heleila exclaimed. "I'd hate to find you gone one day without so much as a goodbye! Aadeya and I would be crushed, absolutely crushed! Isn't that right, Aady?"

Heleila's daughter looked at Keila, then smiled, and nodded her head in agreement.

"I would not leave without bidding a fond farewell," Keila affirmed.

"Maybe we could join you? Imagine! The three of us living off the land somewhere in the mountains! Oh, the very thought just tickles my heart!"

XXII

The Arrival of the Selfa

Zeya stood up in her saddle and looked toward the horizon. She could finally make out the village in the distance. Rolier. At long last, their destination was in sight. At long last, the end of the Venery was near. She tried to push down the fear of failure. It had once again been growing stronger with each step they took east, but it seemed she finally was able to keep it contained.

Zeya looked around at her companions as they rode. They all had smiles on their faces. Strangely, Joreya's expression was one of full bliss. Rolier was nothing compared to the city of Memier, but there must have been something about it that filled Joreya's heart with such joy.

"How are you feeling, Zeya?" asked Meleya.

"Nervous. Relieved. Afraid." Zeya had decided to stop trying to hide her feelings. Her companions were there to help her, and keeping things from them may inhibit their ability to do so.

"Same here," Preza stated. "But at least we now possess another set of eyes to help us search for the male." She gave Joreya a wink.

"I'm not sure how much help I will be, but I will keep an eye out for anything that looks like a man."

"And what does a man look like, Sister?" Meleya asked.

Joreya shrugged. "I haven't the slightest idea."

"Don't worry, that's why we brought the Selfa all this way. It certainly isn't because we enjoy her company!" Meleya teased.

"Oh? Perhaps I will seek out new companions in Rolier, then. Ones that are not solely bound to me by duty, but are able to actually tolerate my presence."

"Nah, you'll miss us too much," Preza countered. "Besides, you'll be hard pressed to find any capable warriors young enough in such a small village. This is the sort of place sisters go to live out what few remaining years they have in peace."

"Can you believe the irreverence, Joreya?" Zeya laughed. "Now you see why the Venery is such a burden for the Selfa. Not only must I make the journey, I must also endure frequent attacks from my companions!"

"I will admit that you three have not quite lived up to my... expectations. I was always taught that the Selfa wielded Vesta's Flame like a sword, and one could feel its heat emanating from her very soul." Joreya suddenly smiled broadly. "I also was told her retinue was made up of zealous sisters who adored her above all others."

Zeya laughed. "Adoration! I demand your adoration!"

"The truth's a merciless wench, ain't it?" replied Preza.

"Hush! We have nearly arrived, and we have a certain image to uphold," Meleya stated with a smirk.

As the Selfa and her companions entered the village, they were surprised to find it rife with liveliness. Sisters were milling about, though many appeared filled with distress. The center of town was full of women trying to sell what seemed to be an assortment of their belongings. Used furniture, pots, blankets, and furs seemed to be the most popular items.

"I think it's safe to say they heard of Memier's fate," observed Preza. "This has panic written all over it."

"Let us just hope none have fled yet. Zeya, you feel anything?" Meleya asked.

"No." Zeya felt her stomach churn as the impact of what she just said hit her. She felt nothing. This village was small, it was barely the size of one of Vulna's smaller districts, and she felt nothing. When she had first felt Vesta's Pull, it led her out of the city and into the wilds. If the male was here, why was she not able to sense him?

"Ah, no matter, I'm certain you will soon," replied Preza.

"How can you be so sure?"

Preza thought for a moment, but was unable to come up with an answer.

"If there's a buck here," Meleya began, "you will find him. If you don't, it was all just a rumor, and there was no male in the first place. You wouldn't be to blame."

"Just because it wouldn't be my fault doesn't mean I wouldn't be blamed," Zeya replied.

"Don't worry about it too much. There's still time for some other Venery to succeed if ours fails," Preza replied.

Zeya appreciated Preza's words, but they didn't really help all that much. It's true, she wouldn't be the first Selfa to fail the Venery. After all, hadn't Selfa Delreza been returning from one before they left?

Still, she knew within her heart that while she wouldn't be the first to fail, she absolutely would be the last.

"Riders! Riders have come!" a villager shouted after finally taking notice of them. Many heads turned in surprise as they witnessed the four women on horseback watching them.

"Hail, sisters!" greeted Preza.

Many villagers returned the greeting, and two approached them.

"Well met, sisters. From where do you travel?" the first woman asked.

"We have come from Vulna. From the Hearth."

The women stared at Preza in disbelief. Zeya saw them searching with their eyes, trying to figure out if Preza spoke the truth. One of them noticed the silver leaf Zeya wore, which created even more bewilderment on her face.

"The Selfa! The Selfa has arrived! Oh, Vesta be praised! The Selfa has come!" This drew many over to them, and a crowd began to form.

"It is as you say," Preza stated. "We wish to speak to Mayor Mitilza, for we have much to discuss with her."

"Is this regarding the fall of Memier?" the second sister asked.

"So, you've heard?" Meleya asked.

"We have, but only recently. Terrible tidings that, terrible," the first replied. "The mayor read the whole village a letter sent directly from Regent Vuleila."

"Where can we find the mayor?" asked Zeya. "We would very much like to speak with her."

"Apologies, but I am not sure. She is likely either at the town hall or down at the docks, trying to keep too many sisters from leaving."

"Leaving?"

"Aye, many villagers have gathered what belongings they could carry and plan on taking the Yeren west to escape the beasts. She threatened to claim their homes for the Sisterhood in order to house any refugees, but that didn't prevent as many from fleeing as she thought it would."

Zeya looked at her companions, who nodded, understanding what she was thinking. If the male was smuggled out on one of the riverboats, they would never find him. They needed to stop that boat from casting off.

"Preza, can you head to the docks and keep that ship from departing?" Zeya asked.

"With pleasure, my Selfa," Preza replied with what sounded like genuine conviction, but she quickly gave Zeya a wink. Preza then turned back to the woman. "You, Sister! Lead me to the docks!"

The woman nodded and began running off toward the river with Preza following on horseback.

Zeya turned to the remaining sister. "Will you lead us to the town hall?"

"It would be my honor, Selfa Zeya," the woman replied with a bow.

* * *

Keila walked through Rolier and watched as many sisters packed their belongings and attempted to purchase supplies. *Madness, all of it*, she thought. *They act as if the Greishic are at our very door!* Keila had had enough of baseless panic. She would leave the village, sure, but she wouldn't risk her precious boy being discovered unless she saw the Greishic with her own eyes. She turned as she heard someone shouting behind her.

"It's right down that way, just go until you hit the river!"

Keila was surprised to see a large sister she did not recognize on horseback head off in a gallop toward the docks. Was it a messenger from one of the neighboring villages? Or perhaps it was a survivor from Memier. No doubt, the woman was seeking the mayor. Keila approached the villager who had directed the rider to the docks.

"Who was that woman?"

The sister looked back at Keila, her face filling with excitement and pride. "That was a companion to the Selfa! Selfa Zeya has come to Rolier! Can you believe it? The Hearth has not abandoned us, far from it! Vesta bless us all!"

Keila felt her knees weaken and she nearly collapsed in shock. The woman continued speaking to her, but she was no longer listening. *How could they know? How in Vesta's name could they know? I was always careful, always so careful. No, wait. I mustn't panic. Just because the Selfa is in Rolier does not mean she knows I have the male hidden.* She realized that the Selfa may only be passing through Rolier on her way to another destination. Coratch, probably. Or perhaps, the Selfa was sent to warn the Eastern Plateau villages of the fall of Memier and provide them with instruction from the Hearth on what to do next. Yes, that was it. She doubted the Selfa would stay in the village for long. Most likely, she would move on to the next town once the message had been delivered. Regardless, Keila decided she should get home and make sure everything was neat and tidy. If she did have unwelcome guests, she had no desire for there to be anything out of place.

Keila headed back through town on her way home but was horrified when she saw three other women on horseback waiting outside the town hall. They were engaged in conversation, so Keila hoped she could move past them without being noticed.

"The mayor's not here, Wombsister," stated one of the women, who stood with her hand on the pommel of her sword. "Let's hope she's down by the docks and Preza is able to prevent the boat from leaving."

"Oh, you know her, I'm sure she'll stop it just fine," the other replied, then saw Keila staring at her. "Hail, Sister!" she called.

Keila pretended not to hear and began walking. She hoped they'd just leave her be.

"Sister, a moment, please."

Keila sighed, then turned. Before her, high on horseback, three women looked down on her. The one who addressed her wore Vesta's Leaf on her breast, the symbol of the Selfa.

"Oh, sorry, sisters. I was not aware you called to me," Keila answered, trying to keep her body from shaking. She could feel the Selfa's eyes on her, she could feel them burning into her, searching her soul for any information on her precious baby boy.

"Can you tell us where the mayor is?" Keila heard the question but did not process it. She couldn't take the Selfa's penetrating eyes any longer. Did she know? Could she really sense that Keila was hiding the male?

"Sister?" one of the Selfa's companions prompted.

"Sorry, what?" Keila asked, trying to pull her focus away from the Selfa's burning eyes.

"Can you tell us where Mayor Mitilza is?"

"Oh, uh... she's down by the docks. Please, excuse me now, I have... I have much to do." Keila turned and continued home. She sighed with relief when she looked back and saw that the Selfa was not following her.

* * *

"Well, that was rude," Meleya remarked, watching the woman walk away.

"Maybe she was just nervous, I know I was when I realized you were the Selfa, Zeya," Joreya replied.

"Yes, that was probably it." Zeya watched the woman until she disappeared from view. Something about her seemed off, but she shook the thought from her mind.

"Do you think we should go to the docks and help Preza?" Meleya asked.

"No, I'm sure she and the mayor have it under control. We should begin searching the village in case I get a hint of Vesta's Pull."

They dismounted and began exploring Rolier's central square. Many of the villagers were occupied in the buying and selling of goods, and few took note of Zeya or Vesta's Leaf. She began to think seriously about the return journey. Whether she found the male or not, they still had a tremendous distance to travel back to Vulna. What if the escort they were to receive from Haralda didn't show up where they were supposed to? While they had made it through the Greenwood once already, and taking the Yeren River would significantly increase their speed and safety, she was still concerned. There could be more brigands waiting to ambush them and steal the male from them. That was a thought that she had never considered before. The male belonged to all of the Sisterhood but her experience on the Venery had made her realize that not all women held true to the Sisterhood's beliefs.

"What are you thinking, dear Wombsister?" Meleya asked.

"The return. You think we'll make it back safely to Vulna?"

"We will. I have little doubt of that."

"Um, can I ask a question?" Joreya requested.

"Ask away, Sister," Meleya replied, smiling warmly.

"What will happen to me? When you find the male and take him back to the Hearth, what will become of me?"

Meleya and Zeya looked at each other. Neither of them had really thought about what fate would befall Joreya once they actually found the male. Taking a refugee back with them to Vulna would surely be frowned upon by the Jurisa. Then again, if they had the male, Zeya was pretty sure all would be forgiven. Besides, the Jurisa might even be joyful that they had saved another fully ripened sister.

Zeya could see anxiety beginning to grow on Joreya's face at her silence. "Whatever you wish, dear Sister. If you want to stay here in Rolier, we won't stop you. But we'd gladly have your company back to Vulna, if you desire to reside there, that is. But Joreya, know that the return will not be an easy one. We will face great danger along the way, and it may be better for you to remain on the Eastern Plateau, even with the Greishic threat."

"Do I have to decide now?"

"No. Feel free to think it over until the time of our departure." Zeya smiled weakly. "And who knows how long that'll be."

"Thank you. You are all so kind to me. You remind me so much of my wombsisters. I hope they got out of the city alive."

Meleya put her hand on Joreya's shoulder and squeezed her gently. "I am sure they did. Don't you think, Zeya?"

Zeya hesitated as the image of the body on the floor in Memier and the memory of Eleza's last breath flashed in her mind. She quickly cleared these thoughts when she saw her wombsister's prompting gaze. "Yes, I'm sure they made it out and are safely in one of the villages by now."

"Thanks." Joreya wiped a tear from her cheek. "I know it's unlikely. So many died in Memier, it seems silly to hope. But I do."

"Hope is never silly. Hope's whole purpose is to keep us going, to keep us believing, to keep us from giving up," replied Meleya.

"I suppose you're right."

* * *

Preza leapt from her horse when she reached the docks. There was a large crowd of women all pushing, trying to get onto a single boat. One of the women, who Preza assumed was the mayor, stood atop a barrel and was shouting at the crowd.

"Sisters! There are far more of you than can fit on this barge. I have only authorized a single vessel to leave port. Please, move back and do not attempt to board!"

"There's still room! More of us can squeeze on!" someone shouted.

"No, the captain has told me she can take no more. Any additional weight will increase the risk of sinking."

"Then let us take another boat. Why should they get to leave, but not us?"

"Only one ship may leave! I have already addressed this. If we haven't heard from the Hearth in three days, I will authorize all riverboats to disembark. This one is full! Return to your homes, this chaos will not be tolerated!"

Preza slowly pushed her way to the front of the throng. Many sisters looked ready to complain of her crowding in, but then thought better of it when their eyes beheld her size. Preza imagined she must have been quite a sight for this small village. She was at least a head taller than any who stood on the dock, which, combined with the battle axe slung on her back, surely made quite the statement.

Preza was nearly to the front of the crowd when a group of women suddenly charged forward and attempted to leap the distance to the boat. Some succeeded, but most landed in the water with a splash.

"Stop! Sisters, please! The boat will *not* leave if it is over-encumbered!" The mayor's words were lost on the crowd as a mad rush began making its way, trying to jump onto the boat.

"Enough!" Preza roared as loudly as her lungs permitted and quickly shoved her way to the edge of the dock. She drew her axe and looked threateningly at the crowd before her. Most were hesitant of this new obstacle, but one sister suddenly broke away from the group and tried to get past her. The handle of Preza's axe met the woman's face with a loud crack. "I said enough! Your mayor has spoken. Your behavior is an embarrassment to the Sisterhood!"

The mayor jumped down from the barrel and approached Preza cautiously. She seemed unsure whether Preza meant her harm or not. Eventually, she found her courage and spoke. "Thank you for your aid in regaining order, Sister. But may I ask who you are and from where you have come? I have not seen you in Rolier before."

"You may," Preza replied, then spoke louder for all to hear. "I am Preza of the Hearth, companion to the Selfa, Zeya, sent by the Hearth to Rolier to find the next male."

Murmurs began rising from the crowd.

"The Selfa is here?" the mayor asked incredulously.

"She is. And I regret to inform all of you that no barge will leave this port today, at least not until the male has been found."

This was met with shouts of both joy and anger.

"Listen!" Preza shouted, attempting to keep the crowd from falling back into discord. "I can see by your panic that you have heard what happened to Memier. It is tragic, but I am here to tell you that there is no immediate danger to Rolier from the Greishic. We were in Memier barely two days past and saw none of the creatures on the road as we journeyed here. After overtaking the city, the beasts fled back into the Greenwood, at least for the time being." Preza felt bad lying to so many, but if the villagers knew Greishic were on the Eastern Plateau, they'd never cease their panic.

Sighs of relief came from the crowd, and the fear in their eyes began to lessen slightly.

The mayor bowed respectfully. "I would like to welcome you, Preza of the Hearth, to our humble village of Rolier." The mayor turned to the crowd. "Sisters! You have heard the words of the Selfa's companion. This changes things. No boat will disembark from Rolier until the Selfa has cleared the village to do so!"

"But I have no male! You told us we could—" The dissenting voice ceased after it was met with a glare from Preza.

The mayor motioned to the helmswoman, who nodded and lowered the gangplank. All sisters who had previously boarded, slowly shuffled off the boat.

Mayor Mitilza turned to Preza. "Please, take me to the Selfa so that I may provide her with any aid that I can."

XXIII

The Gallows

Death. It comes for everyone, and Freila knew she was no exception. She always knew her day would eventually come, but never imagined it would be so soon. There was still so much left to do, so much that she now couldn't do. Freila sat in her cell expecting the door to fly open at any moment. The Jurisa would drag her out in front of the entire city, intending on making a spectacle of her execution.

This was precisely what she wanted. Scholars would look back on her actions and wonder what drove her to make such a decision. Why she chose to risk her reputation, her life, and her daughters' lives. She wanted to make sure they understood why. Her death would be the spark that would light the flame of change.

"Oh, Vesta, give me strength," she whispered to herself.

By now, her daughters should have reached Rolier, or at least be very near it. Although a delay wouldn't affect her plan, she hoped

Zeya would sense and locate the male quickly, for her own sake. One way or another, the Sisterhood was about to change. She prayed it was for the better.

The door creaked open, and two guards entered her cell. "Freila, it is time."

She looked up and was surprised to see Saneza in the doorway holding the chains. Freila bowed respectfully to Saneza and the other guard and looked each in the eye. "Thank you for your humane treatment, sisters. I am ready."

The guards approached and bound her arms and legs with the chains. They then attached another and began leading her out of the dungeon.

"I meant what I told you, Saneza," Freila stated.

"Remain quiet, Prisoner," Saneza replied gruffly.

"Everything I have done was to ensure you, along with all sisters, could have the chance at having a child. A chance at knowing peace."

"Silence!" Saneza commanded.

"I don't expect you to believe me now, but in time, I know you will come to under—"

Saneza slammed her fist into Freila's stomach, sending her to the ground. "The prisoner will remain silent unless addressed. Is that understood, Prisoner?"

Freila remained on the ground, trying to regain her breath.

"Prisoner?" Saneza looked down at her threateningly.

"Yes. It is... understood," Freila managed.

"Good." Saneza yanked on Freila's chains, pulling her from the ground.

The two guards led her up the stairs and out of the dungeon toward the Hearth's courtyard. It seemed a lifetime had passed since she saw her daughters off for the Venery. Zeya had been so afraid. She tried to hide it, but Freila could tell, a mother could always tell. Even Meleya had shown a hint of nervousness. Meleya who was as steadfast as a stone and ready to face whatever the unknown thrust toward her. She missed her daughters dearly, and it pained her greatly to know that she would never see them again. At least, not in this life. Freila wondered how Meleya and Zeya would take word of her death. Hopefully, it would not distract them too much from their journey. And Preza. Vesta had gifted her with a third daughter. What a great woman Preza had turned out to be. *Stay safe, my children,* she thought. *Your trials are only beginning. Remember your path, and follow your hearts.*

Freila was pulled out of the courtyard and onto the city streets where boos and shouts of anger assaulted her ears. She stared at the massive crowd that had come to watch her die and felt great sadness grow in her heart. The number was far from those who had seen Zeya off, but it was still significant. Soldiers lined the crowd with shields up, keeping the mob at bay and Freila safe from their ire. *Safe! I am defended on my way to the grave,* she thought.

"Traitor!"

"You are a disgrace to the Sisterhood! May the end of your wretched life be filled with pain!"

"Blasphemer! You have forsaken the teachings of Vesta! You have betrayed her chosen!"

Some in the crowd hurled rocks at her, but their aim was poor, and the soldiers quickly made an example of any would-be markswomen. While Freila was led toward the gallows, she attempted to prepare herself to be displayed before the crowd. Gilza, Sieyna, and

Cereila stood before her, as well as someone she did not expect. Her friend, Yeleila.

Gilza stepped forward. "Freila, Sister Yeleila has insisted that she be the one to give you the final observances and prepare you to enter into Vesta's Embrace."

"The bitch doesn't deserve any of it," Sieyna muttered with disdain.

"Do you accept Sister Yeleila's offer?" Gilza asked.

"I do." Freila looked at her friend curiously. Had she hatched some scheme to free her?

"Very well, Sister Yeleila, you may proceed."

Yeleila looked at Gilza expectantly.

"Oh, very well. Let us give them their peace." Gilza and the other members of the Jurisa began making their way up to the gallows.

"The guards as well, Gilza of the Jurisa," Yeleila called out. "This is a private moment between mother, daughter, and Vesta."

Gilza sighed. "Guards, give them privacy, but stay watchful."

After the guards and Jurisa moved away, Yeleila spoke. "Dearest sister, what have you gotten yourself into?"

"It appears my suspicions were correct. Glad we had our little chat earlier." Freila smiled weakly.

"Indeed. Were you able to finish your pending affairs?"

"The imperative ones, but there is always more that can be done. No chance you are here to rescue me from my fate?"

Yeleila looked at Freila sadly. "No, my dear friend. I barely received word of your execution. Not much time to plan anything, I'm afraid."

"I understand. I knew the risks involved, and I fully accept the recompense that is owed."

"What evidence did they have against you?"

"Yureza's testimony, beaten out of her. If that was all, I would have been saved from the noose. But Yureza kept my letters, and the writings in our correspondence were far more than needed to have me executed. My only hope is that reading the letters I wrote to her has opened the hearts of the other council members. Well, Cereila, at least." Freila thought for a moment. "It is rather amusing. I had no desire to become a martyr, but now that the opportunity has presented itself, it may work in our favor. My words convinced Yureza to betray the Sisterhood, and they could turn others as well. The words of a martyr can hold great power."

"I will take that under consideration. But regardless, Freila, know that your actions have not, and will not be in vain. Your daughters will succeed, and our plans for the Sisterhood will come to fruition."

"Are you saying that you have already begun to put your part into action?"

"I have."

"At least I go to the noose with renewed hope in my heart. Thank you, Yeleila."

"Your death shall mark a variance in the Sisterhood. Enter into Vesta's Embrace knowing that." Yeleila stepped forward and wrapped Freila in a firm embrace.

Tears began to well up in Freila's eyes. "Thank you, my dearest friend. I wish I was able to return such an embrace, but it is a little difficult given these." Freila held up her bound hands.

"We will see each other again, Freila. Maybe sooner than either of us expects."

"I look forward to it."

"As do I." Yeleila bowed her head and began to pray, "Oh Vesta, hear my words. Take Freila, your faithful daughter into your warm

Embrace. May her soul be reunited with those who have been lost, and so too may those lost in the future swiftly be reunited with her. Guide her safely from this world and into the next."

Yeleila stepped away from Freila, and the guards led her up to the gallows. More booing erupted from the masses.

Sieyna began speaking to the crowd, and she knew just how to get them riled up. "Sisters! As you all know by now, you have been betrayed! This so-called Mother has led, not only the Jurisa astray, but also you of the Sisterhood! This *woman* manipulated us all to ensure it was her daughter who was sent on the Venery. She kept the reports she received regarding the emergence of a male to herself until she could guarantee it would be Selfa Zeya who was sent! She misled us, causing Selfa Delreza to make a fool's journey to Noor. She wasted not only the valuable time of the Selfa but also delayed the coming of our salvation!

"Now, I know what some of you may be thinking. Did we give her a chance to explain herself? Surely she had a good reason for perpetrating such an atrocity. Well, my sisters, we asked her to defend herself, to plead her case. And do you know what she said in defense of her actions? Can you imagine what this ill-conceived woman said? Nothing. She said *nothing*. She offered no words of justification. Why? Why did she not speak up in her own defense? I say it's because she knew of her guilt! She knew that her actions were done purely in self-interest, she *knew* we would pay no mind to her pathetic excuses and decided to save what few remaining breaths she held within her!"

Sieyna motioned to Freila. "Look! Look at her now! She stands with pride, she stands with no remorse, without so much as a modicum of regret! I ask you, is this a woman that deserves to live?"

"No!"

"Kill her! Kill the traitor!"

"Hang her, let the birds gouge her eyes and the worms consume her flesh!"

The guards led Freila to the noose and Saneza slipped it around her neck. Gilza raised her hand, silencing the crowd. "Freila, if you have so chosen, you may now speak your final words."

Freila cleared her throat as she felt the burden of the rope's pull on her neck. She looked out at the crowd as the weight of sadness began to fill her heart. "Sisters! While I do not deny the accusations made against me by the Jurisa—" Angry shouts exploded from the crowd, but Freila waited calmly for them to die down before continuing. "I did manipulate the Sisterhood, I plotted, and I schemed to assure that it would be my daughter sent on the Venery. That is why I presented no defense of my actions. The accusations made against me are not false." Freila paused as more boos erupted from the crowd. "However, what is false is that I did not perpetrate these crimes for my own benefit. Nor did I do so to elevate the status of my daughter. What I did, dear sisters, I did for all of you! The Sisterhood is broken. We are caught in an endless struggle for survival! A continuous loop of doubt followed by hope, followed by despair. I ask you, is this how life should be lived? Is this what we, as women, should be forced to endure? I say no! I say it has gone on long enough. It is time for change. It is time for the circle to break, and it is time for us to live life the way we were meant to live it. Not huddled in our cities and towns waiting to dwindle and die! Not carrying the burden of our unquestionable demise with us in the streets, but living for ourselves and for each other! Expanding, discovering, and *thriving*!"

The crowd remained quiet. They watched Freila carefully, hoping to hear a real solution to the problems they all knew could not be denied.

"Your eyes look upon me now as that of a betrayer. You feel I took what was important to you and tore it down. But my sisters! The time is near that you will look back upon this day, and you will remember my words. You will say to one another, 'Freila truly *was* trying to save us. She helped bring us our salvation, and we cheered as she swung from the gallows.' You will remember that my death marked the beginning, not the end! The beginning of a new period for all humankind. Hail Sisters! Hail the Selfa! Hail to us all!"

The crowd continued to stare at Freila in silence. Many looked at one another, trying to make sense of the words they had just heard.

Finally, Gilza spoke up. "Freila, your punishment for acts of conspiracy and manipulation against the Sisterhood shall hereby be carried out. May Vesta have mercy upon you and accept you into her warm Embrace."

Sieyna walked over to Freila and smiled broadly. "You have failed, Freila. Soon you will be little more than a faded memory, a shadow of a thought in the minds of the Sisterhood."

Freila spat at Sieyna's feet, causing the woman to flinch in surprise. After a moment, Sieyna regained her composure. "Not very lady-like."

Freila looked at her coldly. "I am no lady. I am a woman of my own accord, not bound by your rules of dignity, gentility, or propriety. I will not be humbled by anyone, and most of all, not by you."

Looking at Freila with fury in her eyes, Sieyna raised her hand, signaling the executioner that it was time. Sieyna stood, seething in anger, as the executioner released the trapdoor and ended Freila's life with a crack.

XXIV

The Conclusion of the Venery

Zeya, Meleya, and Joreya continued exploring the village of Rolier. Zeya had sensed nothing within the heart of the village, so they had moved to the outskirts, an area made up of several huts dotting the mostly empty landscape. After word had spread that the Selfa had arrived in Rolier, many sisters had swarmed Zeya and tried to ask her questions that she didn't have answers to. She had missed Preza more at that moment than she ever thought she would. Although, had Preza been around, she probably would have hurt some of the more persistent sisters. At least Meleya was there to help keep them back. Even Joreya, to Zeya's surprise, jumped in and helped keep the mob at bay. Eventually, the crowd had stopped following them around, though it took Meleya threatening to part any would-be disciples with their legs.

"Anything yet, dear Wombsister?"

"No, nothing," Zeya replied.

"Well, there are still a number of huts we haven't approached. I am sure you will feel something from one of them."

"Are you? What if the male was already smuggled out of the village? Or what if he never even existed in the first place?"

"Zeya, I know with every passing moment you become more and more disheartened, but I think it is too early to give in to such thoughts. For all we know, Preza may have found the male at the docks and is searching for us as we speak, ready to show us her prize."

"We can only hope." Zeya wondered if she ever had Vesta's Gift to begin with, or if it was even real. *No, it was real,* she thought as she remembered how it had felt when she was a child. The Pull was so strong, and the fire that took over her entire body was so intense. She touched the silver leaf at her breast as a reminder that there was no way she could have imagined it all. And hadn't both Meleya and her mother seen her eyes glow blue?

"Selfa Zeya," Joreya began, "I know now that a lot of the widespread beliefs regarding the Selfa are exaggerated, but you were still chosen by Vesta to find the male. I know you will find him."

Zeya looked at Joreya and smiled. *I pray you are right, Sister,* she thought. *If only I can remain as hopeful—* "Wait!" she exclaimed as a trickle, then a small wave of warmth began to fill her body. A familiar sensation, it was weak, but she could feel it!

"Wombsister, your eyes!"

Zeya suddenly leapt off her horse and sprinted toward a cluster of huts a short distance from where they stood. The others followed her, struggling to keep up.

"You feel it?" questioned Meleya.

"I feel... something. Hard to say. It's weak, but the intensity grows with each step!" She paused as they neared the huts. The source had to be coming from one of them. She picked a hut and began moving toward it, then stopped as she caught movement in the window of another. Zeya saw a woman peering out her window right at them. When their eyes met, the woman quickly moved back and drew the curtain closed.

"Wasn't that the rude woman from before?" Meleya asked, excitement creeping into her voice.

"I only caught a glimpse, but it may have been." Zeya sprinted toward the woman's hut before stopping in hesitation.

"What's wrong, Wombsister?"

"How do I... do I just barge in?"

"You could try knocking first," Meleya suggested. "Maybe say, 'Excuse me, ma'am, but Vesta has guided me to your door to retrieve the male you have been hiding from the world. Would you be so kind as to bring him out to me, for I would very much like to meet him?"

Zeya smirked. "That could work." She took a few more steps toward the hut, then suddenly felt the warmth overtake her body and collapsed to one knee, gasping.

"Zeya? Are you OK?" Meleya asked and rushed to her wombsister's side.

"Yes," she whispered. "Vesta's Pull, it's so powerful. A flutter in my stomach, a rapid rhythm in my chest, a flame surrounding my entire being. I feel it." Tears began to well up inside Zeya's now blazing blue eyes. "Oh Meleya, I feel it!" She wasn't a failure. She was the Selfa. She had come all this way, crossed the Greenwood to this tiny village, and had found the male! Zeya got up and ran the rest of the way to the hut with blurred vision as tears of joy streamed down her face. She reached the door and took a deep breath. The Pull was stronger than anything she had ever felt before. This was it. The male was inside. She knocked.

After what felt like an eternity, the door opened. Inside stood the same woman from town, staring back at her. The same woman who had acted so strangely in her presence, the same woman that had rushed off as soon as she was able. It was so obvious now. How had Zeya not realized it before? The woman glanced down to Zeya's pin. She stiffened, then gave a clumsy bow.

"Oh, Vesta, be praised! My humble abode has been graced with the presence of a selfa! Never in my life did I think I would receive such an honor!" The woman smiled warmly at Zeya, then looked at Meleya and Joreya. "May I provide aid to the Selfa, or her companions, in any way?"

"Sister, I am here—"

"Please, you may refer to me as Keila," the woman stated, cutting off Zeya.

Zeya stifled her annoyance, then continued, "Keila, I am visiting Rolier on official business from the Hearth, and I would like to politely request to search your home."

The woman's smile did not falter. "Of course, dear Sister. Please, come in. I'm afraid it is rather small, but I will assist you using whatever meager means I am able." Keila retreated into the hut and beckoned for them to enter.

"Quite the change in mood," Meleya murmured as they entered the hut.

The woman was right. Her small home was comprised primarily of a single room. The hut offered a bed, table, small kitchen, and little else.

"Keila," Meleya began, "we have reason to believe you may have in your possession something of great interest to the Hearth. What say you to this?"

Keila stared in surprise. "I would never knowingly hide anything of import from the Hearth! I am but a simple carpenter, now retired. Perhaps if you tell me what it is you are seeking, I can help you locate—"

"Come now, woman, do not take us for fools," growled Meleya. "You know why we have come. Why the Selfa has traveled through the Greenwood to this village. We have come for the buck. We know you are hiding him from the Sisterhood. Bring him to us now, and we may just spare you a painful death."

Keila turned to look at Zeya. "It is true I know what you seek, but I am afraid if you are looking for it here, then you have been mistaken. There is no male here, nor has there ever been. If I were to receive such a gift from Vesta, I would immediately send word to the Hearth so that he would bear the honor of continuing our kind."

"Keila, I am a true selfa. Not some pretender." Zeya stared at the woman with her burning blue eyes. "I have been chosen by the goddess and have been granted her Blessing. Reports from the Hearth have seen us to this village, and Vesta's Pull has seen me to your hut. We will find the male. You may receive a modicum of mercy if you cooperate and either hand him over or tell us where he is. Otherwise, we will have no choice but to tear your home apart looking for him."

The woman kept her eyes on Zeya, considering the words she just heard carefully. Her face flashed with anger, and she threw up her arms in indignation. "Do as you wish, I have nothing to hide! But know this, once you leave, dispirited by your folly, I will be composing an official grievance to the Hearth, demanding reimbursement for any damages you have caused." Keila let out a huff as she abruptly sat on her bed.

Meleya began searching the hut. She pulled open all the drawers and cabinets, removing all of Keila's belongings and throwing them onto the floor. Zeya joined in, searching the remaining cupboards and storage chests that were in the hut. Meleya looked at Keila in anger and moved toward her.

"Get up!"

Keila sighed, then complied and stood, allowing Meleya to search the bed. Meleya tossed the bedding, bent down, and looked under the bed. She rose in frustration.

"I'm going to search outside," Meleya said and went out the door.

Zeya moved back into the kitchen and began to tap on the walls, testing for any hidden cavities.

Joreya looked around the room. She noticed there were intricate carvings on the table and went over to examine them. She traced the carvings with her fingers and smiled, impressed by the designs. She noticed the chairs also had the patterns, then saw similar ones on the bed frame. She moved over to the bed, near where Keila stood.

"Your furniture is beautiful," Joreya said. "You mentioned before you were a carpenter, did you make these?"

"I did," Keila replied curtly.

"I never imagined such talent would exist in a small village. I, too, am a woodworker of sorts, but yours is some of the best I've ever seen. You are truly gifted."

"Many of us originally hail from Vulna or Memier," Keila replied, her tone somewhat softening. "And many were tradeswomen in those cities, myself included."

"Why did you leave?"

"I simply wanted a quiet place to spend my remaining days. Too much noise in the cities for my tastes."

Zeya sat at Keila's table in defeat and eyed the woman carefully. "You can't hide the male forever. Sooner or later, you'll have to bring him out. We can wait as long as is necessary."

"I must repeat to you, dear Sister. I do not have the male, nor have I ever. I am unsure what brought you to my hut, but my suggestion would be to search elsewhere."

Joreya was still admiring the design carved onto the bed. She felt it with her fingers and followed it down to the floor. Suddenly, she froze, then rose quickly. "Zeya—"

In a flash, Keila pulled a knife from her dress and gripped Joreya tightly with the blade to her throat. Zeya immediately took a defensive stance and drew two daggers from her belt.

"Drop the knife!" Zeya shouted.

"How rich. A dog of the Hearth commanding me, a woman blessed by Vesta above all others! The Selfa is *nothing* compared to the one who has birthed the male!"

"You have no alternative, Keila. You are outnumbered, outwitted, and outmatched. Release her immediately and turn the male over to me."

"Why would I do such a thing? The Hearth would take my child, something so innocent and so pure. They would take him, use him, until he's shriveled and spent."

"Release her, and we can discuss this like women. There is no need for anyone to get hurt."

"No one, but my baby boy!"

Meleya burst back into the hut with her sword drawn and surveyed the room. "Find him, then?"

"Not yet, but I think Joreya did."

Meleya smiled at Joreya. "I knew you'd be useful. Don't worry, we'll see you freed from peril soon enough."

Joreya looked back at Meleya, her eyes wide with fright. "Under the—"

"Quiet, Girl! Or I'll spill your blood here and now!" snapped Keila.

"Let's be calm for a moment," Zeya said. She sheathed her weapons and motioned for Meleya to do the same. "There is no reason we can't discuss this in a civilized manner. After all, we are all women of the Sisterhood."

Keila didn't move. "You know nothing of the Sisterhood." Anger flashed on her face again. "The Sisterhood does not consider the immorality of its ways. It only cares for its own preservation and takes whatever it can in order to do so. It would be better for all womankind to cease than to steal the soul of another innocent!"

"What do you mean by that?" Zeya asked, attempting to placate the woman.

"You are far too young to know. Too young to be privy to all the secrets of the Hearth."

"Share your secrets, Keila. I wish to learn."

"The image that the male is worshiped and treated like a king is false. While he is young, sure, the Hearth babies him, ensuring that he wants for nothing. But once he ripens..." Keila trailed off, trying to maintain her composure. "Once he ripens, he is fed herbs to keep his thoughts in a haze and his member hard. He is passed along from sister to sister, and given no rest until his seed begins to run dry, and even that respite is brief. The Sisterhood uses him up, attempting to impregnate as many sisters as possible, hoping it will increase the likelihood of a new male being born. Hoping that, with each generation, the curse will break. It is degeneracy in its purest form."

"And what are we to do?" Meleya asked. "Are we to give up and come to an end? If what you say is true, I am sure the Hearth takes such action because there is no alternative!"

"No alternative? Why should enslaving the pure, the innocent, ever be an option? Perhaps we remain cursed by Vesta because of the way we continue to treat our men? The Hearth has never attempted anything but flagrant rape!"

Through the window, Zeya noticed Preza and another woman approaching. "And what is it you plan to do with the male?" she asked, trying to keep the woman distracted. "Do you plan to keep him to yourself and restrict him from some of the very same freedoms you claim the Hearth inhibits? Do you have no issue with him being *your* prisoner?"

Keila paused, taking Zeya's question to heart. "No, I... I am his mother! I would only keep him safe until he's grown enough to make his own decisions."

"And at what age would that be? 10? 15? 20? 30?" Zeya raised her voice as she called out each age, attempting to keep the woman from hearing Preza's approach. "Not only would you selfishly keep him from reaching his full potential, but you'd also be ruining any chance your fellow sisters would have at survival. Is that what you want? You want to sacrifice our existence just to play mother?"

Keila was visibly shaken. "No, I just want to—"

A loud crash erupted as Preza's axe came smashing through the window. Keila jumped at the sound, nearly dropping the knife. Joreya took the opportunity to slam her head backward right into the woman's face. Keila dropped the knife and brought her hands to her face, and Meleya quickly moved in and subdued her.

"Joreya? Are you injured?" asked Zeya.

"No. The male, I think he's under the bed. I saw some hinges, it should swing up."

Preza entered the hut along with the mayor who looked around, aghast at the events she had just witnessed in her small village.

"Thanks for the help," Meleya said as she held Keila on the floor. "What took so long?"

Preza laughed. "You should be ashamed for letting that woman get the jump on you in the first place."

Zeya moved over to the bed and examined it for a moment. Dropping to the floor, she noticed the hinges Joreya spoke of. She got up and lifted the bed, surprised that it rose without difficulty and swung quietly on well-oiled hinges.

Inside lay a small bundle wrapped in cloth. Bending down, Zeya reached for the bundle. She could feel everyone's eyes as her hands moved toward it, and felt her heart pounding in her chest.

"No, please, don't take him away from me!" Keila wailed. "Don't take my baby, don't hurt my beautiful boy!"

Zeya carefully picked up the child. He was light, far lighter than she expected him to be. His face was mostly covered by the cloth. She gently removed the material from the child's face, gasped, then screamed in horror, nearly dropping the child.

"What? What is it?" demanded Meleya.

"It's... It's..." She couldn't bring herself to speak the words. All of this, the effort, the journey, and the pain, all culminated into this. "It's dead. The male is dead."

The room was silent as Zeya unwrapped the bundle and laid the remains of the boy on the bed. The child's flesh was shriveled in parts and completely missing in others. Pale bone was visible along his little legs. In place of his eyes sat two empty voids.

Meleya approached the bed and looked down at the body. She then quickly turned and covered her mouth, fighting the urge to vomit. Preza moved forward, her eyes filling with tears as she approached.

"Stay away from him!" shouted Keila. "Keep away from my child! Leave him alone, you're scaring him! Can you not hear his cries? He cries for his mother, he cries for me!" She leapt from the ground and rushed over to the body. The others were too in shock to stop her, and they watched petrified as Keila picked up the dead child and gently re-wrapped him in the cloth, bobbing him gently. "Shhh. Fear not, my child, Mother's here."

"It was all for nothing, then," Preza stated after some time. "It's finished. The world ends with us. This thing, it's not even human. It's Greishic." Everyone turned to look at her. "There are deformations in the skull, it doesn't even seem fully developed. This madwoman was probably raped by a Greishic and carried its child. It must not have grown fully inside her womb, and she birthed the abomination stillborn. That's the only way she would have survived."

Zeya stared at the woman clutching the dead Greishic in her arms. Nearby, Meleya sat on the floor, her legs pulled to her chest, head down, and crying. Joreya sat with her, one arm rubbing Meleya's shoulder, and the other wiping her own tears from her cheek.

"The Venery is over," Zeya stated flatly. She staggered toward the door, finding it difficult to breathe. She needed to get out, needed air that wasn't filled with the stench of a rotten baby corpse.

Outside, Zeya stumbled, then fell to the ground, vomiting. Her biggest fear had come true. She had failed everyone. Even though it was out of her control, she was still responsible. It was Vesta's Pull that had brought her here. Even now, she still felt the Pull within her. *Am I going mad? Am I feeling something that's not there? Why does the goddess play with my mind? With my heart?* Zeya cursed the false gift, cursed it for possessing her, and giving her hope when there was none.

"Zeya, the mayor has offered us a place to stay for the night."

Zeya looked up, her vision was blurred with tears, but she saw Preza standing over her.

"What's the point?" She wiped the vomit from her mouth. "If this generation's male died, there won't be another. You said so yourself, we're finished."

Preza knelt down beside Zeya. "I shouldn't have said that. I was shocked, angry, confused. We cannot know for sure. We need to report our findings to the Hearth and prepare for the return journey."

"I still feel Vesta's Flame burning in me. Tell me Preza, are my eyes still blue? Are they?" Zeya demanded.

Preza nodded silently.

"Then that rotting corpse is the male I was *blessed* to find! Vesta cursed me and this journey to end in failure. Vesta has seen to it that the Sisterhood will end." Zeya yanked Vesta's Leaf from her breast and threw it onto the ground. "I wish I had never felt Vesta's Flame. I wish I never left the Hearth, never crossed the Greenwood, and never set foot on the Eastern Plateau. The Venery has brought with it nothing but death and despair."

Meleya exited the hut and cautiously approached Zeya. "Wombsister, the blame lies with Mother's agent. Whoever it was should have made sure that the male was alive and fully human. It is their fault the Venery ended in failure, not yours. If any other Selfa was sent on this journey, the outcome would be the same."

"But they weren't. I was. I was chosen!"

"Mayor! Mayor Mitilza!" a villager shouted as she ran toward them.

The mayor came out of the hut and looked at the villager questioningly. "What? What is it, Eila?"

"Someone has seen Greishic heading straight for us!"

"What? Oh Vesta, have mercy!"

Preza stood. "How many?"

Eila did not answer.

"How many, Woman?"

"They... they said there were too many to count."

Meleya grabbed Zeya's arm and pulled her to her feet. "Your despair will have to wait, Wombsister. We have a village to defend."

"What do we do? Please, Selfa, what should we do?" Mayor Mitilza asked, her voice full of fear.

Zeya didn't answer.

Preza grunted. "Mayor, spread word to any woman willing to meet us at the entrance to town. Tell them to bring weapons or anything that can be used as one. If they wish to live, they will have to fight!"

XXV

Warriors of the Sisterhood

It seemed there weren't very many able-bodied women left in Rolier. That, or the villagers decided to take their chances fleeing. Not more than thirty women showed up ready to defend the village, and most were far beyond their prime. One woman even hobbled around with a cane. A few younger sisters had joined them, but Zeya doubted they had much combat experience. In the distance, a large cloud of dust was approaching the village at a rapid pace. Against the mayor's orders, a few of the villagers had attempted to flee Rolier, only to run into the band of Greishic on the road, and their retreat back to Rolier had drawn the attention of the creatures to the village.

"Remember, the beasts will try and swipe with their claws, so stay nimble on your feet, and if you see an opening, you take it!" Preza commanded. "Leave any Greishic with weapons to us, unless you know how to fight. Focus your attacks on their chest or their head, anywhere else may slow them for a moment, but they'll get you in the end. Try and keep them separated, the Greishic's strength is in their numbers, so isolate them and they are easier to take down! Any questions?"

The small group of women stared at Preza in silence. Zeya could see the fear in their eyes, but for some reason, it appeared to lessen whenever they looked at her, the Selfa, standing alongside them. *Still a symbol of hope*, she thought. *If they knew of my failure, they'd feed me to the beasts with little hesitation. Oh Vesta, bless me with a swift death this day.* Zeya still felt Vesta's cursed Pull within her, though thankfully, it had subsided greatly. Whether it was the distance from the dead infant or the diversion of impending battle, she did not know.

Zeya noticed Joreya standing near the front of the group, listening intently to what Preza was saying. She looked very out of place with the older women, but her face was filled with determination. Someone had given her a sword to use in battle, but the weapon was too large for her.

"Joreya, come here," said Zeya.

The young sister approached Zeya and the determination on her face began to falter. "Yes, Selfa Zeya?"

"That sword, it looks heavy for you."

"It's not. Well, maybe a little, but I've never held a sword before, so I'm not sure what they're supposed to feel like."

"Can you thrust it? Swing it? Show me."

Joreya lifted the sword and swung it through the air. It was clunky and slow, but she managed. She then thrust it forward, but nearly dropped it in the process.

"I can do it, please, don't make me return to town, I can fight!"

"You misunderstand me, Joreya. We need everyone who is willing to fight to defend the village." Zeya pulled one of her daggers from her belt and held it out. "Here. Leave the sword behind. Without training, the dagger will be far more useful to you."

Joreya's eyes widened, and she accepted the dagger eagerly. "It's beautiful. The silver leaf on the handle is so detailed!"

"Mind the blade, Sister. It is sharp. Just stick that end into the Greishic and you'll do fine. Like Preza said, stay nimble. Use your size to your advantage. You're much faster than these slow beasts."

"Oh, thank you, Selfa Zeya! I will return it to you when this battle is over, I swear it."

"As you say. Be sure to call for aid if you need it. There is no shame in asking your sisters for help."

"I will. Thank you." Joreya looked at Zeya with hesitation.

"Yes? Is there something else? Speak freely, Sister."

"I... um... found this outside the hut with the... the hut where the madwoman lived." Joreya reached into her pocket and pulled out Zeya's silver leaf. "I wasn't going to keep it, honest! I was only holding it for when you were ready to take it back." She held it out for Zeya.

"Joreya, I..."

"Selfa Zeya, I know things have not gone as planned, but when I saw this symbol fastened to your chest I had renewed hope, and I know it will do the same for others."

Zeya took Vesta's Leaf and turned it over in her hand. Joreya was right. The symbol meant very little to her, but it meant a great deal to her sisters. She pinned the sigil to her chest. "Joreya, your wisdom far surpasses your years."

Joreya smiled.

"Take up positions, the beasts are almost upon us!" Preza ordered. "You, hunters, begin firing your arrows as soon as they are in range. Take down as many as you can, or at the very least, slow them."

Two women who clutched bows nodded and nocked arrows.

"Take up formation! Remember to spread out, and for Vesta's sake, don't get yourselves killed!"

The villagers spread out in a single line with Zeya, Meleya, and Preza standing at the front. A few other sisters stepped forward and joined them at the forward position. The group of Greishic came close enough for Zeya to see the bloodthirst in their eyes. Their movement made them hard to count, but there appeared to be nearly sixty of the beasts. They did not even slow their pace as their eyes beheld the line of women standing before them. This was it.

"Loose, archers!"

The women began releasing arrows at the beasts. A few hit their mark, but most missed. Four, seven, eight Greishic fell. As the creatures drew near, many of the women stepped backward in fear.

"Stand your ground!" Preza shouted.

The creatures howled and spewed their harsh language at the women as they came closer and closer.

"Vesta, save us," someone whispered.

The beasts spread out, each wanting to take one of the women for their own and rushed forward. The women in the front charged, swinging their weapons at the creatures and cutting some down. A few villagers dropped their weapons and fled. Zeya slashed and dodged and stabbed. She channeled all her feelings: anger, sadness, heartbreak, at the beasts until her mind was overcome by the haze of battle.

Nearby, Meleya was making short work of any Greishic that tried to take her on. All fury, she slashed her sword masterfully. After running one of the beasts through, she quickly moved on to the next. A creature attempted to attack her from the rear, but Joreya moved in swiftly and thrust her dagger into it. The wound did not fell the beast. It turned in anger to attack Joreya, but Meleya twisted and cleaved off its head.

Preza stood swinging her large battle axe, cutting down creature after creature. Two Greishic charged at her, and she kicked one backward, knocking it to the ground. The other beast moved in while she was distracted, attempting to stab her with its rusty sword, but Preza dodged the attack, spun and sliced the creature's body open. The other got up, but she bashed it with the handle of her axe until it finally stopped moving. She brought the blade around and sunk it into the creature to ensure its death. Her face covered in blood, Preza held the visage of a madwoman, and each foe she cut down only served to increase her crazed look.

Most villagers were not faring well. Cries of agony rang out as they were slashed by the creature's claws, and many were silenced soon after. One woman was being dragged by the hair away from the battle. Her screams echoed across the battlefield, but three Greishic stood between Zeya and the woman, preventing her from helping. One of the villagers charged at the captured woman and cut through the creature's arm with her sword. The beast cried in anger and tried slashing at its attacker with its one remaining claw, but the woman deftly avoided the attack and skillfully finished the creature off. She then pulled the sister she had rescued to her feet and ran back to join the battle.

"Keep it up, sisters!" Preza shouted. "Keep it up!"

Zeya saw the woman with the cane, and was surprised that she was managing to survive the battle. Not only that, but she was handling herself quite well. The woman was using her cane to bash any beasts that came within striking distance.

"Will they never cease?" a nearby villager cried out.

"The Greishic do not retreat, they fight till their very last breath! So let's give it to them!" Preza answered.

"Aady!" the woman with the cane shouted. "My daughter, save my daughter!"

Zeya looked in the direction the woman was pointing and saw a woman get knocked to the ground by two Greishic. One of them kicked her in the ribs and she cried out in pain. Another dove on top of the woman and began slashing at her, trying to cut her throat.

"Aady!" The crippled woman began hobbling toward her daughter. Zeya launched a dagger at the creature assailing Aady and struck it in the face. Aady struggled to free herself from the dead Greishic's mass as the remaining attacker moved in for the kill.

"Cursed beast!" Meleya leapt in and sliced through the Greishic. It stumbled back, collapsing to the ground in a heap. She helped Aady up and they both looked around in search of a new target, but no more living Greishic remained.

Less than half the villagers who stood to defend the village had survived. The victory was a somber one, but it was still a victory.

"Oh, Aady! I thought we had lost you!"

"I am here, Mother. I am here."

"Too much risk, I knew there was too much risk allowing you to fight! What sort of mother am I?"

As Aady moved to embrace her mother, Zeya realized it had been her who had rescued the sister being dragged by the hair. *Where did this villager learn to fight so well?* Zeya wondered. Zeya's fury from the battle began to fade as she stood staring at the mother and daughter. Suddenly, she was overcome with heat and fell to the ground.

"Are you all right?" Aady asked, her voice sounding far away.

Meleya quickly rushed over to her wombsister. "Zeya? Were you wounded?"

"No... I... it burns. Oh, Vesta... it burns so much."

"Mother, is she—"

"Hush, Child!"

Zeya's heart beat faster than she had ever felt it beat before. Her head drooped as the unbearable sensation of flame overtook her. *Curse the Pull I feel inside me! It burns so strongly! Why won't it abate? There is no male here!* Zeya slowly raised her head and saw Aady and her mother watching with concern. She looked at Aady with her flaming blue eyes, but she couldn't fully focus on him. *Him?* Clarity washed over, quenching Vesta's Flame in an instant. This was no woman before her, this was no sister.

"You're a..." She found it hard to speak the word. "You're a man." The statement came out more of a question, but it caused Aady to glance around nervously.

"Not a man," Aady's mother spoke. "The last man."

Zeya turned her gaze to the male's mother who stood there leaning on her cane.

"Hello, Zeya. I am Heleila, and we have been waiting a very long time for you."

XXVI

The Return

The Selfa and her companions, along with Heleila and Aady, all sat in Heleila's home. Zeya found it impossible not to stare at the male. That was him. He was the reason for all of this. Thankfully, Vesta's Pull had subsided drastically once she had recognized him for what he was. Zeya could still feel its presence within her, but now it was little more than a warm tingling. Her eyes, too, had transformed to a faded blue, not shining as brightly as they had before. Zeya was unsure if she should feel anger or joy in the male's presence. While Heleila was at fault for not alerting the Hearth to his presence, the man was certainly old enough to make his own decisions and could have done so himself. Zeya couldn't understand why he didn't announce his existence at the first opportunity. His seed could create the next great generation of sisters! While she knew there was truth in what the woman with the Greishic baby had said, Zeya still felt that there was no way that could be all of it. The man was seen as a gift from the goddess, practically worshiped! She had grown up very near to her father's chambers and it didn't seem like women were constantly forcing themselves upon him. Sure, he may have been somewhat a prisoner, but anything he needed was brought to him, wasn't it? Zeya remembered how anytime she was able to get close to her father, she'd see no emotion or recognition in his eyes. So, maybe he really was forced to consume herbs that always kept him in a haze. But he was what kept the Sisterhood alive, and it was his duty, wasn't it? Besides, Yareil had lived for a good many years before he died. Or had he? Zeya realized that, up until now, she never actually thought of her father's age at the time of his passing. But surely the Hearth would do all they could to keep the man healthy and able to continue giving his seed, wouldn't they?

Immediately following the revelation that Aady was the true male, Preza rushed over to him, ready to throw him over her shoulder and carry him right back to the Hearth. Heleila promptly stepped forward, politely requesting to speak with them all privately before they took him away. She swore that once they heard her words, she would not attempt to prevent them from leaving with her son. Curious to the woman's motivations, Zeya had agreed to her terms.

Preza looked from the male to Heleila, then grunted loudly. "Explain yourself quickly, woman. Or I'll cut off your head and drag him back to Vulna."

Heleila looked at Preza and smirked. "I would expect no less of a response from the daughter of Veyna."

Preza's eyes darted nervously around the small hut, startled by her mother's name. "How do you—"

"Patience, Child. All shall be revealed soon enough. What is important now, is that you are here. You survived your journey, and you have a choice to make. One that will not be easy. One that will change the course of the Sisterhood forever."

"And of what choice do you speak? I agreed to hear your words, so speak them plainly," Zeya replied.

"*You* have to decide, Zeya, daughter of Freila, whether or not to take my son, Aadeyo back to the Hearth."

Preza let out a laugh. "You're madder than your neighbor if you think we intend not to."

"As I said before, I will not fight you if that is what you choose. After all, what can a weak, crippled woman, well past her prime, do against four capable warriors?"

"We all saw you on the battlefield. You are far from weak," Zeya replied.

Heleila continued, as if uninterrupted. "I do think, in the end, you will make the right choice. At least that is what your mother thought."

"You pretend to know an awful lot," Meleya remarked. "The Selfa has already agreed to let you tell your tale, but make it quick, we would like to be moving on soon."

"As you wish, Meleya. Here is my tale. I grew up in the Hearth. My mother was a scholar of ancient texts, and she was tasked with finding the means to break the curse set upon us by Vesta many generations ago. She knew it was a fool's errand. Everyone knew, but many in the Hearth still held out hope for a solution that didn't consist solely of remaining complacent until the goddess had a change of heart and decided to lift the curse.

"After I ripened, I followed in my mother's footsteps. We would spend many nights combing through ancient scrolls, tomes, and parchments. We searched and searched for anything hinting at a possible solution. When my mother passed into Vesta's Embrace, I continued the work alone. That was until I met Freila. She was an ambitious sister, and her thirst for power was matched only by her thirst for knowledge. We met often, and she would always ask if I had learned anything of interest since the last time. She held great interest in my work and eventually, in me. We shared many good times together and our bond grew and grew. Eventually, our relationship blossomed into more than just friendship."

"Our mother never mentioned you to us, nor did she ever speak of taking a mate," Meleya replied, indignantly.

"No, she wouldn't have. But I remember when you were born, Child. I remember laying my eyes upon both of you when you were just the tiniest and most helpless of creatures. And Preza, I remember your mother, Veyna, the fearless warrior that she was. I was there when she volunteered to lead a detachment of sisters into the Greenwood and defeat the Greishic once and for all. I was there when so few survivors returned from the crusade, your mother absent among them."

The room was silent as everyone pondered Heleila's words. Zeya knew this woman spoke true, but what did it matter? Strange that someone her mother was connected with would end up birthing the male, and that their paths would cross, but Vesta had played crueler tricks in the past, at least, so she was taught.

"While interesting, your story is not relevant to the Venery. What does this have to do with him?" Zeya motioned to the male.

"I have a name," he replied sharply. "Aadeyo. Please use it."

His voice sounded wrong. Almost as if he was trying his utmost to sound like a woman. Had she been unaware of his surreptitious condition, Zeya never would have noticed. Now that she knew it was no woman who sat before her, his attempt to disguise his masculine voice was obvious.

Heleila continued. "Freila eventually rose to join the Council of the Jurisa. As you know, its members are forbidden from having a mate, and so we were forced apart. Attempting to fill the chasm now left in my heart, I surrounded myself once more with books. I spent every waking moment in the archives, and that was when I found it. I found the truth. The truth behind the lie that has been passed down for generations.

"The story of Diana being cursed by Vesta for her transgressions was false. In actuality, there is very little authenticity to the tale we all know so well. And while I am uncertain how that legend came to be, or why it was taken as fact, it was. The moment our lives changed forever was not due to some curse from Vesta. The point in which we began our current age, one of strife and despair, had little to do with the goddess, but it had everything to do with Diana herself.

"Diana was no ordinary woman, she was a sorceress of immense power. The earliest record I found marked her as good and pure in her deeds. She was known for using her magic to help those in need. She spent much of her life traveling throughout the land, healing the sick, and providing succor to the dying. However, that all changed when she met Lucien. He worked as an apothecary in his village, and he too was kind and pure of heart. Rumor had it that he would not charge his more impoverished patients, even if they insisted he do so.

"Diana quickly fell for Lucien, for she had never met any man like him. Her heart knew that they were meant to be together for all of eternity. There was, however, one matter of great import that kept them apart. Lucien was married. He had been married for some time to a woman named Crystala, and they had four children together, all daughters. At first, Diana tried to ignore her feelings for Lucien. She kept her distance from him whenever possible, but through their mutual work of helping the infirmed, they were often brought together. Eventually, she was no longer able to contain her heart. Diana approached Lucien, confessed her love for him, and begged him to forsake his family and run away with her. He refused. He would not leave his wife and would not abandon his daughters. Not for Diana and not for anyone.

"Over time, the pain of rejection in Diana's heart transformed into hatred, and so she cast a dark spell upon Lucien, one that ensured she would be the only woman he would ever love. Overcome by the sorceress' magic, Lucien abruptly abandoned his wife and daughters and entered into Diana's loving embrace.

"Years passed, and in that time, Diana and Lucien's passion for one another continued to thrive. Eventually, Crystala finally accepted that her once husband would never return to her side. And so, she stopped leaving her home entirely, never setting foot outside again. Crystala ceased eating and spent her remaining days locked in her chamber, oftentimes sitting in complete darkness. It wasn't long before she passed, surrounded by her grieving daughters. They all heard as she called Lucien's name one final time before slipping from this world and into the next.

"Overcome with grief and anger, her daughters blamed their father for abandoning them. They blamed him for leaving their mother and causing her to waste away. Fueled by their outrage, they decided to take action and concocted a plan. They would kill the sorceress and leave their father to wallow in grief just as their mother had. When the day came for them to act, they went to Diana's home under the pretense of wanting to work for her. The four of them entered into

Diana's house, the elder three sisters were searched for weapons, but on that day the guards were lax and neglected to search the smallest daughter, as she was far too young to be perceived as a threat. Upon entering Diana's chamber, they saw their father sitting at her side. No emotion or recognition passed on his face as they approached. The daughters stood in a row and were carefully inspected by Diana to see if they were fit to serve. Diana recognized them, of course, and she had always felt slight remorse over how she had torn their family apart, but it could not have been helped. Lucien was meant to be hers. She continued with the inspection, going from the eldest, down the line toward the youngest. Suddenly the oldest daughter began cursing loudly at Diana. Whirling in surprise, Diana prepared to call the guards and have them all thrown from her home. That was when the youngest sprang into action. Pulling a hidden dagger from her dress, she charged toward Diana and plunged it into the sorceress' back. The child pulled it out and stabbed her again, and again, and again.

"Diana collapsed to the ground, and upon seeing this, Lucien rose up, rushed forth, and in an attempt to protect his beloved from the attackers, slew all four of his own children. He stood helpless over Diana, watching her blood mix with that of his own daughters. Feeling her life fade, Diana tried to use magic to heal her wounds, but she had lost far too much blood. It was then, using every bit of her remaining strength, that Diana reached out to Lucien and channeled the life within him. By sapping him of his strength and life, her wounds began to heal. She now held within her the lifeforce of both a man and a woman, and as such, it would take the hands of both to undo her magic. The spell drained her mental fortitude, and she slipped into unconsciousness. Many days later, she awoke to find herself exiled from the village. The villagers had made it clear that she and her magic were no longer welcome. The massacre of four children was too great a trespass to forgive.

"And so it went that Diana withdrew from the world. She retreated to the mountains that overlooked the Greenwood and with her magic built an immense fortress with walls as dark as a starless sky. In her fortress, Diana remained peacefully away from civilization for a generation. Eventually, pilgrims began to visit her, desiring blessings of wealth and vitality. They had heard of the sorceress who lived in the mountains, and in their greed, they demanded she use her magic to their benefit. She turned them away, every time. Eventually, their jealous anger transformed disappointment into hate. The pilgrims spread word throughout the land that she was an evil witch, one who was responsible for all their hardship and strife. They laid blame for all floods, famine, and disease at her feet. Because of this, the villages sent their strongest warriors to invade her castle and kill her. These warriors were ill-prepared for her powers, however, and she swiftly obliterated them with her magic. This only strengthened their resolve, and they sent even more.

"This cycle continued for more generations until she grew tired of the aggression. She cast a spell using the bodies of all the male warriors she had defeated. A spell on all of humankind. From then on, the world would be cursed and able to birth no sons. Diana only desired to live out the remainder of her days in peace, it mattered not to her that her curse would eventually bring an end to all of humanity. Yet, somehow, seemingly by Vesta's grace, women continued to birth at least one male every generation. As the number of men faded, women took up the sword, the axe, and they took it upon themselves to defeat the sorceress, hoping that it would break the curse. But just as the men had failed, so too did they.

"Eventually a child was born who possessed a strange trait. Her eyes had a pale blue glow about them. No one had ever seen this before, and many thought it was a sign from the goddess. Others thought it was the goddess herself who had come down from the heavens to save them. The child was named Selfana, and as an infant, she was revered by many. Eventually, the glow in her eyes faded and with it, the number of those who thought she had been sent by the goddess also faded. After that, Selfana lived her life as a normal girl until her tenth birthday. That day, she crossed paths with one of the few remaining males. Selfana suddenly collapsed, feeling intense heat as the goddess' fire burned hot within her. Many witnessed the shine of her burning blue eyes and once again started to believe that she was sent to save them.

"Wise women held council to discuss what should be done with this gift. They decided that she, by possessing the goddess' flame within her, would be protected from evil magic, and so they devised a plan. This young girl would be trained to become a great warrior and would be sent on a quest with a male to defeat the sorceress and put an end to the dark art she wrought.

"Eventually, Selfana was deemed strong enough, and was paired with one of the remaining males and sent to the mountains. But the man was old and frail, and he died before they even reached the fortress. Rather than turn back, Selfana decided to continue the journey. She felt that with the goddess' power, she was strong enough to kill the sorceress alone.

"Upon reaching the fortress, Selfana made her way to the witch's inner sanctum and found within it an old sleeping hag. Selfana drew her sword and quickly moved in to kill Diana while she slept, but the hag awoke and shot forth fire from her fingers. Selfana stood helpless as flame surrounded her, but she was not burned thanks to the goddess' protection. This emboldened Selfana, and she once again moved to attack Diana. But the sorceress was cunning. Once she realized the warrior could not be directly hurt by magic, Diana began bringing the walls of her fortress down in an attempt to crush her.

"Dodging the falling stone, Selfana charged toward the witch and managed to pierce her through the heart. Diana fell to the ground and her movements ceased. Selfana went to behead the sorceress as proof of her victory. But as she approached, Diana stood again, her wound fully healed. Selfana stabbed the witch once more, but again, she rose, uninjured. Eventually, the sorceress fully regained her strength and again began pummeling Selfana with magic. Seeing no way to victory, Selfana turned and ran. As she fled, she heard nothing but the sorceress' wicked laugh echoing through the fortress."

XXVII

Decisions

Heleila waited, letting the story settle in their minds. "That is why you must not take Aadeyo to the Hearth. You must take him to Diana's fortress so that he may enter it and together with you, kill her. That is the only way to break the curse put upon us generations ago."

"Well, Pit! I've heard a lot of tales in my day, but this one is deserving of the prize!" Preza exclaimed. "We've heard enough. Let's take the buck and head for the docks right now before any other villagers hear tell of him and start begging for his seed."

"Heleila," Zeya began, "Preza speaks true. Your story sounds even more outlandish than that of Diana which we have all been taught. Why should we believe such a tale? What's more, even if it were true, why would we risk our lives, the male's life, and what would surely be the extinction of the Sisterhood on such a dangerous endeavor?"

"Ask yourself this, Zeya. Why would I risk my child for this tale? Not only is he my only son, but he is also *the* only son." Heleila slowly rose from her seat. "Why didn't I take him and fly when I heard of your arrival? Why did we risk our lives to fight beside you in battle? Why take the time to explain all of this to you if I did not believe in it? Finding Diana's fortress will be dangerous, truly, and that does not even account for facing her in battle. But it is important not to forget, your journey here was also filled with peril. Danger does not preclude success. Everyone knows the Greishic numbers show no sign of abatement while ours wane with each passing day. Let's say you *were* to return my son to the Hearth. Let's say he *would* father a new generation of sisters. What about the next time? What about the time when no male is found? How many more generations do you think the Sisterhood has left? One? Two? This is our chance to save humankind for good. Our chance to put everything back the way it was meant to be."

"I do not doubt the belief you have in your story," Zeya replied. "What I question is the validity of it."

"Your mother believed it. She believed that *you* would believe it. That is why she made arrangements for you to be the one sent here."

"Our mother," Meleya replied, "is very far away. There is no way to substantiate your claim. Truth be told, I highly doubt she would risk her position and in all likelihood, her life, to take part in such a conspiracy."

"Then perhaps a letter from her would alleviate any question you have regarding my claims?" Heleila hobbled to a nearby cabinet and pulled out a roll of parchment. "Here, read it yourself." She reached out, offering the scroll to Meleya. "Go on, take it. You'll see that this has long been your mother's plan, just as it has been mine. It is what

I have been raising and training my son for, and it is what she has been training you for from the moment she saw your sister's glowing blue eyes."

Meleya took the letter and slowly unrolled it while the others in the room watched, waiting intently. "It is written in Mother's hand."

"Read it aloud, Wombsister."

"My dearest Heleila, I pray this letter finds you swiftly. It would seem my suspicions regarding Sieyna were correct. She wants me gone and won't stop until she gets what her dark heart desires. By now, my daughters should be nearing you, and the plan that we set into motion so many years ago finally has some hope of coming to fruition. While I do not doubt they will make the right decision, they may take some convincing. That is why the remainder of this letter is written to them. Be safe, my dearest Heleila and try not to be overcome with worry. They are noble of mind and will choose correctly in the end. I thank Vesta for bringing you into my life, if only for what little time we shared. Alé volás."

Meleya hesitated before continuing. "My dearest daughters, I am sorry I could not speak to you of this in person, but I had my reasons. I am not sure what Heleila has told you up until this point, but I assure you, there is much truth in it. Long ago, while Heleila was working as the Hearth's Head Researcher, she came across this seemingly implausible tale and brought it to my attention. As she no doubt has shared with you, we once shared a relationship that went far beyond friendship. Together, we discussed her findings at great length. After knowing what to look for, Heleila began discovering other writings that reinforced the alleged origin of the curse. Once I was certain enough evidence supporting this revelation had been gathered, we took it to the Jurisa.

"Things did not go how either of us expected. But looking back, we should have known better. A revelation such as this was too great for the Sisterhood, ancient and set in its ways as it was, to have accepted. The other council members dismissed the research harshly. They removed Heleila from her position as Head Researcher and expelled her from the Hearth's libraries. They labeled her findings as blasphemy and threatened to have her hanged if she spread her lies to anyone else. They felt that no woman of this earth could possess the power of this alleged sorceress. 'Only the goddess has the ability to perform miracles,' they said. Since at the time I was the most junior member of the Jurisa, they let me off with a strong reprimand, and forced me to endure further education at Vesta's Temple, but I never stopped believing what I knew to be the truth. Heleila and I grew further apart after that, and it was some time before our paths crossed again.

"One day, while I was volunteering in the Hearth's birthing chamber, she came in, her womb filled with a new sister ready to enter the world. Or so we thought. It was not an easy birth, but as I guided the child from her womb, I nearly shouted in surprise. For you see, her child was male. I quickly covered the boy, fearing one of the other midsisters may take notice of him. I took Heleila to one of the resting chambers and revealed the marvel to her. It was then that we concocted our plan. She would escape the city to a remote village, far from the eyes of the Sisterhood. There, she could raise her child without his identity being discovered, and train him to fight. For my part, I would raise my daughters to be strong and skillful warriors so that they may one day protect and guide the last male to his fate.

"There was only one thing missing from our plan, we needed a selfa. The likelihood of the quest succeeding was low without someone immune to the sorceress' magic. I hoped and prayed for a selfa, both understanding and accepting of this goal, to cross my path. Imagine my amazement when I was given you, Zeya.

Now, the only obstacle we faced was the Hearth. The Jurisa would never allow me to send out a selfa without just cause. So I plotted, I schemed, and I manipulated. All so that you could be sent to Rolier, to Heleila, and to the male. I am fearful that my scheming has been discovered. Sieyna has grown suspicious of me. She claims Selfa Delreza has evidence of my plot and will surely bring this all to light in front of the council.

"That is why, my dearest daughters, this letter must also serve as my goodbye. Zeya, watching you grow into a selfa caused such pride in my heart. My belief in my plans was greatly strengthened when your burning blue eyes first met mine. Meleya, my love for you is matched only by your prowess. I have little doubt you will need to rely heavily upon it on the journey ahead. Remember to protect yourself with the same fervor you have undoubtedly used to keep your wombsister safe. And Preza, you are my daughter, womb, or not. I have always seen you as such and will continue to love you as my own until the final beat of my dying heart. I was blessed to have the honor of raising you and twice blessed to see you grow into such a fine woman.

"If my suspicions are true, it won't be long before I am found guilty of my crimes and executed. I fear that we will not see each other again in this life, but I look forward to reuniting with you all in the next. Hail, sisters. Hail the change! Your ever-loving mother, Freila."

Meleya stopped reading and wiped away the tears that were streaming down her face. Zeya felt a lump in her throat. She was unable to speak. Preza sat quietly, contemplating the words she had just heard, and her eyes too began to water.

"My son is ready to leave whenever you are and as you have seen, he is more than capable in battle. My training saw to that. I have also made arrangements for provisions. It is not much, but it will get you to Coratch where the next phase of your journey will begin."

Zeya looked at the woman, then to her companions, uncertain of what to say or do. She realized everyone was looking at her expectantly, waiting for her to speak. She was the Selfa, after all. She was the one blessed with Vesta's Gift, and apparently that meant it was her decision to choose the fate of the male. No, not just the male. They expected her to decide the fate of the entire Sisterhood. "Heleila, I do not know how much of your story is true, but I do feel something in my heart pulling me toward that path. However, what makes you so sure we will succeed? This sorceress, as you call her, wields power above any foe we have ever faced. If armies perished in battle against her, how can the few of us attain success?"

"Do not mistake my intent, Child. I am far from sure you will succeed. In fact, I feel it more likely that you will die. With that having been spoken, there is more that may aid you on this ill-fated quest than it may appear."

"And of what aid do you speak?" Zeya asked.

"I imagine it has been nearly a thousand years since Diana last felt threatened. Her guard has undoubtedly been lowered greatly. She may even have become complacent in her own defenses. Diana will not be expecting anyone to enter her lair, least of all a man. Secondly, there is a boon that you must acquire before attempting to face her. How it works, or what precisely it is, I am uncertain. It is a talisman that will either mitigate the sorceress' power, or bolster your own. I know little about it, not much more than a description and a sketch, but a friend of mine tracked it down. That is why Coratch must be your next destination."

"This is all sounding a little too much like a children's tale for my liking," commented Preza. "A witch, a magical charm, and a curse that must be broken? In truth, I have heard children's tales that were veritably more believable."

Zeya nodded. "This is sounding more fabricated with each word you speak."

"If we had more time, I would lead you to the Hearth and show you the evidence myself. Just remember that your mother believed. Your mother who doubted and questioned all that her eyes did not see. If someone came to me with a story so seemingly fabulized, a quest completely contrary to my duty as Selfa, and a male who could birth a next generation, I would deem them mad as well. But we all know the world cannot continue this way. Time is running out for us, the end of the Sisterhood is near at hand. We will *not* have another chance at this."

Zeya looked around the room at the others. Everyone stared back in anticipation, even the male. "This decision is not mine alone to make. I would like to hear how each of you feels. I would not have made it this far if it wasn't for you, my companions, my sisters."

Preza nodded solemnly. "I owe my life, my very existence to your mother. If she felt this is the path we should take, even knowing her life would be forfeit, then I say we should go."

Zeya looked at Meleya. "And you, dear Wombsister?"

"I... I am not sure," she replied, stroking her braid nervously. "We have no way of knowing what will happen if we return this male to the Hearth. This could be the generation that breaks the curse, and even if it's not, there is no guarantee we will be wiped out by the Greishic for another hundred years. The soundness of this crusade is questionable at best, and dragging this male on it will surely seal the Sisterhood's fate, likely for the worse."

"And you, Man." The word felt strange on Zeya's tongue. "What makes you so willing to give up your life for this? Or has your mother indoctrinated you into believing that you are destined to be our savior and that not even death can stop you?"

Aadeyo looked at her for a long time before speaking. "My mother has done nothing of the sort. The reason for my willingness is evident in you, Zeya. I have seen the look of foreboding that lives on every sister's face, both from those of this village and those who visit from afar. Everyone has it, just as the four of you have it. It is indicative of the fear that lies within you, the fear that the world you have known, as burdensome as it is, is coming to an end. I do not purport to know the outcome of this journey, but I do know that if we do not attempt it, it would be the same end as if we had failed."

Joreya stood up, looking shyly at the group, then opened her mouth to speak. "I think we should do it. Everyone knows what the Greishic are capable of, but the ones that attacked Memier were different from the stories I've heard. My wombsisters were at the Paling, and they told of a coordinated assault. The Greishic are not only growing in numbers, they also grow in intelligence. It will take more than the walls and valor of the Sisterhood to stop them. It will take numbers beyond compare to anything the Sisterhood can create with the seed of one man."

Zeya looked around at each of them slowly. Her mind raced rapidly as she attempted to calculate the possible outcomes of each decision. *Why me? Why do I have to decide the fate of the Sisterhood?*

The fate of us all? Vesta's Gift? More like Vesta's Curse. She took a deep breath. "It would seem we must either face the wrath of this witch, or the wrath of the Greishic," she stated. "While I am not entirely convinced this quest is not pure madness, Mother did believe it was the right course, Heleila speaks true there. And so, I will take the male to the mountains, find this witch, and help him kill her, even at the cost of my own life."

Heleila and Aadeyo both sighed with relief.

"But," Zeya continued, "I do not wish for any of you to follow me out of duty to the oaths you swore. Meleya, Preza, I will not be making this journey as a selfa of the Hearth." Zeya brought her hand toward her breast and unfastened Vesta's Leaf, placing it on the table in front of her. "I will be making it as Zeya, your sister."

Preza nodded slowly. "And I will accompany you, as your sister."

Zeya's eyes turned to her wombsister. "And you, dearest Meleya?"

"I will continue to be your protector, Zeya. No matter if it is to the center of a Greishic horde or to the mountains on some fool's quest. You are my wombsister, and I will remain by your side, always."

"Thank you, sisters." Zeya turned to Joreya. "Sister, your words were inspirational, and you have been a great asset, but I feel that your part in this journey ends here. Heleila, will you see that she is cared for while we are gone? Set her up with work and a place to sleep? She has lost much and should not be left alone."

"I will, of course," Heleila replied.

"But I want to go," Joreya's voice came out in little more than a whisper before rising with determination. "My mother was wrong. I am not useless. I can help! I can learn to use a sword, maybe not as well as Meleya, but I can! Or I can kill Greishic with daggers like you, Zeya! You saw me in the battle, I didn't run!"

Meleya shook her head. "We have no doubt that you can learn, but there won't be time for any of us to teach you. Do not be discouraged, Sister."

"I... don't want to be... useless," Joreya whispered, struggling to hold back her sobs.

Meleya put her hand on Joreya's shoulder. "Joreya, there will be many times for tears, but this is not one of them."

"My mother can teach you to fight," Aadeyo offered. "She taught me."

"I will, Child," Heleila replied. "There will be a dire need for strong warriors before long. You will be far from useless."

Joreya nodded in defeat. "If that is all I can do to help, that is what I will do."

"When this is all done with, we'll come back this way for sure," Meleya said, smiling.

"Mother," Aadeyo began, "we will find Diana, and together, we will end this curse. I will give you both grandsons and granddaughters." He hugged her, holding her tightly for some time.

"I know you will, Aady, for I feel it in my heart. This is what you were born for. This is why I was blessed by Vesta to carry you, to birth you, and to raise you."

XXVIII

The Change

"Fallen? Are you certain?" Sieyna asked in disbelief at the report Cereila had just read.

"Yes, this message came directly from Regent Vuleila, so there is no doubt. The Greishic breached the Paling and overtook the city," replied Cereila.

"These are dark times," Gilza stated. "Not only has one of our own betrayed us, but the Greishic have overtaken the Paling. Do you know if they managed to intercept the Selfa before she passed through?"

"The message mentions nothing of the Selfa. It is possible she passed through Memier after it fell. It is also possible that she never even made it through the Greenwood. No way to know until we receive a message from Selfa Zeya regarding the success or failure of the Venery."

"Assuming she actually sends us a bird," Sieyna growled. "The traitor spoke of not conspiring against the Sisterhood solely for the glory of her daughter. I fear her plans may be darker than even we can imagine."

"And what of Selfa Delreza? Has she progressed beyond Haralda yet?" Gilza asked anxiously.

Cereila shuffled through the parchments before her. "No. I received word this morning that she and her companions had only just arrived in Solren."

"Very well. Send a missive ahead of her to Haralda, tell Selfa Delreza that Memier has fallen to the beasts and that haste is of the utmost import. They must take the risk and ride their horses through the Greenwood, stopping only when absolutely necessary. As Sieyna said, it is likely the Selfa and her companions have been compromised by their traitorous mother. If we don't intercept them before they leave Rolier, we may never find the male."

Sieyna looked at Gilza in surprise. "Selfa Delreza is skillful, but taking horses through the Greenwood poses a dire risk. Steeds are far from stealthy and they are sure to attract every Greishic within earshot with their pounding hooves."

"If this generation's buck disappears, all is lost. We will have no seed with which to birth another. Selfa Delreza's life is meaningless if the Sisterhood fails. All that matters is finding the male and bringing him back to us." Gilza paused, considering something for a moment. "If he's ripened, tell her to initiate coition with any and all ripened sisters they come across. If he resists, or lacks the virility, instruct her to gather Milk of the Regire. Force feed it to him if necessary and have the sisters force themselves upon him. We need to start increasing our numbers as soon as possible."

Sieyna and Cereila both nodded.

"And what of Memier? Should we not send soldiers to search for survivors? Or, at the very least, aid Selfa Delreza?" Cereila asked.

"Agreed. Have Captain Layna send a detachment of sisters to accompany the Selfa. But make it known that they will be left behind if they slow the Selfa down. Once they make it to Memier, if they believe the Paling can be repaired and the city made defensible once more, instruct them to do so. Otherwise, have them continue with the Selfa until they find the male. We cannot allow him to escape.

"Now, on to our next order of business. Do you each have your lists of qualified candidates to fill the empty seat on this council?"

* * *

The party rode along the road to Coratch, it'd be a few days before they arrived, but once they did, they'd have a much longer journey ahead of them. Zeya's thoughts turned to her mother. Did she still live? Zeya knew, based on her mother's letter, that it was unlikely, but still, she held on to hope. The Jurisa would undoubtedly be sending someone after them if they had learned of her mother's treachery. To counter this, Heleila insisted Zeya send a scroll to the Hearth stating the rumored male was a rotting half-beast carcass being cared for by a madwoman. Zeya had done as instructed, but it hadn't felt right. Strange that stealing the male away on some ill-conceived quest brought her less feelings of guilt than lying did. No, the quest wasn't ill-conceived. Both her mother and Heleila had been planning it for a very long time. Neither of them acted with rashness. The quest was unlikely to succeed, sure, but its planning was sound.

Zeya glanced at the male, and not for the first time. It was so strange. That was *him*. Aadeyo hadn't spoken much since they left the village, and she was about to try and engage him in conversation when Preza began humming aloud.

"That song, what is it?" Meleya asked.

The large woman turned on her horse and smiled. "Not so long ago, you promised I could serenade you after we found the male. Well, there he is!"

Meleya shook her head. "Oh, Vesta. Please, no!"

Preza's smile grew wider and she began to sing:

O' Meleya,
Such a Homely Hag.
No longer young,
How her body did sag.

O' Meleya
Was filled with strife.
'Cause she used only her tongue,
To find a wife.

O' Meleya
She found no one.
For those who drew near,
Would always run.

O' Meleya
Such a Homely Hag.
Lived a life alone,
'Til she looked a dry rag.

"Preza! That was—"

"Beautiful!" Zeya interrupted.

Meleya laughed. "No, I was going to say horrific. When exactly did you have the time to compose such a ballad?"

"It didn't take very long. The words just came to me whenever I saw you."

Zeya laughed loudly. She then checked if the male was sharing in their mirth.

He noticed her looking. "Are you intent on stealing glances at me through this whole journey?"

"No, I..." Zeya felt her cheeks grow warm. "I was just seeing if you liked the song."

"I've heard better. But the interaction has given me much context to the relationship you all share."

"And? Do you approve?" Meleya teased.

Aadeyo nodded. "I hope your cheerfulness will help us through the hard times we surely face ahead."

Zeya smiled. "Can I ask you something, Aadeyo?"

"You may. But you should get in the habit of calling me Aady or Aadeya."

"Oh, that would be wise," Zeya replied. "Um... I'm just curious, you don't really seem all that different from a woman."

"He's different where it counts, Love," Preza stated with a laugh.

Aadeyo grew noticeably red before regaining his composure. "What did you expect me to be? Broad-shouldered, bearded, and possessing a tantalizing musk that emanates from my overly-muscular physique?"

"Silly man, you just described Preza!" Meleya exclaimed.

"He did, didn't he?" Zeya laughed.

"Hey!" Preza shouted, feigning hurt. "That's not an accurate description of me! I shaved before we left!"

Zeya smiled as she looked around at her companions. She knew in her heart she would have had no chance of succeeding on the Venery without them. Being together gave her even more confidence on their new quest. She would succeed, so long as she had her sisters by her side.

Alé Volás

Thank you for choosing to read The Venery. If it spoke to you in any way, please consider leaving a review. Your reviews help independent authors grow and keep sharing their tales with new readers!

Sincerely,

JC Menvielle

www.ingramcontent.com/pod-product-compliance
Lightning Source LLC
Chambersburg PA
CBHW050020120726
47903CB00006B/1840